D0378916

THE
SHANGHAI
FACTOR

Other novels by Charles McCarry

Ark
Christopher's Ghosts
Old Boys
Lucky Bastard
Shelley's Heart
Second Sight
The Bride of the Wilderness
The Last Supper
The Better Angels
The Secret Lovers
The Tears of Autumn
The Miernik Dossier

THE SHANGHAI FACTOR

A Novel

Charles McCarry

The Mysterious Press
New York

Copyright © 2013 by Charles McCarry

All rights reserved. No part of this book may be reproduced in any form or by any electronic or mechanical means, including information storage and retrieval systems, without permission in writing from the publisher, except by a reviewer, who may quote brief passages in a review. Scanning, uploading, and electronic distribution of this book or the facilitation of such without the permission of the publisher is prohibited. Please purchase only authorized electronic editions, and do not participate in or encourage electronic piracy of copyrighted materials. Your support of the author's rights is appreciated. Any member of educational institutions wishing to photocopy part or all of the work for classroom use, or anthology, should send inquiries to Grove/Atlantic, Inc., 841 Broadway, New York, NY 10003 or permissions@groveatlantic.com.

Published simultaneously in Canada
Printed in the United States of America

FIRST EDITION

ISBN-13: 978-0-8021-2127-1

The Mysterious Press
an imprint of Grove/Atlantic, Inc.
841 Broadway
New York, NY 10003

Distributed by Publishers Group West

www.groveatlantic.com

13 14 15 16 17   10 9 8 7 6 5 4 3 2 1

For David Laux

How do I know this is true?
I look inside myself and see.

—Laozi

ONE

1

Those who keep an eye on me think I have a weakness for Chinese women. This is true as far as it goes, but it goes both ways. I am a hairy man, and certain East Asian women like that. My first Chinese girl called sex with me "sleeping with the chimpanzee." Her name was Mei, easy for a chimp to pronounce and remember. We met cute. One day, as I pedaled along Zhongshan Road, she crashed her bicycle into mine. In those days I was new to the life of a spy, so my paranoia wasn't yet fully developed, but I immediately suspected that this was no accident. My first thought was that Chinese counterintelligence had sniffed me out and sent this temptress to entrap me. Then I took a look at the temptress and wondered why I should mind. She was lying facedown, miniskirt awry, next to the wreckage of our two bikes—curtain of blue-black hair, slender legs the color of honey, snow-white virginal panties covering her round bottom. She was in pain—writhing, moaning, sucking in air through her teeth. I crouched beside her and in my stumbling Mandarin asked the usual stupid question. She turned her head and looked at me—starlet's face, unblinking dark eyes filled with tears. I asked the same question again, "Are you all right?" First she heard me, now she saw me. And smelled me. It was a hot, muggy day. I needed a haircut. I hadn't shaved. Chest hair tufted from the open neck of a shirt I had been wearing for three days. Her lips twisted, her eyes blazed. All expression drained from her face. She said nothing. I might as well have been attempting to communicate in American Sign Language. Then she sat up. Her face, her whole person radiating anger, as if I had pinched her in her sleep. Her eyes went cold. She shouted at me. At length. In Shanghai dialect. I understood almost nothing she said, but had no difficulty grasping her meaning. A little crowd gathered. They understood every word, and it made them laugh. When she stopped talking, the crowd drifted away.

The girl got to her feet. Her knees were scraped. She bled from an elbow. She cradled the wounded arm in her other arm, as if in a sling.

Taking great care with the tones, I attempted to say, "Please speak Mandarin so I can understand the insults."

Daggers. She kicked her bike—the front wheel was as bent out of shape as she was—and said, "Your fault."

I said, "You hit me."

"My machine is ruined. Look at the front wheel."

"That proves you hit me. If I had hit you, my bike would be the one with the broken wheel."

"You speak this language like you ride a bicycle. Ugly Chengdu accent. Was that clear enough for you to understand?"

"I think so."

"It thinks!" she said. "I think it had better give me some money for a new bike before I call the police. They'll be here any minute anyway, so hurry up."

"Good. The police will see who was at fault."

"Ha."

In the middle distance I saw a knot of witnesses leading a policeman to the scene of the crime. The girl saw them, too.

"Now you will find out about China," she said.

I didn't doubt that she was right. Getting mixed up with the police was the last thing I was supposed to let happen to me. I was in Shanghai to speak Chinese, not to get the cops interested in me.

I said, "I'll go with you to a bicycle shop and pay for the repairs. But no money."

"*New* bike."

The cop and the witnesses were getting closer. I said, "Let's talk about it on the way."

She smiled triumphantly, lips pressed together. "I ride. You carry my bike."

I picked up the wreckage. She vaulted onto the saddle of my machine, a four-thousand-dollar one bought on the expense account, as if she were leaving Lourdes after being cured by the patron saint of lady bicyclists. I watched her go—her legs and the rest of her, in motion now. She was even better to look at. Dutiful to my vocation, I wondered why would she wear a miniskirt and that skimpy top instead of jeans and long sleeves if she had planned this collision or had it planned for her? Paranoia 101, as taught to novices in a secret installation in Virginia, answered the question: precisely because her handlers knew that her tiny wounds, her lovely face, her shining hair, her sweet body, her sharp tongue, her crackling intelligence, would cause me to think with some other organ than my brain. It was obvious that this girl had been born knowing this.

Oh, she was wily. So were her handlers. Nevertheless—couldn't help it—I thought *poor kid* as she weaved her way through the river of bicycles. Her figure grew smaller and smaller as she pedaled faster and faster. She turned recklessly across traffic into a side street, leaning the bicycle within centimeters of the horizontal, sprocket, pedals and feet a blur. I kissed my bike good-bye. I thought I'd never see it or her again.

I was wrong. A short way down the side street, she waited in front of a bicycle shop. Band-Aids now covered her wounds. She must have had them in her backpack just in case. Inside the shop, bicycles hung from the ceiling.

She pointed. "That one."

The proprietor got it down. It was the very best bicycle available in China, therefore in the world, he said, the only one of its kind in the store, and perhaps in all of Shanghai, since this model flew out of the shops and the manufacturer was in despair because he could not keep up with demand. He named the price. I flinched.

I still held her wrecked machine in my arms. I said, "Wait a minute. What we want is to have this one repaired."

"New bike," she said.

To the proprietor, I said, "How much to fix this bike?" He looked at me blankly but did not answer.

She said, "This man does not do repairs."

"Then we'll find someone who does."

The girl said something to the proprietor in Shanghainese. He went to the door of his shop and shouted. In seconds a very stern policeman appeared.

In English the girl said, "Shall I tell him you assaulted me?"

"And if you do?"

"Investigation."

I didn't reply. She studied my face and apparently saw what she had been hoping to see—profound anxiety. In Mandarin she said to the policeman, "This man is new to our country. He wants to know if this is a good bike."

"The best," the policeman said. "Very expensive. Worth the price."

He left without even asking for my passport. Another little thrill of suspicion ran through my mind. How did this policeman happen to be nearby? Why did he turn himself into a sales assistant? Where was his officiousness? The girl did not trouble to read my mind. She was bargaining with the proprietor. Or seemed to be. They were speaking

Shanghainese, a language I didn't understand. Long minutes passed. The volume rose. At last they stopped talking. Proudly the girl told me the staggering price she had negotiated—a month's pay for a rookie spook. Fortunately, I had just been to the money changer, so I had enough yuan in my pocket to pay the bill. I got out my wallet. She smiled happily, but at the bicycle, not me.

Outside, she said in Bostonian English, "What made you hire a teacher from Chengdu?"

"It was all Chinese to me. Where in the States did you go to school?"

"Concord-Carlisle High School, in Massachusetts."

"Exchange student?"

She nodded.

"Cheerleader?"

"Volleyball."

"College?"

"I came home for that."

"To which college?"

"Questions, questions. What are you, an American spy?"

She was watching my face. I asked her name. "Mei," she said, and in Mandarin asked if I could remember that. She asked my name. I provided an alias. It was a difficult name, Polish with many syllables and odd diphthongs, that belonged to a Hessian running back who played my position for my school while I sat out my senior year on the bench.

She said, "I'm supposed to take that seriously?"

"Why not? Are you some kind of racist?"

"Of course I am—I'm Han. We look down on everybody. I'll call you Dude. It suits you."

"We're going to be friends?"

"Up to you, Dude."

"Fine," I said. "Let's give it a try. One thing I insist upon. Never speak English to me again. You can have your way in everything else."

Apparently this was okay by her. She called me Dude for the next two years. I called her by the only name I knew, Mei. I never asked— never—what her real name might be. Who cared?

On the day of the bicycle wreck, I took her to lunch, then showed her where I lived. Later I took her dancing and, at her suggestion, to a rave where I was the only foreigner. We went for rides on our new bikes, picnicked in parks, found a group to join for morning calisthenics. Soon we were making love three times a night, twenty-six times a month, and sometimes, when the coast was clear, in the daytime. I was twenty-nine. She was five or six years younger, so we were both indefatigable. It was not part of her assignment, or in her nature, to love me. In that we were alike. In bed she was a comic. Everything about copulation, my simian body especially, struck her as funny, and laughter excited her almost as much as fur. She giggled during foreplay, guffawed with joy after her orgasms and made funny noises during them. When we were not going at it, she loved to talk about books and movies and television shows. So did I, so we had a lot to talk about. We watched television and went to the movies, sitting in different rows. She read to me in Mandarin and required me to do the same and get it right before we got into bed. She insisted that I make phone calls to numbers she provided—friends of hers, she said—on the theory that no one really understands a foreign language unless he can understand it over the telephone. For the same reason she taught me songs in Mandarin, and we sang them to each other. Many laughs about my mistakes at first, but my Mandarin improved as my ear quickened in a hopeless attempt to keep up with her. I even learned to flounder around in Shanghainese, a Wu language that is incomprehensible to speakers of most other Chinese tongues.

I was sure from the start that she was on duty, that she reported everything, that she had bugged my room. The funny thing was, she never asked for information, never probed. She showed no curiosity about my family, my education, my politics, my first love, or the girls I had slept with in high school and college and afterward. Probably this was because she had been briefed about these matters by the folks at Guoanbu, the Chinese intelligence service (within Headquarters called "MSS," short for Ministry of State Security) and had no reason to ask. I never questioned her, either. She dressed well, she glowed with health, she had money, she disappeared in the daylight hours, so presumably she had a job or another lover. She explained nothing, never mentioned her primary life, not a single detail, though I did learn that she had gone to Shanghai University, where I was auditing a couple of courses, when I ran into someone who knew her and this person seemed to know about us. Just another inscrutable encounter. I didn't bother to be suspicious. Either Mei was an agent or she was a lunatic. If the former, we were both on duty. If the latter, the benefits were terrific. Besides, I was fulfilling my mission. I had been sent to China to learn to talk like a native, and I was certainly making progress with that. Mei insisted on living entirely in the here and now. That was okay by me. In time we got to know each other very well indeed.

The learning process was wonderful. Liberating. I had never before lived in the total absence of emotional clutter, let alone complete sexual gratification. Nor had I ever imagined it was possible to know a woman this well while knowing next to nothing about her, or that the key to such hidden knowledge was to know nothing about her except what the five senses told you. I wondered if any other American boy, living or dead, had ever been so fortunate. If I did not love Mei, I liked the hell out of her, and I was as mesmerized by her smooth, perfect body as she seemed to be by my Paleolithic one. I certainly did not even want to think about saying good-bye to her and going back to the land of the crazy women.

2

While in Shanghai I was, in the jargon, a sleeper, meaning that I was supposed to wait for instructions, lead a transparent, predictable life, and do nothing that would call attention to myself—such as messing around with a girl like Mei, or buying her a bicycle with a thousand dollars of the taxpayers' money, or getting hammered with strangers at parties where everyone except me was Chinese. I had no contact with anyone in the local base of U.S. intelligence and didn't even know for sure if such an office existed. I hardly ever talked to a Caucasian, though I was accosted by many. I was under orders to avoid Americans, but they were everywhere, and could never discipline themselves to just walk on by when they saw what they thought was a fellow countryman. "You *American?*" Then came the standard student center quiz. It was no different in this exotic place than it had been back home—where was I from, where had I gone to college, how liberal was I? What was my major, did I hate my parents ("You *don't?* Wow!"), was I, um, straight or gay, where did I live, what was my phone number, my favorite band, movie, song, author, microbrew? As Mei and my training had taught me, I provided no answers, asked no questions in return. At first

I pretended to be a Canadian, anti-American to the bone and proud of it. This worked too well. Most American expatriates detested the U.S.A., too, so my progressive gibberish made them want to strike up a friendship. I learned to say I had to run—that cheap Chinese food!

My only American friend was a fellow who went by the fictitious name of Tom Simpson, a nobody like me who worked in Headquarters. Once a month he and I exchanged e-mails. Simpson seemed to have nothing better to do than keep up our correspondence, and it was easy to see he put a lot of work into his messages. Probably he wanted to be a writer when he retired thirty years down the line. Many spies are aspiring novelists, and Headquarters values a way with words above almost everything else. Partly because he was so eager to do well at something that did not matter, I supposed Simpson was low man on the China desk. As time went by, we developed an old drinking buddy joviality, and the correspondence was a pleasure in its way. More important, it told me I had not been forgotten, though someone smarter than me might have hoped for the opposite. The idea—I should say the hope—at Headquarters was that Guoanbu's hackers would read my mail and conclude that I was just another American clod they could safely ignore, maybe for the rest of my life. This is called building cover. In fact it is giddy optimism. Like much else in the practice of espionage, it is built on hope, denial of reality, wishful thinking, ignorance, the tendency to look upon insignificant results as important outcomes, and the Panglossian belief that those who spy by the rules don't get caught.

Needless to say I told Simpson only the barest details where Mei was concerned—the accident, the new bike as an expense account item, that was it. Even to a babe in the woods like me, it was obvious that discovery of my indiscretions would not be good for my career. Yet somehow, the folks back home got wind of Mei. Maybe one of those Budweiser guys I met at the wild Chinese parties Mei dragged me to knew someone I didn't know—such as a case officer from the local Headquarters outpost. It was

Simpson who clued me in. He and I seeded our e-mails with code phrases we called wild cards. "Horny as hell," for example, meant that everything was just fine. "Pain in the ass" meant get me out of here fast. In theory I had committed all these phrases and their real meanings to memory, but even when you're not trying to learn Mandarin, the brain in its infinite playfulness will, as we all know, move memories from one part of the frontal lobe to another. Therefore when I read the words "It's raining possums and rednecks in the Old Dominion" in a message from Tom, I drew a blank. I knew it was a wild card because such phrases were always signaled by a semicolon in the preceding sentence. That archaic punctuation mark was never otherwise used in our correspondence. Of course that made the code easier to spot if you were a snoop, but if you didn't know what the following wild card meant, you couldn't figure it out. It was undecipherable because it wasn't a cipher. Or so the catechism insisted.

Mei arrived moments after I received Simpson's e-mail—a happy coincidence, since what followed for the next two or three hours cleared my mind like nothing and nobody else could do. Mei liked foreplay games. Usually these consisted of a feat of Mandarin recitation performed by myself (with my eyes closed) while Mei messed around. No penetration allowed until my feat of memory was perfectly executed, though unlimited cock teasing was okay under the rules, and that's what Mei liked about the game. A couple of days earlier, she had given me these lines, composed around 200 B.C. by the poet and statesman Qu Yuan:

廣開兮天門 紛吾乘兮玄雲
令飄風兮先驅 使凍雨兮灑塵

In English, the poem, called "Da Si Ming," reads something like this:

Open wide the door of heaven!
On a black cloud I ride in splendor

Bidding the whirlwind drive before me,
Causing the rainstorm to lay dust.

It reads better in the original language. I had memorized these lines as ordered, suffering the usual flashes of agony, and now, while Mei rubbed her unclothed body and fingertips against my Esau-like pelt, I recited it in Mandarin. "Flawless!" Mei said. "You're getting too good. Make mistakes so we can go slower!" I said that rules were rules. Midway through the third act of our daily scenario, my mind awakened and I remembered that "raining possums and rednecks" meant that I was summoned to a meeting with someone from inside the apparatus, and "Old Dominion" meant that Headquarters had reason to believe that I was under surveillance. Of course it did. I had reported this to Tom Simpson weeks before. Instructions would follow.

"Shit," I said.

Between outcries, Mei said, "Speak Mandarin."

Tom's e-mail had told me nothing I didn't already know. I had noticed that I was being watched months before, or soon after the surveillance began. I assumed it was routine, not worth reporting, because I had been forewarned that Chinese eyes would be watching me as a matter of course. I had been told to keep my tradecraft sharp by exercising its rules at all times, so I did what I could to be the Mr. Goodspy I was being paid to be. I studied faces in the crowd in case I ever saw one of them again. This might seem like a hopeless undertaking in China, but in fact the Chinese look no more alike—and no more unalike—than any other people with the exception of Americans, whose five centuries of interbreeding has produced an almost infinite number of countenances. The French, for example, have eight or nine faces to go around, the Germans, the Italians, the Indians, and the Arabs roughly the same number. The Han have only a few more than that. There are subtle variations, of course, but in order to remember a face you have only to recognize its category and remember a variation or two in order to know whether you are looking at a person you have seen before.

It was soon after Mei and I got together that I noticed men and women whose faces I soon began to recognize had taken up positions outside my apartment building. There were twelve of them who worked two-hour shifts as three-person teams. The group watching me was composed of professionals. Seldom did I see the same three faces on the same team, and when they followed me, or followed Mei and me when we were together, the faces changed as they were replaced every block or two by folks from the other two teams. Like almost everyone else in Shanghai, they talked nonstop on cell phones, presumably to each other or a controller. As I was not engaged in espionage and had nothing to hide except a Han girlfriend who had little interest in hiding, I did not mention the surveillance to Mei and she did not remark on it, though it's hard to believe that anyone as wide-awake as she was could have failed to notice. If she wasn't worried, I supposed I had nothing to fear. It was fun in its way.

Headquarters took it more seriously. I heard from Tom again within the week. He told me that the Cardinals were burning up the National League central division, and were in first place with a 7.5-game lead. This hand of wild cards decoded as an instruction to meet a Headquarters man ("first place") who wore a red necktie ("burning") at noon (7 + 5 = 12) on Wednesday next ("central division") at the bar of the Marriott Hotel ("National League") and to use a certain recognition phrase ("game.")

I was followed to the rendezvous as usual, but as far as I could see, no one followed me inside the hotel. At 12:17 P.M. on Wednesday, seventeen minutes after the meeting time dictated by the wild card, a man in a wrinkled blue blazer and a red necktie approached me in the bar of the designated hotel. He was fortyish, tall, skinny, balding, bespectacled, unsmiling. He wore a Joe Stalin mustache.

He said, "Ever been to Katmandu?"

"Not yet," I said. "But I'm hoping to get there someday."

That nonsensical exchange was the recognition code I had been told to use in case of a clandestine meeting with one of our people. The stranger shook hands with me, pressing a fingernail into my wrist. If this too was part of the ritual, nobody had forewarned me, but I responded by squeezing his hand until I saw pain in his eyes. He let go. Dead eyes. The bartender approached. I had already drunk my Coke. The stranger waved him away and said, "Follow me. Don't walk with me. *Follow* me."

He was a fast walker, so I did follow him as he led me through jammed back streets that smelled of sweat and bad breath and rang with shouts to get out of the way. At last we came to a restaurant and went inside. It was almost as noisy and crowded as the streets. He was well known to the host and the waiters, who greeted him with happy grins and bursts of Shanghainese. I was a little shocked by this reception because in my newborn way, I had the idea that seasoned operatives kept themselves to themselves and faithfully practiced tradecraft at all times. For all I knew, that was exactly what this guy thought he was doing.

When we were alone, I said, "What do I call you?"

"Try Steve."

"I'm—"

"Nameless."

The host showed us to a table. He hovered for quite a long time while a smiling Steve bantered with him, ordering lunch for both of us. His mood changed as soon as the fellow departed. He looked me over with his unwavering lifeless eyes, which were slightly magnified by the lenses of his glasses. Beer was brought, then an appetizer. The food was very good. Figuring that Steve didn't care whether I was enjoying my lunch, I didn't bother to comment. Nor did I ask any questions or otherwise say a word. It was obvious that Steve was not happy to be wasting his time on an *Üntermensch* like me. Skinny or not, he was an industrious eater, and when the host came by after each course to ask how he had liked it, Steve reverted to his jollier self, smiling through his mustache. He spoke not a word to me.

At last we came to the end of the meal. I expected that we would now retire to a soundproof room hidden inside a safe house and have a serious talk, but instead, Steve decided to have the discussion right where we were. He had a really loud voice, the ear-splitting kind you hear bellowing at the umpire at baseball games. He talked freely, as if we were indeed in an unbuggable bubble in the basement of an American embassy. The adjoining tables were inches away. This didn't really matter, since everyone else was shouting, too, and maybe because the adage that no one eavesdrops on a loudmouth but strains to hear a whisperer applied in this place. The restaurant was ostentatiously humble but in truth it was upscale, full of sleek, expensively dressed Han who almost certainly went to college in the United States and spoke excellent English.

He said, "So you think you're being watched."

"You could say that."

"It's your job to say it, kid. Yes or no?"

"Yes."

"Why?" He spoke with his mouth full.

"Because I see the same twelve faces every time I go out."

"*Twelve?*"

"Four rotating teams of three."

"Wow. You can remember twelve Chinese faces? Describe them."

I did as he asked. He went back to his fish, all the while staring at me out of that mask. Flecks of carp had lodged in his mustache.

This man was an ass, or for some reason wanted me to think that he was an ass. His behavior, I knew, was meant to discomfit, to intimidate, to gain the upper hand. I had learned about the technique at training camp from a teacher of interrogation and agent-handling methods who took these tricks as seriously as Steve seemed to do. The instructor believed it was a good idea on first contact to let the agent think he was smarter than his case officer. This made it easier to manipulate the agent. I wanted to get out of there, to get myself fired, to go back to Mei. I could teach English like the other Americans did. I was tempted to throw some money disdainfully on the table as my share of the bill and leave with dignity. But even then, green as I was, I had more sense than that. Why would Mei be interested in an English teacher? And even if she was interested, she would be lost to me because her handlers would certainly assign her to another, more productive case.

Finally Steve spoke. "I am instructed to ask you a question and give you a message," he said. "The question is, Why do you think your dirty dozen are watching *you*?"

"Who else would they be watching?"

"Very good question," he said. "You should think about it, turn it over in your mind, see if there's anyone in your life who's more interesting than you."

I said, "I'll work on that."

Steve ignored me. I took this as permission to speak. I said, "If that's the question, what's the message?"

"Good news," he said. "CI is interested in you."

He waited—intent, almost smiling—for my reaction. I probably blanched. *CI?* Counterintelligence was interested in me? My bravado wavered. CI was Headquarters's bad dream. Its job was to know everything about everybody. However, nobody was allowed to know anything about it, including its methods and its success rate. Night and day, in peace and war, the men and women of the counterintelligence division were on the lookout not only for enemy spies, but also for traitors, for sleepers, for the inexplicably nervous, for spendthrifts who couldn't explain where their money came from. They tailed guys who chase women, women who sleep around, homosexuals, neurotic virgins. Their job was to finger the bad guy inside every good guy and banish the sinner to outer darkness. For CI, no holds were barred, no one was above suspicion except themselves, and nobody had the power to do unto them as they did unto others.

Now Steve was letting me know these demons were after me. Was it because I had committed fornication? Or was it something I had omitted to do? I was unlikely to find out tonight. Steve continued to hold me in his contemptuous gaze.

I said, "Gee, that's interesting. Did they tell you why they're interested in some Insignificant McNobody like me?"

"Interested in some what?" Steve said.

"A joke. Forget it."

"You think this is a joke?"

"No, but you're making me nervous. When I'm nervous I make jokes." I thought I owed him that much obsequiousness.

"You should try to overcome that," Steve said. "Answer the original question. Why do you think it's you who's being surveilled?"

"I thought I'd already explained that. Because these people follow me wherever I go."

"You haven't gotten beyond that simple explanation?"

"I guess not. What's the complex explanation?"

"You've got a girl, right?"

"Yes."

"Name?"

"Mei."

"Mei what, or I guess I should say What Mei. I want her full name, or the name she said was her name."

"I don't know."

"You don't know. Have you asked?"

"That's not the way we work. We ask each other no questions."

"She doesn't know your name either?"

"Unless she's a Guoanbu asset on assignment, no."

"How did you meet?"

"She crashed her bike into mine."

"How long ago?"

"Months."

"You saw no need to report this?"

"I reported the accident to my pen pal and submitted an expense account item for the new bike I bought her."

"How much?"

"About a thousand, U.S."

Steve whistled. "But not a word since?"

"No."

"You really are something, kid. No wonder CI is interested in you."

He was sneering. The temptation to make things worse was great, but I resisted it. No response from Steve, but I was used to that by now. The silence was heavy, Steve's manner was disdainful, and Steve such a shit that summary dismissal from the service did not seem to be an unlikely next move.

I said, "So what now?"

"Carry on," Steve said. "Change nothing. Be your usual harmless self. But be careful, my friend. You've got yourself into something you may not be able to get yourself out of."

"And let me guess. I'll get no help."

He pointed a forefinger. "You got it. Lucky you."

He called for the check, paid it with a big tip, kidded around with the host. Then he stood up as if to go. I stood up too. I was taller than Steve, and angrier.

I said, "Is that the message you said you were instructed to give me?"

"No, that was just me taking pity," Steve said. "The message is, you may be traveling soon. Your pen pal will provide the details."

And then he walked out.

3

I had cycled to my meeting with Steve and when I emerged from the hotel garage, wheeling my bike, there they were, well back in the crowd, two men and a woman, ready to leap into the saddle. It was five or six kilometers from the hotel to my place, so they switched riders every click or so. In their clockwork way they always did this just as I turned a corner and they were out of sight for the moment. Then they would pop up again in my mirrors. The bikes were always the same, so a keen-eyed operative like myself was able to keep track of the familiar faces in my wake. Taking advantage of Steve's expert advice to just be my dim-witted fictitious self, I made no attempt to shake them.

It was almost dark when I reached my building. I was warmed by the thought that Mei would soon be home. It had been a hot day. I was sweaty but Mei liked me that way, or so she said—every once in a while she took one of my smelly T-shirts home with her as a nightgown—so I decided not take a shower. She usually arrived at about seven for my Mandarin lesson, and then we would have supper and a couple of beers, and then Mei would test my Mandarin again, and tonight we would watch a DVD of *Destry Rides Again* I had bought on the street because, as I planned to tell her, no one can understand U.S. English properly unless she can unscramble the lyrics when Marlene Dietrich sings "See What the Boys in the Backroom Will Have." That was the routine. I liked everything about it. I liked everything about the life that Mei and I were living—even the tiny pre-Mao apartment I had rented as an element of my cover as a poor, feckless if somewhat overage student. The walls bulged, the concrete floor had waves in it so that the furniture tipped, the sputtering plumbing had air pockets, the electricity came and went.

Waiting for Mei, listening to Ella Fitzgerald sing the blues, I fell asleep. I woke at nine. No Mei. This was a disappointment, but I felt no stab of panic. Sometimes, as when her period started or she had an impulse to skip me for a night, she just didn't show up. I had no phone number for her, no address, no true name, no hope of finding her in a city of twenty-three million in which maybe a million of the females were named Mei and the Mei I knew was almost certainly not named Mei. I waited another hour, spent repeating my memorization for the day (a passage from Laozi's *Daodejing*) into a recorder. By now I was hungry. Because I had no refrigerator, Mei always brought supper with her, collecting exactly my half of the cost before we ate, and since I had eaten the leftovers for breakfast, there was no food in the house. I decided to go out. It would serve Mei right if she arrived and found me gone, though I fervently hoped she'd hang around until I got back.

The night was almost as suffocating as the day had been. Chemical odors, so strong that you could almost see their colors, wafted on a sluggish breeze. The endless waves of humanity rolled by more slowly than usual. On this night they looked a little different, smelled a little different, as if wilted after a day in the glare of the sun. Something else was different—there were no familiar faces. I searched the crowd to make sure I had not missed them. They just weren't there. Why? My watchers had been with me earlier in the day. They had never before deserted me. Had they decided I wasn't going anywhere tonight, and gone home? Had they been replaced by a new bunch whose faces I would have to learn? Were they shadowing Steve? I felt a certain unease. Breath gathered in my lungs. Life as a spook under cover in a hostile country is nagged by the fear that the other side knows something you don't know and cannot possibly know no matter how well you speak the language or how much at home you tell yourself you feel. You are an intruder. You can never be a fish swimming in their sea, you are always the pasty-white legs and arms thrashing on the surface with a tiny unheeded cut on your finger. Meanwhile the shark swims toward the scent of blood from miles away. At any moment you can be pulled under, eaten, digested, excreted, eaten by something else and then something else again until there is nothing left of the original you except a single cell suspended in the heaving darkness.

Oh so melancholy, and no Mei to laugh at me. However, the fact remained that I was hungry, so I set off into the night and walked, only half conscious of where I was going, until I found myself in front of a noodle place Mei and I liked. She called it the Dirty Shirt after the proprietor's soup-stained singlet. I ordered a bowl of noodles and slurped them down. One doesn't savor fast food in China, where everyone except the Westernized elite, seldom seen in this neighborhood, takes care of bodily needs as unceremoniously as possible and gets right back to business. I paid and left and went into another place a few blocks away and gulped a tepid beer. Still no sign of my watchers. When I emerged I saw a face or two I might or might not have seen earlier. I memorized these possibles and decided to take a longer walk to see if they were still with me when I got to where I was going. My plan was to travel in a circle that would bring me back to my building in about an hour. Because there was little elbow room on the street, I had to travel at the same speed as the shouting, spitting multitude in which I was embedded. Nor was there much chance of using shop windows as rear-view mirrors because there were few shop windows and most of them were dark. Now and then I crossed the street so I could look behind me, and sometimes I thought, though I did not really trust my eyes, that I spotted one of the suspects passing through the glow spilling out the door of the open door of an all-night shop. The street lighting on main arteries in this part of Shanghai was dim, and even dimmer in the side streets, which appeared as mere slits of darkness between the gimcrack buildings. I gave them a wide berth. The Chinese plunged into them as if they were wearing miner's caps.

I was almost home when they—whoever they were—made the move. Two men in front of me slowed their pace, the two on either side moved in and seized my arms. They were big fellows for Chinese, not as tall as me but solid meat. There were four of them until suddenly, as I stepped back, thinking to make a break for it, I realized they were six as the two behind me moved heavily against me. I felt a mild sting in the vicinity of my right kidney, then the heat of an injection. I lurched as if trying to break free. The phalanx squeezed in tighter. I might as well have been nailed in a box and there was as little point in shouting for help as if I really were in a coffin. I began to feel faint as the injection took effect. Would it kill me? It seemed possible. I was losing my senses one by one—first to go was touch, then hearing, then sight, and finally taste as my tongue and lips went numb. I could still smell. *How odd,* I thought in the instant before I lost contact with my brain. In Afghanistan, *the last time I thought I was dead, everything stopped at once.* I had never imagined that there might be more than one way to cease to exist.

I smelled cigarette smoke. But I was still in darkness, still in silence, still blind. I felt motion, bumps, mild pain as my kidneys jounced. I began to hear—a whining motor, the sound of the bumps coming quickly one after the other, as if water were slapping the bottom of a boat. I was lying on my back. I was conscious but not really awake.

Opening my eyes I saw darkness, spotted with moving green lights and red lights, and the stronger glow of small white lights. Finally I smelled water—foul water. I *was* on a boat, the boat was moving, I saw stronger lights sprinkled along the shore, heard tinny faraway music and knew the boat was on the Yangtze. Otherwise my mind slept on. I tried to look at my watch and discovered that my hands were bound. Also my feet. If I was taking inventory in this way I must be alive. I wasn't sure.

In Shanghainese someone with a tenor voice said, "He's awake." The tone, somewhere between *la* and *ti* on the diatonic scale, surprised me—a deeper, gruffer timbre would have suited the situation better. Somebody kicked me in the ribs, not really hard but hard enough to make me grunt. This person bent over me and opened my eyes with his fingers. I smelled his breath, cabbage and tofu. My clothes were wet. They smelled of filth. I wanted to urinate—proof positive that I lived.

In American English the tenor said, "Are you awake?"

I wasn't sure I could speak, so I didn't try to answer. My eyes remained open. He said, "*Wide*-awake?"

He and another man stood me on my feet. I fought to keep my knees from buckling but did not succeed. The tenor said, "Oops-a-daisy," and tightened his grip. I staggered toward the gunwale. They understood I wasn't trying to escape and helped me. I vomited over the side. Now that I was fully conscious the water smelled even worse. In the thin light of the stern lantern I saw or hallucinated drowned rats and other nasty things churned up by the prop. The Yangtze smelled like something that had been dead for a long time.

The tenor held a bottle of *maotai* to my lips. I took a sip, then spit it out. He said, "Better now?" His voice was pleasant, his manner easy. There was just enough light to identify him by race (Han), but not enough to make out his features. He sounded like he had grown up in Southern California. His family must have been in Orange County a long time if nineteenth-century baby talk like oops-a-daisy came to him so naturally. The boat bucked. I staggered. The tenor grabbed my arm and steadied me. No special effort was made to restrain me. There was no need. The only move possible for me was to topple overboard into this running sewer with my wrists and ankles chained together.

The tenor put the cork back in the *maotai* bottle and handed it to the other man. Then he said, "You're pretty relaxed. That speaks well for you, given the circumstances."

"Thanks." My voice stuck in my throat.

"No problem."

I gagged, turned my head, hawked, spat. The tenor waited politely for me to finish.

He said, "Can you swim?"

"Yes."

"Good," the tenor said. "Before we go any farther, I want to give you a heads-up. In a few minutes something is going to happen. It will not be enjoyable. However, nobody is going to shoot you or stab you or strangle you or hit you on the head with an ax. You will be given an opportunity to save your own life. That's it. The idea is to teach you a lesson, nothing more."

The tenor's tone was reasonable, sympathetic even, like a friendly hand laid on the shoulder of someone less fortunate than he. He seemed to want me to understand that he was not personally responsible for whatever he was going to do to me next. I wondered what I had done to deserve Steve and this guy in a single twenty-four-hour period, but here I was.

I said, "May I ask a question?"

"I probably won't know the answer. But go ahead."

"Are you sure you've got the right man?"

He spelled my full name and recited my Social Security number. "Is that you?"

I didn't say no. I did say, "Another question—two, actually. What have I done and who have I done it to?"

"I have no idea. Everyone says you're smart, so it shouldn't be hard for you to figure it out."

"Who's 'everyone'?"

"I have no idea."

I said, "Where are we?"

"On the river."

"Yes, but where on the river?"

"Upstream."

"How far upstream?"

"We've been under way for maybe an hour," the tenor said. "Time to get you out of that rig."

He knelt and swiftly unlocked the shackles on my ankles. "Now the wrists," he said. "Please don't do anything foolish."

Doing something foolish was exactly what I had in mind. There were only two of them, and by now I had most of my strength back. I thought I had a chance to fight my way out of this situation. Then the tenor raised his voice and said something in a dialect I did not understand. The other four fellows suddenly appeared. Apparently they had been relaxing belowdecks. That explained the cigarette smoke. Two of them grasped my arms, two more my legs, and the fifth grabbed me around the waist.

Then, as if they were one creature with ten arms and a single brain, they lifted me above their heads, grunted in unison like the acrobats they were, and threw me overboard.

4

The Yangtze was the temperature of body fluids. It was full of dead things and other foul matter. It moved swiftly, it seized me and pulled me under. If, as the tenor had said, this was an opportunity to save my own life, I was in trouble. I am a good swimmer for a man with heavy bones, but as I sank I realized that swimming had little to do with what was happening to me. I kicked, I clawed the soup of turds and piss and the hundreds of condoms that fluttered in the current like schools of albino worms. I willed myself to rise to the surface as I had done hundreds of times before, but I was being pulled down, as if something alive had hold of my foot. I was drowning. I knew this, my eyes stung, I saw nothing but darkness. The acrobats had taken me so completely by surprise that I hadn't had time to take a full breath before I hit the water, and I knew that I would not be able to hold that tiny gulp of oxygen in my lungs long enough to find my way to air. I was dying. Again. Clearly it was my destiny to do that over and over, but there had to be a last time and surely this must be it. I was not frightened. I took this notion as a good sign. Crazily I thought, *Fright is part of the survival instinct. It* *means you still think you can live, that at the last minute some immortal hand or eye will get you out of this.* But I was damned if I would die just because some nameless son of a bitch had decided I should. I swam harder, counting the strokes like I used to count the steps when I ran the football. Breath leaked from my nose, I could not see the bubbles but I felt them leave my body and knew I could not stop the rest from escaping, too.

My head broke surface. Something hard and heavy struck me on the skull. Seeing stars, I reached for it and grabbed hold and hugged it. In the darkness I could tell it was a metal sphere about the size of a medicine ball. I knocked on it. It was hollow, it rang. A container, a mine, a clever Oriental safe full of money or ancient texts? I wondered if my scalp was bleeding, but I was too wet and slimy to tell. I considered the consequences of an open wound in this world of microbes. My sight cleared. There was no moon, there was never a moon over Shanghai. All around me I saw feeble green and red and yellowish white boat lights. It was too dark to see the boats. On one of them the tenor and the acrobats were looking for a man overboard. I tried to put the sphere between me and everything upstream but the sphere was spinning, so I knew I was popping into view every few seconds like a mechanical figure on a steeple clock. There were more lights along the riverbanks now and more switched on in the windows of a wilderness of identical slablike apartment buildings. Using the second hand of the Rolex skin diver's wristwatch I inherited from my father after he shot himself, I estimated that the Yangtze was flowing at about twelve miles an hour. It was five-twenty. I should be in Shanghai proper around six. A splinter of light appeared along the eastern horizon. A slice of the sun followed it, coloring the blanket of smoke and poisonous fumes that overhung the city. A dead baby, white and bloated and wide-eyed, floated by, then something that might have been another. The sun, a misshapen parody of itself, strengthened. Its cantaloupe rays crept across the river. The water shone dully like the rainbow in an oil slick.

In the distance I could see the glittering towers of downtown. A little wind came up. My sphere had been floating in midstream, but now it drifted closer to shore. Up ahead I saw the great Yangtze Bridge. I was as close to dry land as I was likely to get. I let go of the sphere and trod water. I started to swim. Three strokes facedown in this cesspool were all I could manage, so I turned over and backstroked to shore. Several men were fishing near my landing point. Like time travelers from the coolie past they wore big straw pancake hats. Half a dozen plump fish quivered on the mud, slapping their tails as they suffocated. The fishermen gave me barely a glance as I staggered by, vomiting as I went: just another crazy foreigner.

When I got home, I found Mei in bed. She lay on her back, covered to her waist by a sheet, pretty breasts visible, childlike feet with red toenails sticking out below. She seemed to be sound asleep but as I tiptoed toward the bathroom she said, "Why do you smell like that?"

I said, "I fell into the river."

Her face was sleepy. "Ah," she said. "Better take a bath." Catching my full scent, she made a throaty sound of disgust. "Take *two* baths."

In the tiny bathroom I emptied my pockets of money and passport and keys, took off my clothes and shoes, rolled them into a ball, and threw them out the window. The hot water, all ten liters of it, lasted long enough to rinse away some of the oily filth that clung to my skin. Then, shivering, I soaped and rinsed, soaped and rinsed again and again and again, washed between my toes and inside every orifice just as many times, and kept on until the pipes shuddered and the water lessened to a rusty trickle. When I went back into the bedroom Mei awaited me, a bottle of alcohol in her hands.

"Lie down," she said. She rubbed every square centimeter of my body except the male parts, which I protected with cupped hands. As she worked she asked no questions, made no jokes. There was no accusative female "Where have you really been all night?", no jocular "Did you enjoy your swim?" She asked for no explanations whatsoever. She did ask if I had memorized today's material, 春日醉起言志 ("Waking from Drunkenness on a Spring Day"), by the Tang dynasty poet Li Bai, who drowned when he tried to kiss his own image in a moonlit river. I told her I had not got around to it. "Then we can't have our lesson," said Mei. "Go to sleep."

She got dressed and left. No word, no kiss, no smile, no scent except for the alcohol fumes that filled the room. Perhaps I am inventing memories, but it seems to me now that I sensed at that moment that something was unfixably wrong, that things were no longer as they had been, that the Mei I knew was going to change into another Mei, perhaps even the real Mei whom I had never known, that she had a new secret, that she was going to put an end to something, perhaps to everything, that she was wrapped in melancholy. So was I.

Why then, you may wonder, did I not ask her a single question, if only a simple "what's wrong?" or "what's going on?" Why didn't we fight, scream, threaten, accuse, demand explanations? Why didn't we do something instead of pretending that nothing was happening?

Well, Mei was Mei, whoever Mei really was or whoever she was about to become. And my mind was elsewhere. As soon as she was out the door I e-mailed Tom Simpson, no easy matter because there were no wild cards that described my night on the Yangtze. Evidently I came close enough, because Tom told me by return e-mail to get out of China the next day on a certain Delta flight, and to take nothing with me but my passport and the clothes I stood up in.

That evening, to my surprise, Mei arrived on time and brought a better dinner than usual and a bottle of cheap truly awful Chinese

31

chardonnay that we drank warm. I recited Li Bai's poem—I had had all day to memorize it—and the foreplay went as usual. Afterward as she lay on top of me I told her I was going away for a while. That I was leaving the next day. Her body clenched. She rolled off me. I saw something in her eyes I had not seen before. To my surprise, she asked questions—peppered me with them. All of a sudden she burned with curiosity. I had never seen her like this, never known she could be like this.

Where was I going? why was I going? when would I return?

I answered with the truth—America, business, I didn't know.

What kind of business?

Family business.

Was I meeting someone I knew?

Yes, but it was a business trip. No doubt I'd be introduced to strangers.

She turned over on her face, covered herself scalp to toes with the sheet. I went into the bathroom to get a glass of water.

"One more question," Mei called out from the other room. "Exactly how much does this person you're going to meet weigh?"

In my delight on hearing Mei, who never asked questions, ask such a question, I wanted to laugh. Instead I pretended not to hear her. I sensed, rather than saw, that she was putting on her clothes. Because she wore only three garments—skirt, T-shirt, underpants, plus sandals, this took only seconds. When I came back, she was gone.

5

At Dulles International Airport I was met by a pale freckled young redhead. She wore a wedding band on the wrong finger of her left hand. Pointing to herself with that hand, she said, "Me friend. Welcome home. Good flight?" I said, "Dehydrating. A little bumpy over Alaska."

Sotto voce, as if we were down the rabbit hole, the redhead said, "I'm Sally. Follow me."

In the parking lot we piled into a cluttered old Mazda. The load of soda cans and coffee containers and McDonald's and Popeye's boxes and CDs and old newspapers in back shifted and tumbled every time Sally turned a corner or stepped on the brakes. She dropped me off in front of a brick row house on a cul-de-sac just off Spout Run, in Arlington. "Same recognition phrase," she said.

I climbed the steep stairs and rang the bell. The door, gleaming with brass and varnish, opened before the chimes stopped ringing and I was greeted by a rotund, bespectacled Chinese who wore the regulation meritocrat chinos, tennis shirt, blazer, and Docksiders. No socks. He was a little guy, a foot or so shorter than me, and he had to lean back to get a look at my face. I waited for the magic words Sally had told me to expect, but instead of speaking them he let loose a torrent of Mandarin. I answered, briefly, in the same tongue. In the flat English of the Ohio-born he said, "Please repeat in Mandarin what I just said to you." I did so as best I could remember. He said, "That takes care of that. But we've got to go through the motions. Come on in and we'll talk some more. Then you'll meet Mr. Polly."

Apparently this fellow did not bother with cover names, because he neither offered me one nor asked me to supply one. We sat down at the tiny kitchen table. I had the impression that we were alone. The house smelled like a safe house—dusty, untended, empty. Quiet. You could hear the whoosh of traffic on Spout Run, but little else. It was one o'clock in the afternoon. The doorbell rang again. He went to the door and came back with a pizza box. He opened the box. Peppers, mushrooms, black olives. "You hungry?" I nodded. For the next couple of hours, we conversed in Mandarin, the level of difficulty rising as the minutes passed. He spoke the language beautifully. At last he looked at his watch and said, "Almost time for Mr. Polly. Let's knock it off." Obviously this chat had been some sort of test. I asked him how it had gone. "You get an A," he said. "Heavy Shanghai accent, though. But you have an ear, so it'll go away if you hang out with a different crowd." He picked up the pizza box and took it and its fingerprints and traces of DNA with him as he left without saying good-bye.

"Mr. Polly" turned out to be a homophone, a polygraph operator carrying his magic machine, an Apple laptop. He went through the whole rigmarole of recognition phrase, phony name ("Ed"), all the while sema-phoring that he knew things I could never know. He wore a necktie on a Saturday, along with a glen plaid suit that didn't fit around the neck or shoulders and was too tight across the stomach. He sent me into the next room while he set up his apparatus. When I came back, the window shades had been drawn, the lights extinguished. He sat behind me, so I couldn't see his face or his gear.

Being polygraphed ("boxed," in the jargon) is a mixed experience—part Frankenstinian medical exam, part simulated torture, part mesmerism, part fraternity initiation. It bothers most people, which may reflect the truth in the cliché that everybody has something to hide. This was certainly true of me, since I was sure this whole exercise was about Mei, my chief guilty secret. Otherwise, to the best of my knowledge, I was clean. I had never stolen anything or cheated on a wife or sold out to the enemies of my country or felt sexual guilt or believed in God, so they could ask me about anything but my Chinese lover without making the needles jump. I thought that the best thing to do was to think of something besides Mei. I thought about combat—not a good choice, apparently. The polygraph examination went on somewhat longer than usual while Mr. Polly asked his mindless questions.

When the ritual was over, I didn't remember a single thing he had asked me. After he packed up his equipment—it seemed to be okay for me to look at the forbidden object now that it knew my secrets—he handed me a manila envelope, sealed with a two-inch strip of Scotch tape that an enemy agent could have peeled and then resealed without leaving a trace. "Memorize, burn, and flush," he said. "You leave first. I'll lock up."

I walked for a while through the unpeopled neighborhood, then sat down on a bus-stop bench and opened the envelope. It contained a typed note that gave me a phone number to call at precisely 0743 EDT the next morning, a confirmed reservation in a cover name at a motel in Rosslyn, a Visa card in a name that matched the one on the reservation, a cell phone, and twenty crisp new fifty-dollar bills.

6

At 0743 the next morning I dialed the number. A man answered on the first ring and instead of saying hello, recited the number back to me in regulation style. I knew this was the routine, but wondered, *Now what?* He then gave me the same recognition phrase Sally had used. I supplied the response. He said, "Be out front at eight-thirty reading the *Wall Street Journal.*" Click.

The driver of the mud-splashed Chevy that picked me up took me to Headquarters. The destination surprised me. I was not asked for ID at the gate, a good thing because I had none—no plastic card with photo and hieroglyphics to hang around my neck, no nothing. Undocs— undocumented agents like me—never carry official ID. This absence of proof that they're up to no good is their protection. Otherwise, they are warned, they're on their own. If they get themselves into trouble, they'll get no help. If they do well, they'll get no thanks. That formula is, of course, catnip to romantics.

I was dropped at a side entrance where Sally the redhead awaited. Unsmiling, wordless, not quite frowning but by no means aglow, she led me to an elevator. There were no numbers on the buttons. She pressed one of them—no wedding band today—and up we went. We debouched into a brightly lit corridor and then turned left, walking past color-coded doors, Sally in the lead. No one had ever told me what the colors indicated. I still don't know. Sally walked rapidly, heels drumming. I checked her out as a matter of course. She was whippet-thin as was the American style, but after eighteen months of ogling Chinese bottoms, hers seemed broad. She knocked on an unmarked door, opened it, and stepped aside. I walked in and found myself in a space the size of the inside of a small house with the interior walls removed. This vast room was windowless but brightly lighted by buzzing fluorescent ceiling fixtures. Government gray file-cabinet safes lined the walls. Other safes were piled on top of them, smaller ones on top of those. Rolling ladders of the kind used in libraries stood in the narrow aisles. I tried to calculate the collective weight of the safes and failed, but wondered why they had not long since plunged through the concrete floor and onto the heads of the bureaucrats in the offices below. I saw no sign, smelled no odor of human occupancy. The possibility that Sally had locked the door behind me passed through my mind.

Then, as if from very far away, a deep resonant actorish voice—you could imagine it singing "Old Man River" at a class reunion in the old frat house—called out, "This way."

I stepped farther into the room and saw at its far end a desk at which a man was seated. He was gray of hair and skin. He was bony, even skeletal. His skull was unusually large, with a sloping forehead. He wore horn-rimmed reading glasses with round lenses. He was in his shirt-sleeves: red-striped shirt with a white collar and cuffs, bow tie. He wore a steel watch and on his right hand, a class ring. A single thick file folder rested at the exact center of his desk blotter. I assumed that this was my own file, plucked for the occasion from among thousands stored in the safes. Otherwise the desk was bare except for a very bright halogen lamp. No pictures of the wife and kids, no cup of pencils and pens, no appointments pad, no coffee cup—not even the smell of coffee, the signature aroma of American offices. Behind him, on the only segment of wall that was clear of safes, hung portraits in oils of old men I recognized as former directors of the organization.

A single chair stood in front of his desk. In the vestiges of a southern accent, he said, "Please. Sit down."

I did as commanded and almost slid out of the chair. Gripping the seat, I leaned over and looked at the chair legs. The front legs had been sawed off so they were a couple of inches shorter than the back legs.

The man at the desk noted my scrutiny and said, "You are a student of details, I see. Good."

I held my tongue. I was finding it surprisingly difficult not to slide out of the chair. The seat seemed to be waxed. You had to think every minute about keeping your backside in place. This made full concentration on anything else difficult. It was petty, a schoolboy prank, ridiculous. But effective. I realized who this man was. He could only be Luther R. Burbank, Headquarters's head of counterintelligence.

He opened the file, a surprisingly thick one for a small fish like me, and studied it for a long moment, as if absorbed in a novel. At length he looked up—or rather, looked over my left shoulder, and said, "We don't know much about you—yet." His voice, so like a tuba, fell strangely on the ear.

After Steve, after Sally, after Mr. Polly, after all the others except the plump, apparently sane Chinese gentleman I met at the safe house, I really had had enough of this nonsense. I said, "Then tell me please what else you want to know. That might save you some time."

As if a joystick had been manipulated, his eyes swiveled from his mountain of safes to the view over my other shoulder. He said, "I think you misunderstand the situation."

"In that case I'm eager to be enlightened, sir."

"No need to call me sir," Burbank said. "A simple 'you' will do. Relax. I'm interested in you, not suspicious of you."

He lifted his eyes as if to catch my reaction.

Burbank riffled the pages of my file. I expected him to ask me about my swim in the Yangtze, to be hungry for details about this bizarre happening. Instead, he said, "You're not exactly a stranger to me. I knew your father at school. Fine mind, excellent athlete. Great quarterback. All everything in track, scratch golfer, did you know?"

"I don't remember him mentioning it."

A smile. "He wouldn't, of course. Modesty was his style. Must have kept him busy. Handsome devil, gift of gab. Handy with the girls. His death must have been difficult for you. You were how old?"

"Eight and a half. I hardly knew him."

"Meaning?"

"I seldom saw him. He worked at the office all day and well into the night and played golf on weekends."

"You resented that?"

"No. He was the same as everybody else's father, he took the train before I got up, came home after I was asleep. His death was just another absence. My mother wasn't broken up about it. She remarried a year and a day afterward."

"What did you think of that?"

"I was fine with it. My stepfather was a nice guy."

"You look like your father. Taller."

"So I'm told. You knew him well?"

"From a distance. We were classmates, but we were in different categories at school—captain of the team, member of the poetry club. There were no Hessians in those days, and even if there had been they'd have been no competition for him."

Ah, so he knew about my downfall as a starter on the prep school eleven. This was inside dope indeed. He was letting me know he knew a lot more about me than I thought. His school was my school, too, and he was listed as a trustee on the masthead of their begging letters, so he would have been privy to the gossip. My file contained a lot of details. Knowing only the little that I already knew about files, I wondered how much of it was true. By the time our interview was over, I had a better idea. Maybe half of his data were more or less accurate—a surprisingly large proportion, as these rough drafts of reality go. At bottom, a full field investigation is a compendium of gossip, a way of seeing some hapless person as many unnamed others see him. Having heard what they have to say, what to believe? What to doubt? Burbank's snoops had covered the waterfront—my marks in school and college, eight or nine of the girls I had known as Adam knew Eve and one I had impregnated at sixteen in one of the many scrapes my stepfather got me out of with a last-minute five hundred in cash; my male friends, teachers both hostile and fond (mostly hostile), military service, what I read, what my politics were assumed to be, where I hung out, who I hung out with, what I drank, what I smoked, what I tended to say in the candor of intoxication. This had been a far broader and deeper investigation than the standard background check, which hardly ever turns up anything that is worth spit on the sidewalk. Evidently Burbank *was* interested in me, probably because he was so interested in my dead father. I assumed he had flown me back from Shanghai with the intention of telling me something that would knock my socks off. But what? Fire me, hire me, see what I had to spill? I picked up no hints. He played his cards close to his vest—the effect would have been comical had he been somebody else—under the pretence that he was not Torquemada and all this Q & A was just a conversation between two guys who had everything in common except age and wisdom.

"You went to college on a ROTC scholarship," Burbank said at one point. "Why was that? How did you do it? There was no ROTC program at your university."

"I got up early on certain days and put on my uniform and drove to the state university for class and drill."

"Why go to all that trouble?"

"There was no reason my stepfather should have to pay my tuition."

"You didn't really want to be an army officer?"

"Actually, I wanted to go to West Point. Didn't make it."

"Interesting. Not many Old Blues go in for the military life. How did your stepfather take your decision?"

"Stoically. It saved him a lot of money, and he had no reason to care where I went to college, so why would he be disappointed?"

"Well, in its way it was a rejection. He'd raised you. He liked you. He had plenty of money. He expected to pay."

Really? How would Burbank know? He had not asked me a question, so again I did not reply even though clearly he expected a rejoinder. When he didn't get one, he went on as if nothing had happened. He kept up the pretense that we were two preppy old boys chewing the fat—but in fact this was an interrogation. I wished he'd stop demonstrating his omniscience and come to the point. All my life I have hated to be questioned, hated to confide, hated even more to be euchred into pretending to confide.

Burbank said, "Bad luck, your reserve outfit shipping out so soon after you graduated."

"That was the understanding. You took the money and if you were deployed you shut up and went where they sent you."

"Afghanistan in your case."

Again I sat silent in my trick chair. I was getting a little tired of being told what I was and where and what I had been. At this point in our chat Burbank had assigned any number of admirable qualities to me. Few of them applied. It was like listening to an old queen trying to ingratiate himself with the straight kid sitting next to him at the bar.

He said, "You were wounded."

"Yes."

"What were the circumstances?"

"Forgive me," I said, "but what possible bearing can that have on this discussion?"

Burbank sighed. He was not used to having his patience tried. He said, "I am trying to know you."

To what purpose? In fact, he was assessing me and we both understood that.

"Then this line of questioning won't get you home," I said. "I remember almost nothing about it."

"I'd be interested in what you do remember."

"I saw the explosion but didn't hear it. It was so close I lost consciousness halfway through the first second. My identity dissolved. I went under believing I had been killed. When you wake up in a hospital after a bomb goes off in your face, you think you're coming back from the dead."

"You were in the hospital for how long?"

"Seven months."

"You survived and kept your arms and legs," Burbank said. "Do you ever wonder why and for what purpose?"

"Blind luck. Zero purpose."

Burbank looked like he was going to say something, maybe about God's purposes. He looked the type, and he certainly had the voice for it. He was said to know the Bible by heart. Behind me I heard china rattling. Burbank's eyes lifted. Sally appeared, carrying a tray on which she balanced two small bowls, a pottery teapot, and a plate covered with a paper napkin. Apparently it was coffee-break time. It was plain that this was not the part of Sally's job that she enjoyed most, but I didn't think there was anything sexist about it. No doubt you had to have a top secret code word clearance to enter this room and she was junior, so she was it. She put down the tray and went away.

"Have some green tea," Burbank said, pouring the acrid stuff into the bowls. "It's a good pick-me-up." He lifted the white napkin. "We have carrots and celery. And what's this? Tangerine segments."

Was he a vegetarian? For me, this was breakfast. The bitter tea did in fact shock the nervous system and clear the mind. Burbank ate the crunchy tasteless food with real appetite. For some reason, this was sort of touching. To my surprise, I realized that I was beginning to like him. We chewed and drank in silence, a great blessing. After the repast, Burbank—how can I put it?—withdrew into himself. I don't want to fancify. He didn't exactly go into a trance, but he was no longer fully present. His eyes were open but unseeing. I thought he might be meditating—it fitted in with the vegetarianism. He remained in this suspended state for several minutes. I didn't want to stare at him, so I looked at the pictures on the wall, and thinking hard, remembered the names of three or four of the ex-directors in the portraits. I counted the safes. There were 216 of them—three triple-deck rows of 72 each. Did they all have the same combination? Unlikely. But how could even Burbank remember all the different ones, and why didn't he just store his data on thumb drives, and lock them all up in a single safe?

Burbank opened his eyes and closed my file with a thump and came to the point. He said, "Tell me exactly what happened on your night on the Yangtze. No detail is too small."

I complied, leaving nothing out.

When I was done, he said, "Have you asked yourself the reason why?"

"Of course I have."

"And?"

"I haven't a clue."

"But you do. They said they were teaching you a lesson."

"Yes."

"On somebody's else's behalf, yes?"

"That was the implication."

"Does this not suggest that you have offended someone?"

"That's one of the possibilities."

"What are the other possibilities?"

"That the guys who did this don't like foreigners, especially Americans. That they're crazy or under discipline. That they were just having fun on their day off. That they had made a bet. That they were high. That it was a case of mistaken identity. That all of the above apply. Shall I go on?"

Burbank, gazing into space, considered my words for a long moment. Then he said, "In other words, the whole thing makes no sense."

I shrugged.

"You shrug," Burbank said. "Shrugs are the sign language of defeat. They get you nowhere."

True enough. I said, "So what's the alternative?"

He tapped on his desk with a forefinger. "In this work there's only one requirement, and it always applies. Take everything seriously. There is always a reason."

"Always?"

"Always. Our job is to look for the reason, discover the reason, overcome the threat."

"To what purpose?"

"Usually the issue is tiny," Burbank said. "But in certain cases it is an acorn that contains an oak. I don't know how these acrobats, as you call them, could have made that any plainer, or how they could have had any purpose apart from making you understand that this was your last chance, and the next time they come for you, you'll die. Don't you want to know why before it's too late?"

The answer was, Not really. What I wanted to do was go back to Shanghai, find the tenor, and throw *him* in the river. This did not seem to be the right answer, so I said nothing. Neither, for the moment, did

Burbank. He looked beyond me, apparently lost in thought. I guessed that this was part of the technique. The stillness accumulated. Certainly this man had no need to gather his thoughts or choose his words. Even on short, uncomfortable acquaintance I thought his mind was quicker than his behavior suggested, and far more capacious. I was quite sure that mental copies of everything stored in the 216 safes were filed away in the appropriate pigeonholes in his brain. I waited. This interview had already gone on for more than an hour. The strain of keeping myself in the tilted chair was taking its toll. My legs quivered. Abruptly I stood up, staggered a little.

Burbank registered no surprise. He said, "Why don't you take a little walk to the end of the room and back?" Limping slightly at first, I did as he suggested. When I was back in front of his desk, he said, "Do you need a break?" I shook my head, turned the chair around and straddled it, my arms folded across the back. This made it much easier to keep from sliding off. Burbank's expression did not change. He made no comment.

As if the conversation had never been interrupted, he said, "You haven't answered my question."

"I'm not sure there is an answer."

Burbank said, "You don't like questions. This has shown up in your polygraphs."

"And what does that suggest to you?"

"It suggests, among other possibilities, that you aren't easily intimidated. That you're your own man. That you see no need to impress others."

Was he *trying* to be clumsy?

Burbank smiled as though he read the thought. "That seems to be your most noticeable characteristic," he said, pouring it on. "Nearly everyone we interviewed remarked on it." He pointed at the chair. "For example, no one else has ever turned that stupid chair around as you just did, even though it's the obvious thing to do."

I was surprised no one had ever hit him over the head with it, but again I was discreet enough to keep what I hoped was a poker face. Burbank was doing the same, of course, because his masklike mien seemed to be pretty much the only facial expression he had.

"Now I want you to put cynicism aside for the moment," he said, "and listen to what I have to say to you."

I lifted a hand an inch or so: be my guest. It was a disrespectful gesture. Burbank ignored the lèse-majesté and went on.

"I want to put an idea into your head," he said. "What happened to you in Shanghai is significant whether you think so or not or will admit it or not. This is just a proposal for you to consider, no need to say yes or no right now. I have something in mind for you. If you decide to do it, you alone will be the agent of your fate. You will have to be smart enough to get the job done and strong enough, callous enough to live with it. People might die, I will not lie to you. And in a sense you would have to give your life to it also. I don't mean that it's likely you'd die like the others, just that this project would take years, almost certainly many years."

"May I ask who the ones who are going to die might be?"

"Enemies of mankind. You may think what happened the other night is trivial, but believe me when I tell you it is the seed of something that can be large indeed."

"Like what, exactly?"

"You'll know more when you need to know it. Nobody but you and me—nobody—will have knowledge of this operation. Ever. You will work for no one but me, report to no one but me, answer to no one but me."

I didn't know what to say to all that, so for once I wasn't tempted to say anything.

For a long moment, neither did Burbank. Then he said, "Do you know what a dangle is?"

"You bait a hook and hope the adversary takes the lure."

"Exactly."

"And I'm the lure?"

"I've been looking for a long time for someone I thought could handle this, waiting for the opening," Burbank said. "I believe you can handle it, and I also think no one else can."

He did? Talk about the chance of a lifetime. I said, "Why?"

"Because you're a good fit," Burbank said. "Because you keep interesting company. Because mainly you tell the truth if you know it, you're brave even if you choose to deny it, you have a good ear for difficult languages, you're arrogant but you try not to let it show. People trust you—especially a certain kind of woman. Most importantly, if I understand what you've half-told me, you seem to have died at least twice, or thought you did, and you didn't care. That's a rare thing. There's one more reason, out of your past."

"Namely?"

"You want to be the starting running back, as you deserve to be."

7

I was out of Burbank's office in seconds, out of the building in minutes. It was a Friday. Sally had told me as she took me down in the elevator that Burbank had mentioned that I might want to spend the weekend with my mother in Connecticut, then on Tuesday call a different number at a different hour. I called Mother on the way to the airport. Her voice rose by a tone or two when she heard my voice. For her this was the equivalent of a shriek of delight. She collected me at the train station. I was glad of the chance to be back in the country. Summer was coming in, everything was in leaf and color. I breathed more deeply than usual, as if inhaling my native air awakened some earlier self. Mother seemed glad enough to see me. She smiled at me, rose on tiptoes and kissed me on the cheek. She smelled, as always, of expensive perfume and makeup. In the car she behaved as if I were home from school, asking no questions about where I had been or what I had seen in the last year and a half. She drove her coughing twenty-year-old Mercedes with competence. She talked about her forgetful sister, about the wretched political slough America had become with everyone, even the children, turning into bloody-minded bigots, about a grocery store ("It couldn't be nicer!") she had discovered across the state line in Massachusetts that had wonderful produce and excellent fish and very nice cheeses. She was still pretty and slim and dressed by Bergdorf. She had no news. She knew only six people in town by first and last name. Nearly everyone she had known had died or been locked up in a nursing home. She had lived alone since my stepfather died. His name did not arise. Nor did my natural father's name, but he had been absent from her conversation for many years. It had taken her about three days after the funerals to forget her late husbands—probably even less time in my father's case. Men died and ceased to be useful, women lived on. Once a protector could no longer protect, though he was still expected to provide, what was the use of thinking about him? As far as I knew she did not have lovers, but how would I know? Remembering the sounds of frolic that issued from the master bedroom when she and my stepfather were together, I reserved judgment.

I soon fell in with Mother's routine. By day I went for walks so as to breathe as much of the crystalline air as possible. In the evening we read a lot—companionably, each of us in a favorite chair under a good lamp, Mother with her Kindle, me with a thriller from long ago I found in my room. Since my stepfather's departure, Mother had had no television set or radio. She disliked the news, abominated sitcoms and cop shows, thought that pop music was noise. The food was excellent. We made our own breakfasts, always the rule in this house, and a taciturn young woman, a recovering crack addict who had been a chef before she crashed, came in and made the other two meals and put the dishes in the dishwasher. A second woman, a cheerful Latina, came in daily, even on Sunday, and did the housework. On Monday, when Mother and I said good-bye, she patted my cheek. Her eyes were misty. This was not exactly a surprise. Though she had never said so, I knew she had affection for me in spite of the fact that I was my father's child.

Late Tuesday afternoon, from Reagan National Airport, I made the call I had been instructed to make at the minute I was supposed to make it. Same routine at the other end, but this time in Sally's voice. She told me exactly where to wait for my ride. The car that came for me was a gleaming black Hyundai, the luxury model. Remembering the battered motorpool Chevy and Sally's motorized garbage can, I didn't think this could be my ride, but it was and it was as shipshape inside as out. The driver was Burbank himself, who maneuvered through rush-hour traffic to Arlington National Cemetery without speaking a word and parked in an isolated lot. It was too hot to walk among the headstones on this day in early June. Leaving the engine running so that the air-conditioning would go on working, he cleared his throat and in his rumbling basso asked the question.

"Yes or no?"

I said, "Yes."

Burbank said, "You understand what you're getting yourself into?"

"I know what you told me."

He handed me an envelope. I didn't open it.

He said, "Go back to Shanghai. Finish your language immersion. Will a year be enough?"

"A lifetime probably wouldn't be enough, but my Mandarin should get better if I can keep the teacher I have."

"On the basis of the benefits so far, why would you do anything else?"

From another, larger envelope he handed me a blue-backed contract. "This changes your status from staff agent to contract agent," he said. "From now on you'll be working outside, under cover, on your own except for your case officer, me. The contract provides for a one-grade promotion, so you'll be making a little more money. You'll still receive overseas pay and the same allowances, so you should be rolling in dough. If you continue to do well, more promotions will follow. You can also be summarily dismissed, but that's always been so. Read before signing."

The contract was addressed to me in my funny name, the one I had been assigned for internal use only after my swearing-in. I asked about retirement and medical benefits.

"Nothing changes except the title. Contract agents cannot mingle with the people inside. In theory they cannot *go* inside. It will be as I told you. No one but me even has a need to know who you are or what you're up to. You'll be alone in the world."

Just what I always wanted. I said, "One small question. What about the tenor and his friends?"

"Next time you'll see them coming."

"And?"

"Evade or kill."

"Are you serious?"

"Everyone has a right to defend himself."

"I am unarmed and outnumbered."

"That may not always be the case. Buy what you need and expense it as taxi fares."

I read the contract twice and signed it. We talked a bit more. Burbank told me to stop e-mailing Tom Simpson and write to him, Burbank, instead, on the seventeenth day of every month. His name for this purpose was Bob Baxter—impromptu cover names like this one, don't ask me why, almost always began with the same first letter of the owner's true surname. In the envelope I found a list of new wild cards. Also my e-ticket and ATM and credit cards on a bank different from the one I had been using. I was to go back to Shanghai tonight and go on as before, living the life I had lived, playing the amiable dumb shit, hanging out with the Chinese, absorbing as much Mandarin as possible, staying away from other Americans and Europeans, especially Russians and Ukrainians and people like that.

"Speaking Mandarin as well as you do, with your war experiences and the resentments they'll assume those experiences generated, you'll be a natural target, so somebody, even an American, may try to recruit you. Just laugh and tell them to get lost. And let me know in the next e-mail if this happens, with full wild card description of the spotter and his friend who makes the pitch."

"Any exceptions?"

"Listen with an open mind to any Chinese who approaches you."

"And?"

"Let me know immediately. The person who hired the tenor and the acrobats may try to befriend you. Will try, probably."

"And I'm supposed to welcome the overture?"

"'Tis a consummation devoutly to be wished," said Burbank.

With that Burbank gave me a searching look, our first prolonged eye contact, and backed out of the parking space. It was a silent ride to the nearest Metro station, a silent parting. No wasted handshake, no "Good luck!"

It wasn't until Burbank had dropped me off and driven away that I realized I had neglected to ask what happened, what I was supposed to do, if he died before I did. He had transformed himself, I realized, into my only friend.

8

When I got back to Shanghai, I found no sign or scent of Mei. A ripple—come on, a tsunami of anxiety passed through me. I could tell she had been in my room after I left. The bed was made and all signs of bachelor disorder had vanished. She had sprayed the room with air freshener, a new touch. Did that mean she'd soon be back or that she had gone a step beyond wiping off her fingerprints and was erasing her own scent and that of the two of us, and this was good-bye forever? The second possibility seemed the more likely. Mei had a talent for exits. After six days without her I was very horny. But maybe she simply had had enough of the hairy ape. These thoughts were uppermost, but also I longed to speak Mandarin and had no one to talk to. My instincts told me she was gone. I'd never see her again. I had always expected this to happen—all those unasked questions, and maybe too much lust, had broken the back of our relationship. There would be no second bicycle crash. We could live in this teeming city for the rest of our lives and never bump into each other again. There was nothing to do but go out for a bowl of noodles and get on with my life. After eating the noodles and passing the time of day with the woman who sold them to me, I went home, read as much of the stoutly Communist *Jiefang Daily* as a political agnostic could bear, and fell asleep. About an hour after I drifted off, Mei—her old merry wet naked self—woke me up in the friendliest fashion imaginable. It was possible, even probable now that I had begun to see the world as Burbank saw it, that she was just carrying out her assignment as a Guoanbu operative, but if this was the case, 'twas a consummation, etc.

I spent the next twelve months in Shanghai unmolested by the tenor or anyone like him, exploring Mei's body and as much of her mind as she chose to reveal. We still arrived separately at parties, almost never dined in a restaurant or showed ourselves together in public, never sat together at the movies. We saw the local company of the Peking Opera— same performance as usual. I met more of her friends. Always, I was the only American at the party. Only one category of Chinese attended, *taizidang* as they were called—"princelings," the children of the most powerful of China's new rich. Strictly speaking, the title applied to the descendants of a handful of Mao's closest comrades in China's civil war, but Mei's friends, the B-list, children of the new rich, qualified for the honorific, though in quotes.

It took me a while to figure this out. Most of these people were smart in all senses of the word, brainy and absolutely up-to-the-minute when it came to fashion of any kind—clothes, movies, slang, books, ideas, dangerous opinions, music, dances. They behaved as if freedom of speech was revered and encouraged by the Communist Party of China. How could they feel so invulnerable? Easy—they were the children of the high leadership of the Party who were the new capitalists. As long as their fathers were in favor, they were immune from the police, from informers, even apparently from the most powerful components of Guoanbu, since they were openly living la dolce vita and denouncing the stupidity of the Party instead of building communism in a labor camp. Since Mei was one of them, she too must have a power dad. Like Mei, they had all done well at good schools and universities, in China and abroad. At least half of them were Ivy Leaguers. They all spoke English, often very rapidly, to one another, as if it were a kind of pig Latin that only they could understand. They never spoke English to me—Mei's rules, I guessed. In their cultishness they reminded me of American elitists, but less narcissistic and romantically paranoid. Unlike their Western counterparts, they did not have to pretend that they lived in a bogey-man, crypto-fascist, totalitarian state whose ruthless apparatus could mercilessly crush them the moment their fathers fell out of favor, or for no apparent reason at all. They understood that the absolute power and the absolute corruption of their rulers was their reality, knew as a birthright that the worst could happen tomorrow or an hour from now. So they ate, drank, and were merry.

Not that they didn't have serious moments or hidden agendas. The princelings didn't address one another by true name in the usual Chinese way, but instead used nicknames. I was called Old Dude, in English. Mei's nickname was Meimei, or "little sister." That nickname can also mean "pretty young thing," but in the next lower stratum of slang it translates as "pussy," so I didn't really get the joke or the insult. Just before my last year of living Chinese came to an end, a member of the cohort who was called Da Ge, or "big brother" took me aside. Mei was particularly friendly with Da Ge. He was as handsome as she was beautiful—in fact they looked a little alike. Naturally they paired off. They spent hours together in corners, giggling and confiding and holding hands. This looked a lot like flirtation, though they never danced together or made eyes at each other or nuzzled. In the back of my mind I thought he might be her case officer. Or the lover I suspected she saw when she wasn't with me.

One night, out of the blue, Da Ge asked me, while everybody else was dancing to the din of Metallica, if I would like to meet his father, who was CEO of a Chinese corporation that did a lot of business with American and European multinationals.

I was taken by surprise. I asked Da Ge why his father wanted to meet me. He said, "He is interested in you." Where had I heard those exact words before? Was Burbank at work here? Was this the first phrase of a recognition code to which I had not been told the response? Not likely. There was only one way to find out what was going on. With as much nonchalance as I could summon, I said, "Sure, why not?"

After all, I was following orders, because Burbank had told me what to do in a situation like this. Da Ge named a date and time and said a car would come for me. He didn't have to ask for my address. Next day I ordered a good suit and a couple of white shirts from a one-day tailor and bought a necktie and new shoes. I told Mei nothing about this.

The car turned out to be a stretch Mercedes shined to mirror brightness, Da Ge in the backseat. We were driven through traffic at a snail's pace to a grand private house in a posh neighborhood I had never before visited. Da Ge made the introduction—"My father, Chen Qi."—and disappeared. Chen Qi's appearance took me aback. I saw in him, to the life, the father who had died a quarter of a century ago. Ethnic characteristics were erased. I did not know how a Chinese could so strongly bring to mind a dead WASP whom I barely remembered, but the resemblance was startling. Chen Qi was the same physical type as my late parent— tall, muscular, handsome as an aging leading man, possessed of a smile that pleased but gave away nothing, abundant dark hair with streaks of gray, skeptical brown eyes projecting wary intelligence, perfect manners, bespoke clothes, an almost theatrical air of being to the manor born. Of course both men were the recent descendants of peasants, so maybe that was the key to their patrician manner. Before dinner Chen Qi and I drank four-ounce martinis—three apiece. These, in larger quantity, had been my father's favorite cocktail. The gin quickly made me drunk. The dinner itself, served by a drill squad of servants in tuxedos, was not the endless parade of Chinese banquet dishes I had anticipated, but instead the sort of twentieth-century faux French meal one gets, if one is rich enough, in a three-star restaurant in Paris or London or New York—four courses artfully presented, small portions, terrific wines. My host led a conversation that in its good-natured triviality mimicked banter. Again like my departed father, Chen Qi smiled his concocted smile seldom, but to great effect.

Over espresso and brandy in what I think he called the drawing room—a Matisse on one wall, a Miró on another—he came to the point. "My son speaks highly of you," he said.

"That's kind of him."

"Kindness has nothing to do with it. He has been brought up to be truthful and to keep me informed about his friends. Through him and others I have been aware of you for some time."

I said, "Really?"

"Yes, almost since you first came to Shanghai," Chen Qi said. "Not many foreigners get on in China as well as you do, let alone penetrate our life as you have done." He inserted a barely perceptible pause before the word *penetrate.*

"I've been fortunate in my friends."

"Indeed. And you had the right introductions. That's very important. Also you speak Mandarin very well—almost too well, some might say. Do you get on as easily with Americans and other Westerners as you do with the Chinese?"

"Mostly," I said. "But I've also met people everywhere who didn't exactly fall in love with me."

The smile. Chen Qi switched to English. "So have we all," he said. "Now I would like to come to the point."

Thereupon he offered me a job in his company. He explained that he did a lot of business in America, which, even though he was speaking English, he called by its Chinese name, *Meiguo,* the beautiful country.

I was startled by the offer. Chen Qi saw this and said he had long been in search of a young but experienced American who knew both China and the United States and could move comfortably between the two and help him and his corporation to avoid unnecessary misunderstandings with its U.S. partners and other Westerners. He understood I spoke good French and fair German and thanks to the army, a certain amount of Dari, was this correct? I would work directly for Chen Qi, taking orders from no one but him, and if I succeeded, as he fully expected I would, the rewards would be appropriate. My starting salary would be $100,000 a year before bonuses and stock options, with a substantial raise after a six-month period of probation. I would have free occupancy of an apartment in Shanghai owned by the corporation and an expense account. The corporation would cover the full cost of medical care for any illnesses or injuries that might occur anywhere in the world. I would have six weeks of vacation a year but no Chinese or American holidays except October 1, National Day, which celebrates the Foundation of the People's Republic of China, Christmas, and lunar New Year's. This job, Chen Qi said, was a position of trust, and he would expect my full professional loyalty.

9

"**So what was your response?**" Burbank asked.

"I told Chen Qi I needed a week to think his offer over and I'd give him my answer when I got back from the States."

"How did he react to that?"

"He seemed to be okay with it," I said. "He asked why I was going home."

"And?"

"I told him I was going to visit my aged mother."

"Then you'd better make sure you visit her," Burbank said. "The eyes of China are upon you."

I had gotten off an airplane less than an hour earlier and had spent every moment of that time giving Burbank a detailed report of my conversation with Chen Qi. Burbank and I were seated in a Starbucks in Tysons Corner, Virginia. The place was almost empty at this time of day.

Burbank sipped his milky coffee and made a face. It must have seemed insipid after green tea. Disdainfully he slid the paper cup across the tabletop until it was out of reach. My news had had a visible effect on him. This was something new. Clearly this bolt from the blue gave him something to think about, and I supposed that thinking was what he was doing now. He had fallen into one of his mini-meditations. I waited for him to come back to this world.

After a minute or two, a shorter interval than usual, Burbank revived and said, "What was your reply to the bit about full professional loyalty?"

"I asked if my loyalty to him was supposed to supersede my loyalty to the United States."

"And he said?"

"That that particular issue would never arise."

"Even though it has already arisen. You are no longer a dangle. You are a penetration agent. He's taken the bait."

Or maybe *we* had. I left this thought unspoken.

Burbank said, "What questions did he ask you about your background, your qualifications?"

"None. I assumed he must already know everything he needed to know."

"A reasonable assumption. They've been assessing you for two and a half years—maybe longer, seeing that you majored in Chinese and your teachers were Chinese, no?"

"Some of them were," I said. "Neither they nor anyone I met in Shanghai ever asked me a personal question."

"Of course they didn't," Burbank said. "Chen Qi, or whoever in the background put him onto you, probably had some New York law firm run a background investigation on you. Perfectly legal, forever confidential under American law—attorney-client relationship."

"Why would they be interested?"

"Because you're a catch. You've got potential. Especially for them."

"A multibillion-dollar Chinese corporation wants to pay a hundred thousand a year for potential?"

"They do it every day. To them, if in fact it's them paying the bill instead of some shadowy third party, a hundred grand is chicken feed."

"You think Chen Qi is a puppet?"

"I think Chen Qi is a loyal Party man who has done extremely well for himself and would roast his own mother on a spit to keep what he has."

"In short, we're dealing, in your opinion, with Guoanbu."

"If we're lucky," Burbank said.

I was lost. Burbank was going to order me to take this job. He was going to order me to go to work—actually, pretend to go to work—for Chinese intelligence. I knew this before the sound of his voice died. I needed a moment to get myself together. I could tell by the look of him that Burbank wanted to get out of Starbucks, wanted to go to some bleak location, park the car, and condemn me to my fate. I had long since drunk my double espresso. After the flight, after forty minutes of Burbank, I needed more caffeine. I said, "I'm going to get another coffee. Want anything?"

He said, "God, no. Order the coffee to go. We can't continue this conversation here."

At least he was predictable. While I was at the counter, Burbank made a phone call. It lasted maybe five seconds. Inside the immaculate Hyundai he said nothing. Now he seemed to be meditating and driving at the same time. I slept, waking up when he braked or made a sharp turn, then going under again. We took country roads, one after the other, and somewhere west of Leesburg, he pulled up to an isolated barn that had been converted into a house. It had a keyboard lock. Burbank entered the combination and we went inside. It was cool, nicely furnished, the walls hung with large hyperrealistic paintings that looked like the next stage of photography. All were depressing—mournful swollen pregnant girls whose fetuses were visible as in sonograms, curly-haired, beautiful brown children wearing prostheses, ruddy workers in hard hats, faces frozen in terror as if watching a mushroom cloud in the last nanosecond of their lives.

"Not very cheerful," Burbank said. "The caretaker is the painter. Believe it or not, she sells this stuff for good money."

By now it was early evening. To my surprise he poured drinks—single malt scotch—and shook unsalted nuts from a can into a bowl. Like the methodical spy he was, he turned on the stereo to defeat listening devices that one really would not expect to be present in a safe house. All the more reason, according to the unwritten manual, to take precautions. Believe nothing. Trust no one. Every lock can be picked, every flap unglued, every seal counterfeited, every friend suborned.

Burbank crossed his leg, thin ankle resting on bony kneecap. He said, "Can you stay awake?"

"Possibly."

"Try. This meeting may go on for a while. We have a lot to talk about. Let me know if you get to the point where you can't concentrate."

"If I fall sleep, that's the signal."

Burbank did not acknowledge the pleasantry. "For starters," he said, "let me ask you what you think of Chen Qi's offer."

"I think it's genuine in its way," I said. "He has some reason for hiring me. His offer was bizarre. I think he knew that I saw what he was up to, or wondered what he was up to, and that he wanted me to draw certain conclusions from it."

"Like what?"

"Like the offer actually came from Guoanbu, that he *was* Guoanbu, that I was caught in the flypaper."

"He was threatening in manner?"

"Far from it. He was as civilized as they come, on the surface. He reminded me of my father."

Burbank lifted a palm. "Explain."

"There are physical and other resemblances."

Burbank gave me a quizzical look but asked for no details. I wondered if I had been wise to feed him this psychic clue. Burbank seemed to be wondering the same thing, using his own unique terms of reference. I was too tired to regret my words or worry about their effect on him.

At 6:00 P.M. exactly Burbank stopped asking questions, turned off the stereo, and tuned into the evening news. Drinking scotch and chomping on nuts, he was absorbed by today's recycling of yesterday's stories. I hadn't watched American television for a long time, and almost never the news, so I recognized neither the anchorperson nor the hot topics. In minutes I went to sleep. An hour later, when Burbank switched off the set, I woke up and stumbled into the bathroom. When I came back I saw no sign of him. Was he in another bathroom? A long time passed. I looked in the master bath. He wasn't there. I called hello. No response. I turned on the outside lights. The Hyundai was gone. It was raining, sheets of it. Well, if he didn't come back, I could always go back to sleep. I was hungry. I looked in the refrigerator. Lettuce, celery, carrots, low-fat yogurt, red and yellow Jell-O, a lemon with a strip of peel removed, an unripe melon, two minibottles of water. In the freezer, two frozen organic dinners (vegetarian). I was looking at the demented paintings again when Burbank came back, a six-pack of microbrew lager in one hand and a bag from a sandwich shop in another. I smelled hot tomatoey American food. He put his packages on the kitchen table and said, "One tofu with sprouts, arugula and roasted red pepper, one meatball with provolone, red onions, hot peppers, and black olives. Which do you want?"

"The meatballs."

"Sit ye down," said Burbank.

To the prodigal home from China, the meal was at least as delicious as the mixture of canned pork and beans and canned spaghetti that Nick Adams, just back from epicurean Paris, mixed together, as I remembered it, over a campfire in Hemingway's "Big Two-Hearted River." Fearful that the beer would put me back to sleep, I drank the water, stealing the second tiny bottle for good measure.

When we finished, Burbank tidied up, putting the debris back into the sandwich bag, washing his beer bottle and my water bottles with soap, presumably to erase our fingerprints, brushing the crumbs into his hand, then into the bag, wiping the tabletop with a sponge, then with a paper towel. He looked happy. Apparently the indoor picnic had been as much of a treat for him as for me.

He brewed some green tea for himself. I drank instant espresso. We remained at the kitchen table. I was glad not to be in the same room with the caretaker's paintings. Burbank waited for his tea to cool, then drank it in a single thirsty gulp.

He said, "What really do you make of this offer of Chen Qi's?"

We had already discussed this in mind-numbing detail, but I went along, as I was paid to do. I said, "As you said, Guoanbu comes to mind."

"Why? Do you suspect that girl who's teaching you Mandarin?"

The answer, of course, was yes, but I didn't want to betray Mei to the likes of Burbank. If *betray* was the word. More than once the thought had crossed my mind that she was being run not by Guoanbu but by Burbank. Her objectives were his objectives: be my crammer in Mandarin, put me in touch with young Chinese who might someday be useful, fuck me cross-eyed to keep me away from sexual technicians from Guoanbu. Just as often, I told myself she could not be working for anyone but Guoanbu. If the usual rules applied, she had been setting me up all along for Chen Qi's recruitment pitch. Only at certain moments did I think she was nothing more than a lusty woman who just happened to have a thing about hairy Americans.

To Burbank I said, "What do *you* think?"

"I think it's a golden opportunity," Burbank said.

"For whom? To do what?"

"For us. To do what we do."

"You don't think it's a trap?"

He snorted in amusement. "Of course it is, in the opposition's calculations," he said. "But that can be an advantage for our side. Some of the best operations we've ever run involved walking into a trap—or, to be more exact, by pretending to be stupid enough to do so. The idea is to demonstrate your low IQ, move the trap, change the bait so the trapper goes looking for his missing trap and steps on it himself and has to chew off his own leg to escape."

Burbank's face positively glowed as he imparted this wisdom. As the animal for whom the trap was being baited and set, I found it hard to join in his enthusiasm. And yet I was learning something. He was showing me his mind, or more likely the fictitious mind he had invented for the purposes of this conversation.

Burbank said, "What do you think the opposition's purpose might be?"

The answer that sprang to mind was, *Same as yours—to own me, to ruin my life.* What I said was, "To recruit me, to compromise me, to double me, to expose me, to pump me out for the utterly trivial things a nobody like me knows. To embarrass the United States, and if I'm lucky, to swap me in due course for some Chinese agent of greater value."

"To surround us, in short. Do you play *weiqi?*"

He meant the Chinese game called Go in Japan and in the West. In Mandarin *weiqi* means "the game of surrounding." I had often played it with Mei, who always skunked me. I said, "After a fashion."

"Work on it. You can't understand them if you don't understand *weiqi.*"

"Do you know the game?" I asked.

"No one does unless he's Chinese. I play it. It's hard to find partners. Chen Qi is a *weiqi* man. The game is a passion with this guy. We know that about him. Work on it. Get a teacher, get good enough to play him. Beat him if you can. He'll think all the more of you if you do."

These were orders? What next? Who knew but what *weiqi* was the basis of Burbank's technique as a counterspy. Certainly I felt surrounded. It was time to change the subject.

I said, "I'm curious about something."

Burbank lifted his eyebrows. I took this for permission to go ahead.

I said, "Why do you have all those safes in your office?"

He thought this over. He saw what I was trying to do and decided to humor me.

"You think I should digitize all that information and store it in a computer?"

"Why not?"

"Because safes are safe," he said. "Because they contain things I need to know, need to keep in secure storage, one copy only." He was spacing his words as if teaching me some arcane truth in a language I did not fully understand. He continued, "Think about the origins of the word *safe,* the meaning of that term to the collective subconscious, think of what the concept of being safe has meant to mankind over millennia. We are weaker than the other carnivores. We fear other tribes of our own kind with all our hearts and souls. Our existence depends on our being safe from the Others, capital *O.* We are obsessed by it. The lust for safety is the reason why clubs and spears and gunpowder and nuclear weapons were invented. If experience has taught us anything in recent times, it is that computers are *not* safe. Computers are gossips, they are compulsive talkers. Touch them in the right place, with the right combination of digits, and they swoon and spread their legs. That's what they're designed to do—disgorge, not safeguard. That's what they do. Safes have no brains, no means of communication, therefore no such vulnerability."

I said, "They can't be cracked?"

Burbank ignored the question. He said, "You have reservations about this opportunity." No question mark.

"Serious ones," I said. "Don't you?"

"Of course I do. There are always reservations. Think about landing on the moon in that LEM. It might as well have been made of papier-mâché and it was built to fly in a vacuum, but Armstrong and Aldrin showed that it could be done."

Excellent analogy for the equipment for this mission, I thought. I said, "I have no wish to be an Armstrong or an Aldrin."

"You won't be. Others have gone before."

Yes, and never came back. I said, "Suppose we go ahead with this, whatever it is. What would it accomplish?"

"Nothing, maybe. But maybe a lot more than we imagine." Burbank said. "There are no certainties. There never are. But you'd be on the inside, and. . . ."

"Inside what? A corporation."

Burbank said, "A corporation, please remember, that is a wholly owned subsidiary of Guoanbu."

Burbank sounded as if he had taken it for granted that I would be as enthusiastic about this operation as he seemed to be, that I would be as unconcerned as he was about the risks that I, not he, was going to take. To myself, I was one of a kind, new to the world, never to be born again or otherwise duplicated. To Burbank, I knew, I was just one stone, black or white, it didn't matter which, waiting on one of the 361 squares on his *weiqi* board for his finger and thumb to move me.

"Penetrate the corporation and we penetrate Guoanbu?" I said.

"Mighty oaks from little acorns grow."

"And I would do what to make that happen? Please tell me."

"Build a network. Let them discover it."

"Who would be crazy enough to sign up?"

"The friends of your girlfriend." His voice was calm, his manner urbane, and he showed other signs of madness.

I said, "You're serious?"

"It doesn't have to be a real network. The Chinese just have to think it's real and eliminate it."

Yes, he was serious. I said, "And how do you propose I create this thing that does not actually exist?"

"The usual methods," Burbank said. "Befriend, befuddle, betray."

We studied each other's faces for a time. Finally I said, "Guoanbu will kill those people."

"Very likely," said my new chief. "I told you that from the start. But Guoanbu will never know if they killed everybody. Think about it. They'll lose face on a catastrophic scale. They'll be looking over their shoulders till the end of communism, which may be quicker in coming if we pull this off."

I said, "May I ask what gave you the idea I would go along with something like this?"

"Well, for one thing, it's what you're trained to do and paid to do," Burbank said. "Besides that, you have a chance, a reasonable chance, to slay the dragon. That would be a great service to your country. To China and all its people. To mankind. You will be remembered."

Remember by whom, I wondered, if only Burbank knew what I had done? I said, "I am at a loss for words."

After a long pause he said, "So?"

I know, I knew then what I should have said. But a new Faust is born every minute, so what I did say was, "I'll sleep on it."

10

I slept for two days in my old bedroom in my mother's apartment on the East Side of Manhattan. On her sixty-fifth birthday, a summery night, I took her to dinner at the Four Seasons. She had been to the hairdresser that day. She looked lovely. She wore a new dress, her large but not too showy diamond rings, her jewel-encrusted Cartier watch, her ruby and sapphire necklace, her sable coat. My late stepfather had been a generous expense-account tipper, so the maître d' remembered her and gave us a good table. The waiters fussed over her. She had a lovely time. Oysters, lobster bisque, grilled sea bass, Roederer Cristal throughout, dessert that made the liver thump, not a serious word spoken.

Mother was thinner, much thinner, than she had been the year before—pancreatic cancer, she told me the next morning with her usual absence of affect. The oncologist couldn't be nicer. I wasn't to bother about the situation. Her executor, my stepfather's old partner, would handle arrangements—cremation, no clergy, no eulogy, "just a simple brief sniffle at graveside," she told me. I needn't come all the way from

China to be present, if that was where I was when it happened. I wept, dumbstruck that she was mortal. Mother watched tears roll down my unshaven cheeks with a faint sympathetic smile, but did not touch me or speak to me. Just like old times.

For a couple more days I walked the streets or wandered through the Metropolitan Museum—thinking of Mother, yes, but mostly grappling with the Chen Qi/Burbank dilemma. It was almost impossible to believe that I was dealing with reality, but the fact is, I was in the grip of temptation, with all the fears and hesitations that go with it. I had felt this way before when, for example, I contemplated seducing the hot new wife of a clueless friend. She had married what she could get, not what she wanted, and reading her signals I knew she wouldn't say no if I made the move. But what about afterward? What about the tricks of fate, the unpredictability of women? What about remorse? What about death—my death, final and real for a change, at the hands of the man I had betrayed? Then as now, I had no one to talk to. Mother was not a candidate for confessor and wouldn't have been even if she had been in the best of health. The urge to confide in someone, to spill everything, to make this chimera go away by drawing a picture of it, was very strong. Standing before a Titian in the Met, I felt a compulsion to turn to the stranger beside me, confess my dark secret, and ask for advice. I restrained myself—this poor guy from Iowa, in the city for the weekend, would think, more rightly than he knew, that I was a nut case. A bartender would do—in one ear, out the other, another wacko on his fifth scotch. Nobody could possibly believe the grotesque truth. Passing a Catholic church on Saturday evening, I decided to go inside. People, mostly women, were lined up for confession. I joined the queue. I had seen confessional boxes in the movies but, not being a Catholic, had never entered one. Except for weddings and funerals, I had seldom before been inside any church or even heard prayers spoken aloud, let alone whispered them to the Almighty. As a child I was given no religious instruction. The name of Jesus was unfamiliar to me until I went to school. When I asked questions, Mother advised me to make up my own mind about God. She herself didn't think there was one. The fairy tales in the Old and New Testaments couldn't possibly explain the grandeur of the enterprise—just look at the stars, just imagine the infinite and eternal universe rushing across time and space to who knew what destination. (Her exact words: she talked to me like that when I was seven years old.) She hadn't baptized me, a fact that created misgivings years later in Headquarters when I was being cleared for employment by friends of the Savior. Did this guy have a comsymp for a mother, or what?

Outside the confessional, my turn came. In the dimness on the other side of the box (is that where the nickname of the polygraph came from?) sat a priest with bushy black eyebrows. I cleared my throat, but I didn't know the drill, so I said nothing. Sounding like a gruff cop near the end of his shift, the priest said, "Speak!" I just couldn't do it. The safe was locked, there was no key. I said, "Sorry." The priest said, "No doubt you should be. What have you done?" I said, "I can't do this. I took an oath." In a weary voice the priest said, "Then hell is your destination. Beat it."

On my way out I remembered something helpful. Mother, thinking no doubt of my father's peccadilloes and maybe of her own, liked to say that people did what they wanted to do. Always. They might say they did what they had to do, or that they had no choice, or that they were helpless in the grip of circumstance. They might even struggle against the inevitable. But the truth was, *they did what they wanted to do* even knowing that it would end in self-destruction. It was as simple as that. It was in the DNA.

In my case, at least, she was right. On the steps of the church, I called Burbank on my cell phone and said, "The answer is yes." The next morning, early, I said good-bye to Mother and received the two air kisses I knew would be the last she would ever give me. Smelling her Chanel No. 5 and noting the threadlike wrinkles beside her eyes that she probably would have had fixed by a plastic surgeon if terminal cancer had not intervened, I felt the fond amusement that was her idea of love instead of the pointless grief she would not have forgiven.

11

I went back to Shanghai. No Mei was there to greet me, there was no sign or scent of her in my room. This time her absence was permanent, but I had expected that. Her work was done.

Chen Qi, now the boss, no longer the genial host, welcomed me to my new job with a hard handshake but no smile. When I accepted his offer, his eyes were cold. He had bought me. From now on, like everyone who worked for him, I would address him and speak of him as Chen Zong, or when speaking English, "CEO Chen." There was no longer any need for him to be charming. I was given an office with glass walls on the same floor as his, a great honor. Thereafter, on the first day of every month, the sum of $8,333.33 was deposited to my account in the Bank of China. As Chen Qi had promised, I moved into a fully furnished apartment a dozen floors below the corporate offices, and commuted by elevator. It was a nifty but sterile place, something like a suite in the Hilton, with maid service and a fine view of the boundless city floating in its pall of smog. Of course the apartment was wired just as my office was wired, and probably equipped with cameras. I didn't incriminate myself by looking for bugs and lenses. Anyone who wished to do so could observe me to his heart's content. Why should I mind? It was nice, in a way, to be of interest, to be present in someone else's imagination, as Mei was in mine. I caught glimpses of her ghost every day.

At first I was given trivial work to do. Pointless though they might have been, these assignments were heavy with importance because they came directly from Chen Qi's office by hand of messenger. I hardly ever saw Chen Qi himself, and almost never saw him alone. Sometimes when he was receiving an American visitor, he summoned me. The other American was usually disconcerted to see the likes of me working in a place like this for a man like Chen Qi. Though they all smiled and shook hands and repeated my name in hearty tones, few such visitors were friendly. What was an American *doing* here? It was okay to do business with these greedy Communists, money was money, but *work* for them? Be their *underling*? Once or twice a week in the elevator or the corridors I ran into a princeling Mei had introduced me to. It was the same with them, and there were quite a few of them. They averted their eyes. They didn't speak, nor did I. Needless to say I was no longer invited to their parties. I never had been invited by them, of course, Mei had just brought me along as a curiosity. Without her, I was isolated, of no interest, and besides that, a potential menace because I saw Chen Zong, heard his voice, and if I did not actually touch him, I touched papers that he had touched. Did this bode well or ill for the fictitious network of agents and assets that Burbank imagined? Who knew?

I had expected to be used as an interpreter, but there was no need for my services because Chen Qi spoke serviceable English. Besides, he had a whole corps of interpreters. One of them, a jolie laide named Zhang Jia, worked in the office next to mine. At first she ignored me, then she was indifferent, then sometimes she nodded when we passed in the corridor. Gradually this mock foreplay escalated. Meaningful looks were exchanged through the glass wall that separated us. When I asked her to dinner she accepted without hesitation and spent the evening with me in a restaurant on a lower floor of the tower. Judging by the stares, interracial couples were uncommon in the restaurant. This did not seem to bother Zhang Jia. We spoke English to each other. Hers was flawless and ladylike, something like Mother's Miss Porter's elocution with a faint Chinese counterpoint. Unlike Mei, Zhang Jia talked about herself, providing her entire curriculum vitae as if reading from a script. This was regarded in CI circles as the likely sign of an agent regurgitating a cover story. No surprise there. Zhang Jia said she was from Beijing, the daughter of workers who had wanted a son but being kindhearted, refrained from drowning her when she was a baby. When she was twelve and a star pupil, the revolution discovered her and took her to its bosom. She went away to a boarding school in another part of China, where she learned English. She was an alumna of Wellesley College and Beijing Foreign Studies University. We dined alone in her apartment. She was an excellent cook, a pleasant companion. We played tennis on the courts in the basement. She was a fine player. I was out of practice and out of shape. She sometimes beat me and probably could have beaten me more often than she did. She had been good enough to play on the Wellesley varsity. We went to the movies in the tower's theaters and sat together. We played *weiqi.* She was unbeatable. Through all this chaste fraternization we mostly spoke English. One night, in her apartment, we got into bed, Jia leading me by the hand, and switched to Mandarin. She was a more decorous lover than Mei, but skilled.

After that first night together, we never spoke English again. As time went by, my Mandarin got better and better. Zhang Jia taught me etiquette, a subject Mei had neglected. For a long time I learned very little besides that and Mandarin and *weiqi,* but millimeter by millimeter, second by second, that changed. Zhang Jia was like a wife. She dominated, or thought she did, by submitting. Her job, apparently, was to manage me. She was diligent. We began to see Chinese couples socially—encouraging news for Burbank. They all lived in the tower and worked for the corporation. They were different from Mei and her friends—more real, more serious, more sober. Nicer. Clean as whistles politically. Children of the proletariat. They seemed to like me, but they could not possibly have trusted me. In accepting me, or making believe they accepted me, they were almost certainly doing what they were told. How could such behavior be otherwise explained?

Except for Zhang Jia, I was never alone with any of them. But in its way my friendship with her was almost beautiful. So was she, I realized, as her face gradually became as familiar as my own.

12

Sluggishly, time passed. Burbank had reminded me more than once that truly great operations took a long time to come to fruition. Espionage was a molasses waterfall, he said, it was brain surgery performed while wearing boxing gloves, it was like really having to urinate while following a subject who was walking on the roofs of cars in a traffic jam. "They'll watch you for a long time, years probably, they'll place temptations in your way," he had warned me. "If you make no false moves, the inevitable will happen."

At the office, things went well enough. Gradually, CEO Chen gave me more significant work. I saw signs, tiny signs, that he was pleased by the way I did it. At the end of the six-month probation period, my pay increased by 20 percent. I was given a larger office, even nearer to his. I welcomed this perk because it meant that the wifelike Zhang Jia would no longer be next door, watching me day and night. My affection for her was considerable, but it owed something to the Stockholm syndrome, and there were days and nights when I longed for Mei, who used to drop in for noodles, Mandarin, sex that was always new, and movies and chatter, and then vanish for the next twenty-four hours. My sex life with Zhang Jia was adequate—she was nothing if not dutiful and expert—but it was a routine that never varied, first the clever hand, then the clever tongue, then the slippery prize. Her idea of conversation was close interrogation, another sharp change from life with Mei. I fought exasperation and often lost. Zhang Jia throbbed with curiosity. Although our transparent offices no longer adjoined, she found ways to keep me under observation. Who was that on the telephone when I was so animated? Why was I so often away from my desk, and when I was out of sight for ten minutes, what had I been doing at the mystery destination or destinations? I wondered if she had an earpiece concealed beneath her thick gleaming hair so that a hidden interrogator could feed her questions, as a television producer feeds them to the perky blonde with the microphone. Even though there was no such thing as an empty space in Shanghai, I fantasized running into Mei in an elevator where we were alone. She would hit the red emergency STOP button, ignore the cameras, and say hello as only Mei could. The weight would lift from my chest. Empty dreams.

Chen Qi began taking me with him on trips abroad. He traveled in the company jet, I flew commercial, leaving a couple of days earlier to make sure all was as it should be on his arrival and he would not waste a minute. In private he was still distant, chilly, curt. However, in the company of American customers he treated me as an honorary equal. As the money rolled in from Sino-American joint enterprises, I was better accepted by the doubters among my countrymen, who seemed to conclude that I was in it for the bucks, too, and therefore an okay guy. At meetings, Chen Qi would sometimes let me make the presentation. This happened more often if the people we were meeting were new to him. His English was good but not perfect, and he was wary of embarrassment. He understood almost everything the Americans said, of course, but often he would interrupt a conversation and speak to me in Mandarin, as if asking for a clarification. We were always on the up-and-up about what we said in Mandarin in the presence of Americans. Who knew but one of those smart young people sitting against the wall understood the language? Cunning, these ever-smiling Yanks. Half of the along-the-wall crowd were women, and some of them were babes. I had been away from American females for so long that I had become as sexually curious about them as I used to be about Chinese women. I remembered the sulks and the accusations, but couldn't quite remember how they smelled, how they looked and behaved with their clothes off. The urge to ask one of them to go dancing was strong, but like the asset under discipline that I was, I resisted. My American date would almost certainly be mistaken by Guoanbu for a Headquarters asset, and because the whole world believes that American spies are everywhere, there was no possibility whatsoever of evading observation. Unlike others from the tower who could only go outside in groups of two or more when on foreign soil, I was allowed to walk alone wherever I was. But I was under instructions always to carry a mobile phone so that Chen Qi could always get in touch. The real reason for this protocol, of course, was that the GPS in the phone told CEO Chen's security people exactly where I was at all times. I was under no illusion that I was ever alone.

American businessmen, I discovered, were just as paranoid as spies. I learned a lot of secrets while traveling with Chen Qi, but they were business secrets, which accounted for the Americans' suspicions. How did they know that I hadn't been planted on Chen Qi by some rival U.S. company that was paying me to conduct industrial espionage? They would pour me drinks and interrogate me—all the standard questions, always getting around to how come I spoke such good Chinese. Where had I learned it? "In bed," I would reply. They would laugh as if they actually believed the lucky dog.

It never occurred to me to report what I learned to Burbank. For one thing, though neither Chen Qi nor the American executives would have believed it, Headquarters was prohibited by law from spying on American citizens, and it took this taboo seriously. For another, reporting anything to Burbank meant being in contact with Burbank—the last thing he or I wanted.

I had last seen him a year before, at Mother's graveside service. Somehow she managed to live almost a year after our dinner at the Four Seasons. Because she didn't want anyone who knew her to watch her die, or to look at her wasted body after she died, I never saw her again. Twelve people attended the obsequies, as she called her burial rites—my dotty Aunt Penny, the anorexic recovering addict who had been Mother's cook and gardener, the Guatemalan cleaning lady, three women Mother played bridge with, an assistant undertaker, my stepfather's former law partner, me—and, lurking behind the monuments, Burbank. Naturally no clergyman was present. Aunt Penny, in good though quavering voice despite the November cold and the wind and the graveside mud on her shoes, read an Emily Dickinson poem—the one about Death driving his passenger in a carriage to the next world. The law partner spoke about the beauty and grace and unfailing kindness of the deceased, and about her brilliant, almost Olympian horsemanship as a young woman. The gravediggers waited some distance away, hidden, except when they peeked around a corner, by a marble crypt the size of a delivery van. As Mother's coffin, the urn of ashes inside, was lowered into the grave, Aunt Penny said in a loud voice, "I hope Sis didn't insist on being buried with her jewels. Those fellows just steal them. Strip them off the corpse's fingers after the family has left."

When it was over, everyone except me drifted away. I stayed beside the grave for a while, giving Burbank time to saunter among the headstones and take himself out of sight. I followed and saw a car—not the Hyundai—parked with the motor running, Burbank at the wheel. I got in.

Burbank said, "Do you have a cell phone on you?"

"No," I said. "Do you?"

"No," Burbank said. "No GPS in this car, either."

Dusk was upon us. Until nightfall we drove aimlessly on country roads, going nowhere, saying nothing, spotting no surveillance. Back in the village, we parked three blocks from Mother's house and walked the rest of the way by separate routes. Tradecraft to the max was the rule of the day—everything but chalk marks on utility poles. Because these techniques were a dead giveaway, I hadn't used them for more than two years except when I was in the United States. Burbank got lost, of course, as spies sometimes do because they're concentrating on what's behind them instead of where they're going, but eventually he found his way to the door. I let him in, threw the dead bolts, and led him past furniture covered by sheets to the windowless basement, where on weekends my stepfather used to watch ball games on television. The room was soundproof, so as not to bruise Mother's eardrums with the roar of the crowd and the babble of the announcers. It had a well-stocked bar and a microwave and a cabinet filled with canned chili and other guy food. Burbank sat at the bar. I went behind it, unplugged the telephone, and poured two glasses of Laphroaig. I drank mine at a swallow, poured myself another, and handed him his.

Burbank lifted his glass and said, "I'm sorry for your loss."

Was he now? As usual when I was with Burbank, words it would be wiser not to speak came to mind. However, I lifted my glass in thanks, and this time sipped rather than gulped the sublime, peaty varnish.

"So," Burbank said. "How's it going?"

"Imperceptibly."

He nodded as though that was precisely the word he had been hoping to hear. He smiled with his lips together. He commiserated. He understood. He had often been bored himself when operational. It was part of the game. It made the good moments better when they came, as they always did. He said, "Some guy wrote that the craft is like being in love—long periods of frustration, suspicion and loneliness, punctuated by brief moments of intense gratification, or words to that effect." He changed the subject. There were housekeeping details to discuss. I had been promoted to GS-13 ("It's a bit early in the game, but you're a special case"), not that it mattered, aside from the honor of the thing. Because Chen Qi was paying me more than twice as much as my government salary, and I was being allowed for cover purposes to keep that money for the time being, Headquarters's bookkeepers had offset my official salary against my cover earnings, so I was being paid nothing by the government. So far the bookkeepers had not come up with a way to compute the dollar value of my benefits, which admin regarded as part of my compensation.

I said, "You mean I'm going to owe you money when all this is over?"

"Of course not," Burbank said. "It will be written off, but admin wanted you to be up to speed on the technicalities, as they put it. They have no idea who you are or what you're doing. They just go by the book."

Burbank pointed to his glass. I poured him another whisky. He was unflustered. He was supposed to be. Agents got upset. The drill was to radiate calm and assurance, to reassure them, to set their minds at ease, to suggest but never say that a vast, powerful, invisible force was looking out for them every minute of the day and night, and you were personally making sure that the force would keep them from harm no matter what.

"Enough trivia," Burbank said. "What exactly have you been up to since the last time we met?"

With some omissions and some additions, I told him what I have already told you. As usual, he paid rapt attention. You could almost see the 1s and 0s, or whatever binary code the human brain employs, combining into data and speeding to their various destinations inside the vault of Burbank's bony skull.

"It sounds like things are working out pretty much as we hoped," he said. "Do you agree?"

"I see no sign of progress, but maybe I'm too close to it. It's not easy to know what Chen Qi and friends are up to. It's tricky enough, keeping a grip on your sanity, locked up in a tower with a bunch of people to whom you look and smell like an ape."

"You believe that's really the way they feel?"

"The Chinese are racists like everyone else, only more so," I said. "They see nothing wrong with it. I overhear remarks. I see the looks on faces. I know how I smell to them because they let me know."

Burbank was examining me with a new look on his face "Beware paranoia," he said.

He was telling *me*? Burbank was director of paranoia for the most hated intelligence service in the world. He lived and breathed paranoia. He was Headquarters's therapist, never dismissing the possibility, nursing the hope that his worst suspicions might turn out to be justified. The reality was, Burbank would have been a pretty poor chief of counterintelligence if he wasn't paranoid.

He refused a third whisky. I didn't ask if he was hungry. It was early still, and remembering the tofu sandwich, I guessed he wouldn't be much interested in what my stepfather's ghost had to offer. For long moments, he seemed lost in thought. Then he said, "You didn't mention getting laid."

"Should I?" I asked.

"Everything is relevant. For example, are you still screwing that wild woman you met on the Bund?"

I said, "No, but I miss her. She was good for the mission. She taught me Mandarin. Also *weiqi*. You advised me to concentrate on both."

"Then you and I have reason to be grateful to her. Her name again?"

"Mei."

"Surname?"

"I have no idea."

"Why not?"

"As you know, we exchanged no personal information."

"Just secretions."

I said, "That's disgusting."

Burbank said, "What word would you choose to describe an agent under discipline and deep cover who slept with a foreign woman for two and a half years and never officially reported that fact to Headquarters?"

"Discreet. I thought you must be running her. Now I'm even more suspicious."

"You are?"

With a smile (*"I'm joking!"*) I said, "If I never mentioned her, how would you know about her?"

"Many matters come to my attention." Burbank waved a hand—weakness noted, subject closed, sin locked in the appropriate safe. Let's move on.

"So what are you doing for poontang now?" he asked.

"For what?"

"Pussy—pardon the twentieth-century slang. This wild woman is not welcome in the tower, I assume."

"I have never seen her there. Or anywhere else since I got back to Shanghai. As you know, because I have reported it, I now sleep with a somewhat more conventional female."

"The Wellesley girl? The one who works for Chen Qi?"

"Yes."

"Was provided by Chen Qi?"

"That's my assumption, unless you know otherwise."

"Have you chosen the next bedfellow?" Burbank asked.

"I didn't choose the other two," I said. "I'm hoping for yet another nice surprise."

Suddenly Burbank laughed, a bark followed by a snort. It was startling to hear such sounds issuing from this mirthless being. Then, in his sudden way, he shut up and got lost in thought. For a moment I thought the conversation was over.

But it wasn't. Burbank's eyes refocused and he said, "About the Chinese ladies, enjoy yourself. I think your dingus may lead us in an interesting direction."

We talked a little more, pleasantly enough for a change, just passing the time of day. Before Burbank left by the cellar door, he wiped the fingerprints from his whisky glass, then dropped it into his coat pocket. Mother would not have been pleased. The glass was crystal with the Dartmouth coat of arms engraved upon it, a present from her, and my stepfather had been very fond of it and the eleven others—now ten—just like it.

13

On my return to Shanghai, Zhang Jia, sitting in a straight chair with her knees primly together, told me that she had met a prospective husband, a civil servant who was a fellow graduate of her university in Beijing, and that our friendship must come to an end. She wanted to have a child. For the sake of its future, its father could not be an ape. Her prospective husband was intelligent, upstanding, the son of workers, a loyal Party member. Wifely to the last moment, she cautioned me against being too much alone after she left. Until I found another woman, I should have lunch and dinner in the cafeteria. The food was nourishing and there were plenty of nice, educated people to talk to. Her friends would welcome my company. Perhaps I would meet another girl while shoveling noodles. At the very least, communal dining would be good for my Mandarin. I was speaking so much English while traveling with Chen Qi that I was beginning to make small but unfortunate mistakes in syntax. I needed to converse with people who would correct my errors in a friendly way. If the overwhelming relief that consumed me on hearing the news of her imminent departure showed in my face, Zhang Jia gave no sign that she noticed. When she finished her presentation she stood up, bowed ever so slightly in my direction, as if animated by some genetic memory of female submissiveness, and walked out. We did not hug or kiss. We had never kissed. Zhang Jia just left, closing the door quietly behind her. It was the most civilized breakup I'd ever had.

Not long after that, CEO Chen called me in and told me that he had decided that he needed a personal representative in Washington, and I was his choice for the job. My assignment was to keep in touch with his American customers. I should travel around the United States as much as necessary, keeping an eye out for new business opportunities, new American ideas, and the tides of American politics. Sometimes he would ask me to join him in the States or in other countries. The corporation had an office in Washington, and I would have a desk there but would not belong to that office. I would continue to report directly to him. I should avoid fraternization with the other people in the office. Chen Qi would keep in touch by telephone and e-mail. I would be provided with a new smart phone to be used for communicating with him and for no other purpose. I should carry the phone on my person at all times. After Chen Qi told me this news, he dropped his eyes and went back to what he was doing. To him, I was now invisible. Minutes later, when I was back in my office, a man I had never seen before brought me the new phone and an Internet confirmation for an Air China flight two days hence to New York. No one in the tower said good-bye to me.

A car took me to the airport. Another met me at Dulles. In the corporation's offices on Connecticut Avenue, a stocky, plain young woman with china-doll bangs and buttonhole eyes who introduced herself as Sun Huan, my assistant, showed me to my office. No one else made an appearance. All other doors were closed. The made-in-China Scandinavian-style furniture in my corner office was handsome in its way. The room was a most desirable space, filled with light. Someone—my first in-house enemy, no doubt—must have been moved out to make room for me. Sun Huan gave me the keys to my apartment, located a mile up the avenue, and told me the doorman's name. Very convenient, Sun Huan said. She lived in the same building and walked to work every day with her roommates.

Now that I was back in my own country, where only the FBI, the NSA, and various agencies of the Department of Homeland Security read other people's mail, I sent Burbank a handwritten letter, using an accommodation address I had memorized at our last meeting. I received no reply. No pay phones that worked remained in Washington, a serious loss to spies, whose three essential qualities when on the sidewalk were said, in pre–cell phone days, to be an accurate watch, a strong bladder, and a pocketful of change for coin telephones. One evening I took a chance, rode the Metro to Bethesda, and paid cash for a cheap throw-away, no-GPS cell phone in a shopping mall. On another day I took the Red Line to the zoo, and from the men's room called Burbank's old contact number. It rang twelve times. Nobody answered. I tried again a couple of hours later. Again, no reply. I flushed the phone's memory card down the toilet at the zoo and dropped the rest of it, wiped as clean as if Burbank had done the job himself, into a trash can in a movie the-ater miles away. Very wasteful, the clandestine life.

There was nothing to do but wait. Burbank knew where I was. When the situation began to explain itself, as in his philosophy it must, he would make contact. Or maybe not.

Evenings and weekends, I worked on re-Americanizing myself. I had half-forgotten how to live in my own country while I spent one-fourth of my life blundering around Afghanistan or lying in army hospitals or living a lie as every honest secret agent must do, or reducing my mind to rubble by speaking nothing but Mandarin and screwing Chi-nese women whom I could not permit myself to love without breaking my solemn oath of loyalty to my country and my craft. In my absence, everything had changed just slightly—the slang, the food, the music, the clothes, the drugs, the etiquette or such potsherds as remained of it, the conscience of the nation and its hopes and fears, the president, the Constitution. The educated class, always less happy than it deserved to be, was deeply, maybe incurably peeved. Many who died on 9/11 were people like themselves, who were not supposed to die in American wars. Now that the taboo was shattered, something worse could happen with even more disconcerting results. No one was safe, no matter how many diplomas he or she had, no matter how special he or she might be. Suicide bombers could not be far in the future—in fact, they should have started blowing themselves up in America long ago. This loss of immunity, this end of specialness, was somebody's fault, probably a hidden somebody or more likely a vast conspiracy of hidden somebodies. Mother had been right, America was askew. Anger was the fuel of politics. In her opinion, the atmosphere was worse than the sixties. Now as then, the nonconformists only succeeded in being all alike— same thoughts, same vocabulary, same costumes, same delusions, same cookie-cutter behavior masquerading as rebellion. Coming home to this country on the brink of a nervous breakdown was like waking from a coma and seeing two moons in the sky.

CEO Chen kept me busy running around the country to talk to harried executives who made time for me with the greatest reluctance. These were tough customers. They listened to my presentations with wandering minds. A deep recession was in progress. Business was slow. They had no interest in spending more money than they were already spending. Still, the work was not without interest. These entrepreneurs explained that they were biding their time until a new business cycle began. I had no MBA, it was true, but surely even I could understand that. Creative destruction was taking place. It happened at intervals in a free enterprise system. After the wrecking ball had done its work, something more profitable always resulted. Like Chinese philosophers of old, they believed in constants. The capitalists had their own scriptures, just like the Communists had had Marx and Lenin in their blood-drenched heyday. One irascible executive in Texas, his store of politeness exhausted and three drinks under his belt, reminded me that multinational capitalism had accomplished in a decade that which blundering international communism had failed to do in almost a century of effort—it had unified the world in the service of a single idea without murdering a single soul. The motivating force for this great revolution, he said, tapping on the gleaming conference table to emphasize each word, was the God-given love of money. That, he added, was the difference between an idea that harnesses human nature and one that denies it. "It woke up a billion-plus Chinese to their true nature," he said. "They're a nation of compulsive capitalists, always have been, and if they had channeled the energy they put into the Cultural Revolution and the rest of that Maoist bullshit into good old-fashioned business, they'd be running the world." I was sorry Chen Qi was not present to hear this, but then again, if he had been, the words I heard would probably never have been spoken.

Right after this meeting, I flew back to Washington. An American Chinese gentleman was seated beside me on the airplane. After an hour or so of silence, I dropped something on the floor. As I bent over to retrieve it, so did the Chinese gentleman. Our heads bumped. I wasn't much affected, but he was a small man, and he had a lump on his bald skull. He seemed so dizzy and out of it that I rang for the flight attendant and asked for ice. She brought it and told him, as if she were a trained nurse, not to go to sleep in case he was concussed. "*Concussed?*" the gentleman said. "Is that a word?" He held the plastic bag full of ice to his skull and soon recovered, though he must have had a bad headache. We began to talk about nothing. He spoke rapid colloquial English with a deep southern accent. He told me all about himself. I knew what that might mean, in terms of the craft. He was a third-generation American, born in Tuscaloosa, Alabama. He had served a hitch in the U.S. Navy as a gunnery officer on a destroyer. His children were all going to good colleges—Brown, William and Mary, Stanford. He himself had gone to Auburn.

He gave me his card. I told him I didn't have one of my own on me—I'd given them all away on my trip. This didn't worry him. Business comes first, he said. He said, "Do you like Chinese food?" He got out a pen and on the back of his card scribbled the name of a restaurant on Connecticut Avenue. "Excellent," he said. "The chef is from China. So is everybody else. Nobody but the owner speaks English, so you have to point at the menu. If you like Peking duck, his is the best in town. Very prettily served, too. I advise you to order it even if you don't like it, to enjoy the show."

14

The next day Chen Qi summoned me to London. He was accompanied by two Chinese in Italian suits. They were about my age. I had never seen either one of them before, but there were sealed floors in the tower, so there was nothing to wonder about except that they were now being revealed to me. Chen Qi always traveled with a couple of bodyguards, but these new types, comfortable in their suits and ties and quick to demonstrate how smart they were, were not members of the bodyguard class. They spoke good English, and to me, nothing but English. For a week, in meetings, they did the talking and the interpreting while I sat by, silent but tempted to raise my hand when something was garbled in translation. Chen Qi would not have noticed had I done so. Not once during the days we were together did he rest his eyes on me for as much as a second. I wondered why I was there.

After the final meeting, Chen Qi satisfied my curiosity. He drew me aside in the lobby of the office building and told me in Mandarin that this was my last day as an employee of the corporation. My return fare to the United States had already been paid. I would receive six months' severance pay. I could remain in my Washington apartment for one month. He had no criticism to make of me. I had performed my duties in an entirely satisfactory manner, but unfortunately I was a speck in the eye of the corporation. My presence made others uncomfortable. I spoke Mandarin too well. I copulated with a Chinese woman on company property. My ways were not China's ways. The authorities had noticed me and my unfortunate habits. I should go back to America, work in America, be an American. With my language skills and my experience of China, I should have no trouble finding a job even in these difficult times. He handed me an envelope. Then we were done. He turned on his heel without a word or a change in expression, and walked away. The hotshots followed. They would never give me another thought, and why should they?

There went Burbank's fictitious network—or so in my innocence I supposed. I felt a rush of relief but also, I confess, a certain sour disappointment. I may have loathed the mission, but I also wanted to accomplish it. All my life I had been given Everests to climb—beat up the bully, make the team, make the girl, get into a college I could mention with nonchalance at a cocktail party, and in the army, take that hill, kill that stranger, hold that position, recover from those wounds. Something was up. Something worse would come next.

Half a day later my flight landed in New York. I took the shuttle to Reagan National Airport, the Metro to Dupont Circle. Walking home, dragging my carry-on suitcase behind me, I passed the restaurant the Chinese American gentleman with whom I bumped heads on a different airplane had recommended. For months I had walked by the place every day without giving it a second glance. It was still open at 11:00 P.M. I stopped, read the menu, and went inside. The host, who spoke monosyllabic English, led me to a booth. I ordered a beer. I wanted noodles. Like my friend on the airplane, the host looked pained and recommended Peking duck. "You will like it," he said. "Trust me."

The duck was a long time in coming but finally it appeared, borne on a tray by an almost unbelievably beautiful Chinese girl. Smiling shyly, she showed me the glazed bird. It was whole and nicely displayed. She donned transparent plastic gloves, showed her perfect teeth again, picked up a razor-sharp Chinese knife, and carved the duck. She had a knack for it and she disjointed the bird and sliced its breast in minutes, arranging the pieces on a platter as she went. There was three times as much duck as I could eat, plus the usual mountain of rice.

When she set this feast before me, I spoke to her in Mandarin—a compliment on her deftness. Up to this point she had not looked at me. Now she did, with wide, startled eyes. Then she fled into the kitchen, heels clattering, raven hair flying.

A Chinese man, lean and saturnine, wearing jeans, Nikes, and a plain black T-shirt had just been seated in the opposite booth. He watched the girl go and caught my eye. No smile, but he had an intelligent face. He was unmistakably a native Chinese.

In English I said, "What was all that about?"

He said, "You speak very good Mandarin. Possibly she's an illegal. She probably thought you were an immigration agent."

"If I were, I'd certainly never deport her."

"You've lost your chance," he said. "By now she's in a car on her way out of town. Bad luck for the restaurant. She was an attraction."

He ordered a bowl of noodles. He switched to Mandarin. We had a polite conversation about Laozi. We quoted the sage's famous sayings back and forth. I asked my new friend what his favorite lines were. He said, "The one about a small fish being spoiled by too much handling." I said I liked the one about water, a soft thing, always overcoming iron, a hard thing. "Laozi is always relevant," he said. He quoted another passage:

"Why are people starving?
Because the rulers eat up the money in taxes.
Therefore the people are starving.
Why are the people rebellious?
Because the rulers interfere too much."

I said, "You sound like a Republican running for president."

"No. Laozi sounds like Laozi."

His noodles were delivered. He stopped talking. I left first. My friend, eating with his bowl under his chin, paid no attention. He had not divulged a single detail about himself except that he seemed to have memorized the whole of Laozi. This told me something—perhaps. Maybe he was a follower of the Dao. Or someone like me.

Trudging up the hill toward bed, I was too tired to care what he was or what that meant. *To be worn out is to be renewed,* according to Laozi.

15

The entry code at the corporation's office had been changed, so I had to ring the bell. Sun Huan came to the door and without a word or a smile, handed me a brown grocery bag containing my personal belongings. I gave her the CEO Chen–only mobile phone that had been issued to me in Shanghai. She received it solemnly, wrote a receipt, and shut the door in my face. Back on the street, I checked my bank balance at an ATM. The full six months in severance pay plus the dollar value of unused vacation time had already been deposited. This considerable sum, added to the banked salary I had not spent while I was in China, made me quite prosperous. I wondered how much of the windfall the Headquarters admin types would find ways to pilfer. Until they figured that out, I could afford to pay cash for a Maserati. I didn't have to look for a job because I already had one, or so I assumed in the absence of information to the contrary. What now? Should I just wait for Burbank to show himself, or should I try again to make contact? Was I under any obligation to report my news? The last time I tried to keep him posted he ignored my letter and stopped answering the telephone. I felt a twinge of resentment. Should I just forget about Burbank, draw out my cash, walk away from my contract, find an American woman to marry, have kids, live an American life as Chen Qi had recommended, and when the end came, be tumbled into the grave with a rattle of dry bones after every last penny and every drop of life had been squeezed out of me by the system and the wife and kids?

Although I had consumed no alcohol since the Chinese beer I drank with my Peking duck the night before, I felt slightly drunk—woozy, reckless, beckoned I knew not where. I decided to go to New York. Now. I had inherited Mother's apartment there, along with the house in Connecticut, some stocks and bonds, and all her belongings including her jewelry, which she had not worn to her cremation after all. The expense of maintaining the apartment and the house was considerable. I couldn't sell them because of the slump, so why should I pay rent? I withdrew a thousand dollars from the ATM, went back to the apartment and packed my belongings, which fit into one large suitcase and one carry-on, and took the Metroliner to Penn Station. While still in the station, I bought yet another cheap unregistered cell phone and dialed Burbank's number. The result was the same as before—a dozen rings, no pickup. Maybe he too had been fired, or been stricken with cancer, or died when a safe fell on him. Everything Burbank said or did was classified, so it made sense that his death would be stamped top secret. On the way uptown in a taxi operated by someone from central Asia who was just learning to drive, I sent him a text message, telling him in wild cards what had happened and where I was. Again, silence. I shrugged and went on with my existence. I had done what I could, and thanks again, pal, for wasting five years of my life. I thought about the future. Maybe I could become a banker. Or better because even more uninteresting than banking, get a Ph.D. and become a professor of Chinese.

It was good to be in Manhattan, where I had spent the winters of my boyhood, the summers having been daydreamed away in Connecticut.

I immersed myself in the city's money-gulping culture—museums, concerts, theater, movies, basketball games. I joined a gym. I visited bars I had liked when I was a kid, but they were full of kids and drunks, so I drank at home—four ounces of the Macallan before dinner, seldom more, never less. I didn't enjoy dining alone at the bar in loud restaurants at one hundred dollars a plate and being treated like a mendicant, so I usually had a mock-gourmet dinner delivered to the apartment. I didn't want company, and when women struck up a conversation in a public place, I was polite but distant. Nothing had happened to my libido. The problem was, I was looking for a Mei in a world where there was only one Mei. I wanted my Shanghai life, stage-managed though it almost certainly had been, to come back. Maybe I just wanted someone to talk to, certainly I wanted a particular face to look into while making love. My Mandarin, I knew, was flying away. Sometimes in midtown I overheard phrases on the street that I didn't really understand. In dreams I saw a Chinese woman in Central Park who usually turned out to be a Mei who didn't know me from Adam. If it was the real Mei she probably would have told me I should learn another Chinese language. "It's ridiculous to speak only one Han language," she would say in her dream-woman voice, which croaked a little, like Jean Arthur's English. "You should perfect your Shanghainese and learn Yue."

One night in spring, after seeing a play on Forty-fifth Street, I decided to walk home. The weather was warm, the air was still. As I emerged from the theater, I noticed a young Chinese couple. Half hidden in the crowd, they walked along behind me for a few steps, the woman talking on a cell phone. At Sixth Avenue I turned left. The couple kept on going east. There were few pedestrians on the avenue. The yellow moon, almost full but flattened on one edge, hung overhead between two tall buildings. I gazed at it, my head bent far back. This posture was slightly dizzying. For once I was content, free of exasperation. I had enjoyed the play, I was glad to see the moon in such a beautiful phase. Because of the pollution and the glare of electric light, it was a rare night when you could see any of the lights in the sky over Shanghai or any other city in China or for that matter, anywhere else in the world unless you were in the Sahara Desert.

A man's voice said, "Be careful. You're walking into traffic."

I woke up, and I unbent my neck. He was right. I was inches from the curb. I said, "Thanks." But I was on my guard. He was smaller than me, but he might have a gun or a knife or maybe Mace, which was as often a robber's weapon as a victim's defense. There was enough light to see that he was Chinese, like the young couple that might have been following me outside the theater.

He moved into the light of a store window. He wanted me to see his face. He waited for me to recognize him. I did so immediately. He was dressed as he had been the last time I saw him, in that Washington restaurant, but now he wore a leather jacket over his black T-shirt and a baseball cap. What was he doing here? I didn't know whether I wanted him to know I remembered him.

He refused to play the game. "I thought it was you," he said. "The Peking duck. The young lady in distress."

"And Laozi," I said. "I remember. How are you?"

"I'm well, thank you. What are we doing in New York?"

"I was wondering the same thing," I said. "You first."

"A long story," he said. "Shall we walk together?"

If nothing else, this was an opportunity to speak Mandarin. I thought I knew what he was, why he was here, whom the Chinese woman had been talking to on her cell phone. I said, "Why not?"

Neither of us mentioned Laozi again. Nor did we exchange names. For two or three blocks we didn't exchange a word. As before, my companion asked no personal questions, volunteered no personal information. A person who offers no information is the reverse image of one who offers too much—follow the logic? After ten minutes or so, I broke the silence. How did he like New York? It was the greatest city in Christendom, he said. I didn't think I had ever before heard that particular word spoken aloud. He began to talk. Small talk. My new friend was a basketball fan. He watched the Knicks on television and liked a pickup game. So did I, I said. Then I said, "We haven't answered your question."

"What question was that?" he asked.

"'Why are we in New York?'"

"I live here," he said.

"So do I."

"Really? I took you for a man of Washington. A civil servant, perhaps."

We marched on. He was exercising, not strolling. I asked if he knew a lot of civil servants.

He said, "Far too many. I work at the United Nations."

"As U.N. staff?"

"No, in China's delegation," he said.

"Do you find the work interesting?"

"Not especially," he said. "The U.N. is an artificial thing. It makes a lot of its great purpose, but in fact it has no purpose except to be the choo-choo toy of Washington."

"Then what's the point?"

"Someone must protect the small fish from too much handling," he said.

At last we reached my building. Though he may have regarded the address as valuable information, he barely glanced at it, as if he already knew where it was.

He said, "Do you play basketball?"

"I used to. But I'm older now and not as nimble as I used to be."

He handed me his card. "I have access to a gym," he said. "If you feel like playing a little one-on-one, give me a call." He didn't ask for my card. I didn't offer one. I was pretty sure he already knew who I was, that this encounter was not accidental.

I said, "I'm sure you'd beat me."

"Who knows?" he said. "Games are in the lap of the gods. I'm shorter and older and not especially interested in winning. We can bet on the outcome—a dollar a game."

I said, "Maybe we should play *weiqi* instead. Then you'd be sure to win."

"That's an idea," he said. "Also for money?"

I said, "Now you're making me worry. Are you a ringer?"

He knew the outdated slang, he caught the double meaning. I could see it in his eyes. He smiled a disarming smile and, without answering, lifted a hand and walked away, moving even more swiftly than when we had been walking together. I looked at his card. The Chinese characters gave his name as Lin Ming. His title was "economics attaché." Read "Guoanbu." What next?

I didn't call him. Making the first move would be the wrong move. There was little doubt in my mind that there would be, in due course, another chance meeting. I made no change in my habits, so as to make things easier. A couple of days later I realized I was being watched—four mixed-gender, all-Han teams of three people each, just like in Shanghai. Here, they stood out a bit more even though they stayed farther back and there was nothing unusual about seeing three Chinese scattered in any New York crowd. I pretended to be oblivious to their company. Since the goal of tradecraft is a natural appearance, why not just be natural? The adversary will watch you whether you know he's there or not. Let him watch, for who knows who watches the watchman? Just the same, remembering Burbank's lecture on the right to self-defense, I started carrying a can of pepper spray and a short fighting knife, and was careful not to let anyone get too close to me when I went walking after dark.

One afternoon a month or so after bumping into Lin Ming, I stopped at a sandwich shop that served excellent meatball sandwiches, then went to the movies. I saw a Woody Allen film, a very enjoyable one set in Barcelona—amusing story, good acting, beautiful ardent women. I wondered if Mr. Allen realized how much better his movies had become since he stopped casting himself. Lin Ming was far from my mind as I walked, still smiling, out of the theater. I had stopped in the men's room, so the rest of the audience had scuttled away by the time I reached the sidewalk. It was raining—a downpour. Darkness was falling and the cars had their headlights on and their windshield wipers thumping. The rain blurred the scene, you couldn't read the signs on the buses or make out faces. I waited under the marquee for it to let up. After a moment or two my eyes adjusted. A few feet away, also under the marquee, stood Lin Ming, smoking a cigarette and watching the traffic. When he saw me, he dropped the butt, ground it out with the sole of his shoe, and said, "Hello there." No smile of delighted surprise. Meeting by chance in a cloudburst in the middle of a city of eight million was the most natural thing in the world, of course it was.

"Hello yourself," I said.

Lin Ming did not explain himself. In some not so very elusive way he reminded me of Burbank. I imagined telling Burbank this and watching his reaction. The comparison would tell him something about Lin, something about me, something to lock up in a safe.

To Lin Ming I said, "Let me guess. You just happened to be passing by and there I was, coming out of the movies."

Smiling at last, the winner of the game of wits, Lin Ming said, "Actually, yes. I was just getting out of the rain and you appeared as if beamed down like Captain Kirk." How did he know these things? He was carrying a gym bag. He said, "Basketball?" Pointing at my Keds, he said, "You're wearing the right shoes. The gym is right around the corner." I shook my head and smiled regretfully.

The rain was letting up. Lin Ming shifted his gym bag from one shoulder to the other. He looked at his watch. "I'd better go or I'll miss my time," he said. "It was nice to run into you. Big city, small world. Long odds."

"Odds can be odd," I said.

He walked away.

Feigning impulse, I called after him, "Wait up. I could use some exercise."

An hour later, panting and drenched in sweat, I owed Lin Ming three dollars even though I was five inches taller and years younger than he was. Under the basket he was quick, deceptive, a deadeye shooter. He played in the same way that he walked—fast, silent, no expression whatsoever on his face, no movement of the eyes or body to tip off his next move. Besides, I had let him win.

I went home to shower, and as hot water washed away sweat and unknotted muscles, I wondered where and when I would run into my new friend next. And how long it would take him to pop the question.

16

Every week or so I cleaned out the mailbox. The usual yield was a large accumulation of junk mail addressed to my mother, sometimes a bill her executor had forgotten to pay, and almost always, several appeals from dodgy strangers who wanted her to give them money. Mother subscribed to the *New Yorker* and *National Geographic* and most of the other genteel slicks that people of her generation and kind displayed for a while, then threw away after looking at the pictures. She also received a couple of beefcake magazines as well as some soft-porn publications. Rifling Mother's mailbox I learned secrets she never meant me to know, and this evidence of her humanness caused me to love her a little more. It also brought back those long-ago female howls from the master bedroom.

A few days after I ran into Lin Ming under the marquee, I found a small envelope addressed to me in a nymphet hand—the kind in which the letter *i* is dotted with a little circle. This puzzled me, since no one knew I was here except the doormen, Lin Ming, and maybe Burbank in his omniscience. I waited until I was alone in the apartment to open the envelope. Inside was an invitation from Dr. Brook Holloway and

Mr. Henry Smithers to the christening of their infant son, Stanley Austin Holloway-Smithers, at the Church of Saint Luke in the Fields on Hudson Street at ten o'clock in the morning of the coming Friday. Business attire, no gifts, please. Friday was two days away. As I had never known anyone called Holloway or Smithers, I surmised that this was a summons from Burbank. That meant that the place named was a cover name for another place, the day and time likewise. The problem was, I didn't know what the wild cards meant, and therefore I couldn't possibly get to the right place at the right time. There was no RSVP phone number. The return address was a post office box with an Upper West Side zip code. Of course I had the number for the phone that Burbank never answered, but even if someone picked up, I could hardly ask to be told over an open line, in plain English, what "the Church of Saint Luke in the Fields" stood for, what the actual time of the meeting was, and what was the significance, if any, of those tin-ear aliases. I looked in the envelope again and found a smaller card inviting me to a reception following the baptism at an address on Washington Square. Was it possible that at some point in my life I *had* known a Holloway or a Smithers, or both, and that the invitation was puzzling because it was genuine? After playing a few hands of solitaire on my new laptop, I decided to go to Saint Luke in the Fields at the time indicated and see what happened.

Wearing one of my Shanghai suits and a shirt and tie and buffed-up leather shoes, I showed up at the church at the precise time indicated. The doors were locked. I lingered for a few minutes, another breach of protocol, since the unmet agent is supposed to consider himself under observation by the adversary and to slink away without delay. No one approached me. I took a cab to an imaginary address on Eighth Street, loitered until the hour of the reception, and tried to find the address on Washington Square. It did not exist. The amount of time wasted every day by spies of all nations on comedies of errors of this kind would provide hours enough for a terrorist cell composed of two illiterate brothers and a cousin living in a cave to build a nuclear device. By now it was well past eleven. I decided to take a walk around Greenwich Village. Maybe someone would follow me, tap me on the shoulder, and explain this fiasco. It would be easy to keep me in sight. It was Friday, so I was almost the only guy on the street wearing a suit, and as usual, I was taking no noticeable countermeasures.

On Fifth Avenue, a young man was handing out leaflets, but only to men. With each leaflet he shouted, "Here you go, dude, get laid! Only twenty bucks." I gave him a wide berth. This offended him. He yelled "Hey!" and ran after me, then walked backward in front of me, red-faced and shouting, spit flying. Was I too effing good to read a leaflet about the crimes of the secret elite? Was I some kind of effing right-winger? Did I effing love it when some effing American assassin murdered innocent Muslims with an effing Hellfire missile? I stopped in my tracks. He walked toward me, crazy-faced. When he was close, he murmured, "This one is special for you." He handed me a leaflet. I took it. Up close he was a nice, clean kid with freckles who smelled of shampoo and whose loving parents had paid for about ten thousand dollars worth of work on his teeth. He said, "Read this, it will show you the way to the Lord."

As I walked away, I read the leaflet. It was a plain piece of paper on which was printed, in block letters, "LOBBY OF ALGONQUIN. NOW." I was back in touch.

I folded it up and placed it in the inside pocket of my jacket, which closed with a button. On the way uptown, I reflected for the thousandth time on the absurdity of the life I was leading. I asked myself why I stayed with it, how all this nonsense could possibly lead to a result that would change the fate of the world by so much as a milligram, why I had wanted to get involved in the first place. Of course I knew the answers to all these questions. As much as I was tempted to put an end to this farce, to quit, to forget it and try despising some other walk in life, the truth was that I had become a secret agent because I could not bear for another minute the pointlessness of life in the real world. To go back to it would be no escape. It would be a surrender to the destiny I fled when I went on the lam. If the craft meant nothing, at least it was done in something like absolute privacy, as if everything was happening in another time, another universe, another state of consciousness. Its joys were palpable. For years I had been left alone to enjoy the pleasures of learning to speak and read an ancient and beautiful language and the company of a brilliant woman who loved sex. If that wasn't a blessed state of being, what was? What difference did it make if the work I did meant nothing, accomplished nothing, burned up money on an epic scale? What human endeavor was any different?

As the cab pulled up to the curb on Forty-fourth Street, I knew I was kidding myself, but at least I knew that escape was a dream and knowing that for certain was a terrific joke on me, on everybody, and for the moment I was a happy man. Of course, I hadn't yet gone inside.

17

It was lunchtime, so every seat but one was taken in the shadowy lobby of the Algonquin. My stepfather, a *New Yorker* enthusiast who loved this place, used to tip the waiter who worked the room fifty dollars per visit to make sure there would always be a table for him and the people he brought in to commune with the ghosts of the Round Table. I looked around for Burbank. No sign of him. He was the quintessential gray man you might not see in a crowd the first time you looked, so I looked again. This time I recognized the person who was waiting for me. He lifted a hand and smiled. He was dressed like a diplomat in a dark pin-striped suit and the rest of the rig, including cuff links. No wonder I had missed him at first glance. Not only was he not the man I had been looking for, but this Lin Ming didn't much resemble the Lin Ming in jeans or sweats I had known before this moment.

He must have laid a satisfactory tip on the waiter, because the man was at our table before either my host or I had had time to speak a word. I ordered mineral water. Lin Ming was drinking tea. He wore round rimless glasses.

I said, "How come you shoot baskets so well if you're nearsighted?"

"Contact lenses. It's kind of you to come on such short notice."

"The invitation was imaginative," I said.

"I'm glad you thought so."

People were finishing their drinks and drifting toward the dining room across the lobby. The din of their conversation made it difficult to hear Lin Ming. He waited until the people at the next table vacated. Then he said, "I apologize for the charade." He pronounced *charade* as a French word, an odd little flourish.

I said, "No problem. I wonder, though, why you went to so much trouble when all you had to do was waylay me the next time I went to a theater."

"Do you have a theory about that?"

"I have an idea, but I'd like to hear your story."

"Very simple," Lin Ming said with perfect composure. "You have avoided tradecraft so assiduously for the whole time I and certain friends have been interested in you"—that word again—"that you have made these people want to know you better. One would have to know tradecraft and know it well in order to fake its absence. Or so my friends assumed."

"'Tradecraft?'" I said, as if the word were new to me. This was an amateurish move.

Lin Ming thought so, too. He was deaf to the interruption. "Today," he said, "tested our assumption."

"And did I pass or fail?"

"Well, here you are. Why don't we have some lunch?"

We were seated at a good table. Clearly they knew Lin Ming at the Algonquin. He ordered a salad composed of many raw vegetables. On the twenty-year-old recommendation of my stepfather, I had a club sandwich—my first, as far as I could remember, since he took me to lunch here when I was sixteen. Strangers were inches away from us on

111

all sides. Lin Ming talked no business. He had been to a Knicks game since the last time we met. It was enjoyable even though the Knicks lost. Basketball was better when you could hear the players cursing at each other, when you could see the sweat fly off their bodies and smell it. Did he particularly enjoy the smell of sweat? At basketball games, yes. The smell of each race was different. Also the sweat of men and women. Had I noticed?

Lin Ming paid the bill in cash, with a knowing but not showy tip. He played by the rules, as an operative is supposed to do as part of the camouflage. We went back to the lounge. It was deserted now. The waiter brought us coffee and disappeared. "Everyone has gone back to work," Lin Ming said. "So we have the place to ourselves."

He sipped his coffee. Lin Ming noticed that I wasn't drinking mine. He asked if I would prefer something else.

"No, thanks."

"Then I will come to the point," he said in Mandarin. "You speak our language with remarkable fluency. You know our country."

"Only Shanghai."

"No one knows the whole of China. Anyway, that's not a requirement of the job."

"What job? I was just fired from a job in China."

"That's not really the case. Better to look at your situation as a transfer."

"I don't follow."

"I want to offer you a position. The salary would be somewhat higher than your former position paid—and perhaps, depending on results, much higher, and totally tax free. It would require a change in your lifestyle."

I thought, *Here it comes.*

I said, "Like what?"

"You wouldn't be living in China. At least, not right away. Perhaps in the future, if the job requires it."

Lin Ming was going slow. Why, if he was so sure of me? Or sure enough, at least, to organize this morning's charade. Of course it hadn't cost much—little more than whatever his people had paid the crazy kid to hand me the message. Probably they had shown him a photo of me and given him his leaflets and a fifty-dollar bill. Or more likely, a twenty. Or maybe he was an unpaid true believer.

"I don't mean to be pushy," I said, "but what exactly is this job, and who exactly would I be working for?"

Lin Ming said, "Let me tell you that as a whole, rather than in fragments."

"Fine. But you're making me nervous. I think the moment has come to lay the cards on the table."

"Or the stones on the board. We must have that game of *weiqi*. Soon."

We seemed to be having it now. If his purpose had been to take me by surprise, he had succeeded. I could hardly have felt more surrounded, even though this scenario was playing out as though Burbank had written the script. Lin Ming seemed to read my thoughts—with something like a twinkle in his eye. He drank a little more coffee. I didn't think he liked the stuff any better than I did.

Lin Ming said, "Let's be frank. I think you know what the job is. You know what I am and what I am doing, and therefore you know who you would be working for."

He was telling me that this was the moment to break off this conversation if I wasn't interested in what was coming next. It was the moment to save him from embarrassing himself.

I said, "Go on."

"Very well," Lin Ming said. "Here is the proposal. We believe that you are sympathetic to China and interested in China's future in the world as it is intertwined with the future of the United States. You have unusual skills and useful contacts."

I started to interrupt. Lin Ming cut me off. "Please. We wish to work with you. We believe you already have a job, a confidential job, and that is the job you have been doing for the past few years, including all your time in Shanghai. We want you to go back to that job, to go inside and work closely with Mr. Burbank. We will make sure that Mr. Burbank has good reason to be pleased with your work. We will help you. We will provide you with information that will be of great interest to Mr. Burbank and his organization. It will be reliable, truthful, valuable information. In return we would hope that you would offer us your services as a consultant, including the provision of certain information that is likewise interesting and trustworthy. We would handle your situation with great care. Very likely you will be promoted and honored by your agency—and honored and rewarded, with the utmost discretion, by us also. By me. We would work together. For the good of both our countries."

I said, "'Us' being who—Guoanbu?"

At the sound of this word, Lin Ming winced. He said, "The moment has not yet come to discuss details."

I said, "You must be crazy."

"You think so?" Lin Ming said. "No one else has ever suggested that."

"Listen to me. I bled for this country. I'm an American to the bone, descended from generations of Americans. Under no circumstances, none, would I ever consider betraying the United States of America. Or worse, betraying my ancestors."

That outburst, as I intended, was theatrical. But Lin Ming had been acting, too. He still was. Now he exhaled, as if expelling his surprise at my rudeness. As the book of tradecraft prescribed (the manual is the same in every language and in every epoch), he waited for me to calm down. He was a professional, keeping his head, playing the game, doing his thing.

"I understand," he said. "Mei will be very disappointed."

I said, "She will? What's that supposed to mean?"

"The plan was that she would come back to you."

"Why?"

"Because she wants to be with you. Because she would be helpful." He smiled. "Because she would give you the opportunity to speak Mandarin with an intelligent person."

Ah, the bribe of bribes. The thing I wanted most in the world! The clumsiness, the nerve, the contempt, the "Roll over, Rover!" The bastard! But oh, what an opportunity. Using the Method like a Brando, I summoned things that had made me mad in the past—Wojciechowski the Hessian, the brainless coach who recruited him, my father's selfish death—until my face reddened with anger. In a furious silence, I walked out of the Algonquin. Minutes later, as I was turning onto Fifth Avenue, Lin caught up. Walking along beside me, looking up at my profile, he said, "You haven't said no."

"Then I'll say it now. No."

"I can't hear you over the traffic," Lin Ming said. "Wait. Think. Take your time. Let's meet for a game of *weiqi* when you've had more time to consider this new opportunity, and talk some more."

He stopped walking. We were in front of Brooks Brothers. As I strode away, I looked into the store window and saw Lin Ming's reflection. He was lighting a cigarette.

What insouciance. Or, more probably, a signal to his sidewalk people.

18

Counterintuitive though it may seem in a time of terrorism, most employees of Headquarters who still have landline home telephones are listed in the directories for Washington and its suburbs. True, you have to know their names or their wives' or husbands' or bedfellows' names before you can look them up or call them up or blow up their houses or cars, but once you've identified them, the next move is yours. Therefore, walking in on Burbank wasn't an impossible mission. I looked up Burbank, Luther R., in the anywho.com white pages. There he was on Forest Lane in McLean, Virginia, complete with driving directions. I knew there was no point in calling him at the number listed, so I changed into jeans and a sweater, stuffed a book and a sandwich and a bottle of water and a change of underwear into my backpack, then took the bus to Broadway and the subway to Forty-second Street, walked to the Port Authority bus terminal, and took a bus to Washington, last passenger aboard.

It was about midnight when I arrived on foot at Burbank's house. Dark sky, sleeping neighborhood. The downstairs lights were on. I assumed that a state-of-the-art alarm system and surveillance cameras would be in operation, so I just walked up to the front door and rang the bell. No one answered. But I heard someone inside the house, a young woman from the light-footed sound she made, running rapidly up or down stairs. Through the glass above the door, I saw a moving shadow. I heard a dial tone, a low female voice. In an astonishingly short time, two McLean police cruisers pulled up at the house, strobes flashing. Four large cops got out of the vehicles and approached me. All carried nightsticks, each had the other hand on a holstered handgun. Whoever was in the house switched on the outside lights. These included several powerful floodlights that bleached the cops' skin.

The lead policeman, a burly sergeant, assumed the stance of authority and said, "Lemme see some ID." I gave him my passport, in which nearly every page bore incriminating stamps and notations in Mandarin and other unreadable languages. He asked for another government-issued picture ID. I handed over my District of Columbia driver's license. Was the address on the license my current address? "No, officer." Then what was my current address and why hadn't I reported it and gotten a new license? Because I didn't have a new address in D.C. Did that mean I was homeless? I explained that I was staying in New York for the time being. Then what was I doing on foot in McLean, Virginia, at this time of night? Where did I work? I admitted I was jobless. At that, the questions ceased. The sergeant cuffed me. Another cop frisked me while a third read me my rights. I was placed under arrest on suspicion of trespassing in the night. Nobody asked me if I knew the people who lived in this house, and I couldn't have answered the question even if it had been put to me, because I wasn't sure I did. For all I knew, the residents were some other Burbanks—the real ones, and the Burbank I knew was really a Brackenridge or a Bumstead. Or maybe this was a Potemkin house and Luther and family, assuming he had one, had never lived here at all. Also, I was sure that anyone who came to the door, especially Burbank himself, would say that they had never seen me before in their lives. Local cops weren't cleared to know that I knew Burbank or that he knew me. Strictly speaking, they weren't cleared to know me in true name. But now they did.

Other cops booked me at the police station, strip-searched me, confiscated my belongings, including about five hundred dollars in fifties, a drug dealer denomination, and put me in a cell. I asked if I could keep my book. A desk officer examined it carefully for hidden razor blades or poisonous pellets or explosive pages, and to my surprise, handed it over. The cops told me I was entitled to one phone call. I said not right now. I had no one to call except Lin Ming.

An hour or so later, a jailer told me I had a visitor. He opened my cell and led me down the hall to a small windowless room. A well-nourished sleepy-eyed gray-haired man in yesterday's rumpled suit sat at a table. He said, "The bail was three hundred dollars. I posted it. Do you have that much with you?"

"I did when I arrived. Who are you?"

"Your lawyer." He stood up. He was in no mood to be friendly. I asked him what time it was. "It's three-thirty," he said. "A.M. Let's go."

I followed the jailer while my lawyer settled the bill. At the desk, my belongings were returned to me. Everything was there. I signed a receipt.

In the lawyer's car, a well-broken-in, entry-level BMW, I said, "Now what?"

"Now you owe me three hundred dollars."

I counted out the money and gave it to him. He stuffed it into the breast pocket of his jacket and started the car. I said, "What about your fee?" He didn't answer the question.

He said, "The bail money will be returned to you by the police. Eventually. The owner of the house where you committed trespass has decided not to press charges, so you're a free man, no hearing or trial, except that you now have a rap sheet, a public record under what I presume is your own name, that puts you on his doorstep at a specific time and date, with four police officers as witnesses. I advise you to observe the speed limit in Virginia from now on."

I said, "Do you want me to get out of the car now or are we going somewhere?"

"I'll tell you when to get out of the car."

He drove me to a house in a sleeping suburb. Another digital lock. He punched in the numbers and let me in. He followed me through the door and turned off the alarm system. Did all safe houses have the same entry code so that agents wouldn't forget them in the same way they used to lose keys? The lawyer said, "Someone will come to see you." He was still disgruntled. As if I had asked a question, he said, "No, I don't know when. Until they get here, stay put. Do not answer the phone. Do not *use* the phone. Do not memorize the address. Do not open the door if the doorbell rings. Do not order pizza. You can use a bed, take a shower, jerk off, eat the food if you find any. Do not go outside."

Where would I go? I had no idea where I was. All suburban housing developments look alike, and besides, every Yankee who ever crossed the Potomac except Ulysses S. Grant got lost as soon as he reached the Virginia side. I couldn't have found my way to the nearest 7-Eleven.

The lawyer left. I locked the door, turned down the heat, drank a glass of nonfat milk, and microwaved some packaged macaroni and cheese I found in a cupboard. *Busy day,* I said to myself and to the listening devices. I found a puffy recliner chair in the basement television room, sat down, covered up with the Burberry, pulled the handle, and went to sleep.

Burbank arrived after dark the next day. I smelled him coming before he even opened the front door because he was carrying a bag of sandwiches—tofu for him, meatball for me, same as before. How could he remember the meatballs? It had been months. Did he take notes? I was too hungry to ask questions. Apart from the mac and cheese, I had found nothing to eat in the kitchen except a couple of Snickers bars, frozen solid. Burbank brought two bottles of microbrew beer, and this time I drank mine. For fifteen minutes, no noise was heard except the sound of chewing. Burbank had no more small talk than he'd ever had, which was to say, none. He was his original muffled self—no *hello* or *good to see you* or other fake camaraderie, no handshake, not the smallest smile. He was a man who lived without the niceties. *Admirable,* I thought. I wondered if he was the same way at home—silent cocktails with his wife if he had one, mute dinners, wordless copulation. If he was upset by what had happened on his doorstep the night before, he didn't say so. My visit had been a serious breach of security. Maybe his silence indicated displeasure. Maybe he thought the tongue-lashing could wait until I finished my sandwich. It was even possible that he thought I must have had a good reason for doing what I did. That was no excuse for having done it.

When we finished eating and Burbank had stuffed the sandwich wrappers back in the bag and gone though his routine of wiping our fingerprints off everything we had touched, he took from his pocket a small remote, like the ones used for keyless car ignitions, and clicked it. I thought he must be turning the listening devices off or on, because he now began to talk.

"About last night, my apologies," he said. "I wasn't home when you called. The au pair was frightened. She was alone. She's from Colombia, so she tends to be a bit nervous after dark."

I said I hoped the girl was all right now. Burbank said, "So what brings you to town? I assume you have something that won't wait."

Apparently he hadn't gotten my text message or had been too busy to read it. I told him what I had written, in detail. As before, he listened intently and seemed to take it for granted that I was leaving nothing out, since he put no questions to me. He took a photograph from his pocket and showed it to me. It was a very good likeness of Lin Ming, taken outdoors on a New York street. Lin Ming was wearing sweats and a Mets cap. Burbank said, "Is this the man?"

If he hadn't received my texts, how did he guess? I said, "Yes."

"What contact have you had with him?"

I told him about the "chance" encounter in the Washington restaurant, about bumping into him on Sixth Avenue. "Also, we ran into each other last week. . . ."

"Jehovah at work. Where?"

"In the rain, outside a movie theater, and then we played one-on-one basketball at a gym."

"Who won?"

"He did."

"A little guy like that beat you?"

I nodded. "And day before yesterday he tried to recruit me."

"Details?"

I provided them for the second time.

Burbank said, "I wonder why he gave you so much detail. Usually the Chinese are stingy with information."

"You know who he really is?"

"*What* he really is, more or less," Burbank said. "It really doesn't matter whether the name he was born with was Chang or Wang or Wu or Xu or what benighted village he comes from. He hasn't been his original self for a long time. We've caught glimpses of him. He's been posted to Tokyo, Paris, London, always under diplomatic cover. He's cordial, social. It's easy to take a liking to him, as you found. He's baptized an impressive number of sinners."

"Was his method the same as with me?" I asked.

"No. His M.O. is to be quiet, slow, discreet. The question is, why was he not the same as usual with you?"

"Don't ask me."

"I'm not asking you."

"Then let me ask you something. What now?"

"Suspicion," said Burbank. "Prudence. Deception."

The three muses of the craft. Burbank was watching me as if he expected me to say something and I was taking too long to say it.

At last he said, "Tell me, what was in your mind when Lin Ming was making his pitch?"

"Self-congratulation because I thought I had read him right. Although I had always assumed that Mei was on duty, I was surprised—startled—when he revealed that he or his friends controlled her."

"You believed that?"

"I believed he wanted me to believe it."

"A natural reaction, but watch yourself. What else?"

"Having revealed so much, he was coy about being Guoanbu."

"Maybe he isn't Guoanbu. Maybe he's military intelligence, like Alger Hiss's Russian case officer. Or something else we're not aware of."

"Like what?"

Burbank waived the question away. He said, "I feel that there's something more. Something you hesitate to put into words. Am I right about that?"

"Okay," I said. "Yes. What he was offering was so close to what you told me you hoped for from this operation that I wondered if it was a case of great minds, his and yours, running in the same channel."

Burbank blinked, like an actor on cue. He said, "Why ever would you think a thing like that?"

"Sometimes I have unworthy thoughts."

"Thanks for the compliment," Burbank said, getting to his feet. "Interesting mind you have. Keep using it. Go back to New York. Play this fish a little longer. Keep your knickers on. Then we'll see."

And that was all I got out of him. He gave me a new phone number to call, a different accommodation address to write to, and a mobile phone to use when I called so the caller ID would be recognized. All this reminded me of CEO Chen. Why did I keep making these comparisons?

19

Two weeks later I was walking in Riverside Park when I saw Lin Ming on the path ahead, bouncing toward me, arms swinging as though in training for a power-walking marathon. He wore a sweatband with a Knicks logo. I sauntered on. I expected him to thrust out a hand, smile broadly, pause to chat. Instead, eyes front, concentrating on technique, he strode right by me. Snubbed! Would I ever recover? I resisted the temptation to turn around and watch him jounce away into the distance but kept on walking, avoiding designer dogs, trying not to stumble over the shrieking brats in designer rompers who swarmed the path while their nannies gossiped in Spanish and half a dozen other languages.

A week or so after that encounter, I found another invitation-size envelope in the mailbox. It contained a card with a Chinatown address typed upon it in red, along with the following message: "Sorry to be in such a hurry the other day. Nothing personal. Hope Saturday is a good day to play *weiqi*. 6 o'clock? Afterward we can have dinner. *Very* good Sichuan chef." The card was signed, also in red, the color of happiness, in an unreadable scrawl.

The meeting place turned out to be upstairs over a restaurant called Sichuan Delight. A sleek young man with a patch of hair under his lower lip was posted at the door. He said, "Please follow me, sir. When he opened the unlocked door, bright ceiling lights switched on, revealing a steep flight of stairs. I smelled China. The young man told me to knock on door Number 8—one knock only. Because it sounds in Mandarin like the word that means wealth, eight is a very lucky number. I knocked. Lin Ming opened the door. Like me, he wore sneakers, jeans, and a T-shirt, his displaying 機, the character for "opportunity." He smoked an unfiltered cigarette—not his first. The room was blue with smoke. Behind me, the hallway lights clicked off. Lin Ming said, "Come in from the dark. The landlord doesn't like to waste electricity."

The stage set was complete. The *weiqi* board was already set up. So was the teapot. A large poster of Three Gorges dam hung on the wall—meant perhaps to remind me, unsubtly, of the beautiful Yangtze. We sat down immediately, and after drinking tea, began to play. As I had expected, it was the village idiot versus Bobby Fisher. We played three games in less time than it usually takes to play one. Lin Ming tried hard not to humiliate me, but I was so bad he could not find a way to let me win. There was plenty of chatter, almost entirely Lin Ming's. He had given up hope for the Knicks, but the baseball season had begun. Maybe the Mets would surprise themselves and make it to the playoffs.

Minutes after we finished our final game of *weiqi*, a waiter arrived from the Sichuan Delight with a staggering load of dishes. Lin Ming had not overstated the chef's skill. After supper—seconds afterward, Lin Ming must have had some sort of hidden bell under the table or carpet—a busboy came and took away the debris. Lin Ming took out his pack of Camels and offered me one. I shook my head. He drank very little of his maotai, but Chinese host that he was, kept my glass topped up. The genteel American has not yet been born who will not go to almost any lengths to avoid being disrespectful of a foreigner's culture, no matter how silly it seems, no matter how transparent the foreigner's contempt for that American's monkey-see monkey-do behavior might be. Foreigners will spit out our food and drink in disgust, challenge the intelligence of every idea we express, look amazed when we act according to our own etiquette instead of making the hilarious mistake of mimicking what we mistake for their own good manners. In this we are alone among the great powers of history. Ancient China laid its disdain on lesser peoples with a trowel, and modern China does the same. Timur the Lame did not make nice to conquered peoples by acting like a Han or a Turk. When the British or the French in their palmy days Gatling-gunned a few hundred Chinese or other racial inferiors, they didn't apologize. They just told themselves that the slant-eyed beggars obviously placed no value on human life, and had a drink.

I was playing the supine American with this Chinese intelligence officer who was trying to suborn me to treason because that was what I thought he expected. For the moment Lin Ming had stopped making conversation. Glowing Camel between his lips, he looked at the ceiling. He tapped the ash from his cigarette at the last possible moment and put it back between his lips. Squinting through the smoke he said, "Have you been in touch with Mr. Burbank since last we met?"

I told him the truth.

"By telephone?"

"No, I took a trip to Washington."

"Ah. And was he glad to see you?"

"Surprised, I think."

Lin Ming ground out his cigarette in the overflowing ashtray. He said, "May I assume that you told Mr. Burbank about my offer of employment to you?"

"Of course I did," I said.

"In what detail?"

"I told him everything. How else could I keep his trust?"

"You wish to keep his trust?"

"Isn't doing so the whole point?" I asked.

"Excellent," Lin Ming said. "Very, very good. You know how to think ahead. That's very rare. I'm proud of you."

He lifted his maotai glass and wet his lips. Supinely I did the same, striving to stay in character, hoping that I was winning *his* trust, but not betting the farm on it.

Lin Ming's mobile phone rang. He looked at the caller ID and left the room to answer it. A long time passed. He did not return. I took the hint and left. As I descended the stairs, the blinding overhead lights went out. In a Fu Manchu movie, the sinister young cashier would have stepped out of a hidden compartment and driven a dagger into my spinal cord. In this humdrum real world, however, I found the fellow waiting for me in the street below, smilingly holding open the door of the taxi he had fetched for me.

20

I had recorded my conversation with Lin Ming with a dirty-tricks cell phone. When I got home after my evening in Chinatown, I extracted the chip from the phone, placed it in a small plastic pillbox I found in Mother's medicine cabinet, put the pillbox in a padded envelope, addressed it in fictitious name to Burbank's post office box, and dropped the envelope down the mail chute. One of the oddities about the explosion in espionage technology is that the computer has rendered snail mail the least vulnerable of all methods, apart from the cleft stick, for the transmission of secret communications. What geek would ever guess that a letter flying around in plain sight might be less easy to hack than an imaginary byte?

The next morning I took a train to Westport and drove to the house in Mother's decrepit Mercedes, which I had left in the station's parking lot. She had called it her new car because it was new to her. She had driven junks exclusively. When a car stopped running she would call up her used car dealer and ask him to bring her a replacement priced at no more than a thousand dollars including removal of the worn-out vehicle. Both my father and my stepfather had been crazy about fast, costly European cars, and I guess her fondness for derelict vehicles was one of the ways in which she expressed her delight over the expiration of her promises to love, honor, and obey.

Like her mother before her, from whom she learned about men and soils and seeds and fertilizers, Mother had been a keen gardener. Now, with the arrival of spring, her flowerbeds were coming back to life. I visualized them as I drove. I had kept Mother's cook, the recovering crack addict, on as gardener and caretaker, and when I arrived at the house she was kneeling in the backyard, transplanting seedlings. She wasn't a bad-looking woman. It was a sunny day—hot, for the hills of New England—and she wore a sensible gray sports bra and denim shorts. She was barefoot. Her fine hair was escaping strand by strand from the rubber band on her ponytail. The knobs along her spine were prominent, but she had a good body, nice legs, pretty breasts. When she recognized the Mercedes she stood up—her bare knees were muddied—and pulled on a T-shirt. This further tousled her hair. She didn't bother to tuck it in. I waved in a nice-guy way and parked in the driveway. She didn't move a muscle. I walked across the garden, which was a carpet of jonquils and other early flowers whose names I didn't know. She tracked me with a sentinel's eyes as if expecting me to trample something. If she recognized me she gave no sign. She definitely wasn't the smiley type. For a moment I thought she really might not know who I was—I had hired her at the cemetery, and she had seen me only a couple of times before that and then briefly—so I took off my baseball cap and said something like, "Planting flowers, I see." One expects such inanities to be understood as gestures of good intentions. No chance of that from this poker-faced militant. I told her I was sorry to arrive unannounced. In the first sign that she had identified me, she said, "It's your house. You can arrive whenever you feel like it."

Her message was clear. I could send her a check every two weeks if I wanted, but that didn't require her to be agreeable. Had I any orders? I told her to go ahead with what she was doing. She nodded, fell to her knees, and went on with the spring planting.

After using the bathroom—I carried no luggage because I had the clothes and razor and toothbrush I needed stowed away in the house—I sat in the sun and read a book in Mandarin about Shanghai between the world wars. It was refreshing because it barely mentioned the hapless foreigners who were the featured characters of most other histories of that time and place. After a while the garden nymph finished what she was doing, stacked her empty flowerpots, and disappeared into the greenhouse. Water pipes howled. Mother had equipped the outbuilding with a shower and required all grimy people to use it to prevent dirt from being tracked into the house.

Soon the young woman emerged with wet hair pasted to her head. She was now dressed in jeans, sandals, and a clean shirt unbuttoned to her cleavage. She walked over and stood beside my chair. She gave off the odor of Ivory soap. I hadn't smelled it since I made out with Mary Ellen Crowley when I was in the eighth grade. I didn't speak or look up. After a long silence that was the equivalent of a staring contest, she said, "You read Chinese?" I closed the book, marking my place with a finger, looked into her cold eyes, and said, "Are you calling it a day?"

"That's your decision," she said. "If you want dinner I can cook it."

"Good idea. What's on the menu?"

"Tell me what you want and I'll go get it and cook it."

"Anything?"

"Anything Stop & Shop has." I knew it had a lobster tank. I said, "Lobster. The rest is up to you. I'll get the wine from the cellar."

"Fine."

She held out her hand, palm up. I gave her an inquiring look.

She said, "Money."

I gave her two fifties. When she saw my bankroll, the look of proletarian disgust I had noted earlier came back into her eyes. Her upper lip twitched in contempt. The reaction was understandable. Nobody loves the rich, and how could she know that I was okay because Communists had made me rich?

She said, "Do you know how long you'll be staying?"

I told her I wasn't sure, but I'd like it if she made supper every night. She nodded, put the money in her pocket, and remained where she was. She seemed to be thinking something over. I thought she would now turn to go, but she hung where she was. She said, "May I ask a question?"

"Sure."

"Are you here because of my message?"

I said, "No. I didn't know you'd left a message."

She said, "Then I'd better repeat it. Somebody broke into the house."

I flinched, as if I had just seen my name in print on the crime page of the *Shanghai Daily*. I said, "Are you sure?"

She said, "Otherwise there'd be no reason to mention it, would there?"

After a moment I said, "Let me rephrase. How did you become aware of the break-in?"

"A pane of glass in the kitchen door had been broken and replaced."

"Replaced?"

"That's what I just said."

"Tell me more."

Wearily—why hadn't I listened to her message?—she said, "When I let myself in with the key, I noticed broken glass on the kitchen floor—not much, only a few slivers. They glittered in the sunlight. Then I smelled putty and saw that it was fresh and the glass was new, not wavy like the old glass."

"You're a good detective." No answer. I persevered. "Why would they bother to replace the broken windowpane, but leave broken glass in plain sight?"

"I have no idea."

"Did you call the police?"

"That never crossed my mind."

"Why not?" I asked.

"Because I've got a criminal record, possession of crack cocaine. I probably would have been booked as a brain-damaged drug addict looking for something to steal and sell."

"So what did you do?"

"I looked around and saw that the burglars had left other signs of their intrusion."

"Like what?"

"They'd violated everything—stripped the beds and remade them, opened all the doors and drawers in all the rooms, looked under the rugs, took the telephones apart, opened the pill bottles," she said. "They tried to put everything back exactly as they found it, but working in the dark, they didn't always succeed. A lot of things were slightly not where they should be. Also, you could smell them."

"How did they smell?"

"Male sweat. Drugstore aftershave. Urine and fecal matter in the bathrooms."

"They didn't flush the toilets?"

"The stink was in the air, and there were smears in one of the toilet bowls. I also smelled plaster dust, very pungent."

"Plaster dust?"

"This is an old house. The walls are plaster, not Sheetrock."

Obviously she had an uncommonly good sense of smell. I kept the thought to myself. By now I had learned to pay this woman no compliments.

"Anything missing?"

"Your mother's letters and papers," she said.

"All of them?"

"Everything she kept in boxes in the attic. Also her photo albums. Maybe other things, like keepsakes I didn't know about."

"Nothing of value, then."

"She valued what was in the boxes. She kept an armchair and a lamp in the attic so she could go up and read them. She kept her stocks and bonds and CDs in a safe in her closet. But as far as I know she got rid of everything like that before she went into the hospital for the last time."

"Got rid of that stuff how?"

"She put it in a safe-deposit box. Maybe some cash, too."

"Who's got the key?"

"I don't know."

"Did she give you anything before she died?"

"An antique topaz brooch set in opals. A thousand dollars in cash. A pat on the cheek."

"She must have liked you."

No response.

This was food for thought. This burglary was a curious crime. It might not have sent her mind racing as it did mine, but even to a smart amateur, if that's what she was, it had to seem peculiar. I *knew* what it meant—a search team, a very clumsy search team, had conducted what they thought was a clandestine sweep of the premises. They had committed a number of basic mistakes—they hadn't put things back in the exact place where they had found them, they had taken things away instead of photographing them as the rules dictated. These characters apparently assumed that a few old boxes from the attic wouldn't be missed, which meant they thought they could bring them back into this empty house with impunity another night. They had forgotten that you can't assume a damn thing, that you have to stick to the rules, that you should never, ever leave behind the slightest trace of your entry.

"One more thing," the chef said.

"Yes?"

"I found a dozen tiny piles of plaster dust."

Now we were getting someplace. I said, "Did you sweep them up?"

"No. I watch TV. I didn't touch anything that might be evidence."

"Show me."

She led me to my bedroom, to the living room, to my stepfather's basement hideaway. Sure enough, tiny heaps of plaster dust—about a quarter-teaspoon each—lay on the parquet next to the baseboard, as if a mouse or an insect had chewed its way through the wall. But no mouse or termite was guilty of making this mess. What I was looking at was the dust left by a small, fast, super-sharp drill—the kind used by technicians who install electronic bugs. I said, "Hmmm. Have you ever seen a mouse in this house? Or a carpenter ant?"

She said, "No."

I looked at my watch. I said, "You must want to get going to the store."

She said, "I should. What time do you want dinner?" Her voice was softer now, even borderline friendly.

I said, "Seven-thirty?"

"Every night?"

"Yes."

She nodded and left without uttering another word. It was quarter after four. It would take her at least an hour to get to the supermarket through rush-hour traffic and do her shopping and get back to the house. That gave me time to do what I had to do next.

Once again I was in no doubt that I was being listened to and watched as I worked, but I had nothing to lose because the team that did this sloppy job almost certainly belonged either to Burbank or Lin Ming and both of them already knew that I was a spy who recognized spyware when I saw it. I dug five itsy-bitsy cameras and seven audio bugs out of the walls. These I ran through the kitchen disposal to send the message that there was a price to be paid for blatant amateurism. Not that I believed that this was truly the work of amateurs. The blunders were a little too obvious. Maybe what I had discovered so far were decoys. The real bugs would be properly concealed. A good technician can drill through a very thick concrete wall, vacuuming up dust like a dentist as he goes, and stop at exactly the point where nothing remains between the drill and the opposite side of the wall except a coat of paint or the wallpaper. Why anyone would go to so much trouble to bug the empty house of a dead widow who had nothing to hide I could not guess. But maybe I was chasing the wrong suspects. Who knew but what the FBI or some other zealous feds had done this work? I called it a day. There would be time enough tomorrow to check it out.

Dinner was fine—just the right amount of grape-seed oil and lemon in the dressing for the lobster salad, excellent sautéed veal, fresh peas, big Peruvian blackberries with the proper crunch and sweetness. From the cellar I had chosen an Alsatian pinot gris—Mother had liked her glass of wine, and what she saved on automobiles she spent on the grape. Also I found out that the chef's name was Magdalena. She made it plain that no diminutives were allowed. She looked less bony in dimmer light and now that the sun was down smelled faintly of a perfume whose aroma another far more agreeable girl had given me cause to remember.

21

Next morning I arose at first light and resumed my inspection. Sure enough, I spotted the backup bugs and cameras, taking care to look like a guy wandering aimlessly around the house sipping his morning coffee. I let them be. Let my watchers think I had fallen into their trap, that I had mistaken their decoys for the real thing. I had no plans to hold operational meetings in this house or mumble secrets in my sleep. There was no reason why these clowns, whoever they were, or for that matter why the whole world should not watch me shave, cut my toenails, chew my granola, read my books, eat my supper, fix a faucet—even, if there was a merciful and compassionate god, watch me nail the fair Magdalena one moonlit evening after she had done the dishes. Imagine her, imagine mismatched us as infrared images, imagine the moans, the gasps, the rest of the pornography. It had been a long time since Shanghai.

I stayed in the house for a week, and at the end of the week decided to stay a little longer. It would be a good thing, I reasoned, to give Burbank plenty of time to mull the choices offered by my tape of Lin

Ming's recruitment pitch, and for Lin Ming to pile a few more stones on the *weiqi* board. The change of scene not to mention the sense that I was not, owing to Magdalena's daily appearances, all by myself, was good for me. Gradually I stopped seeing the frowning gardener she used to be and started noticing the woman she was. There were things about Magdalena—many things—that made me think there was more to her than she thought she was letting me see. As her behavior softened, my curiosity grew. This was not part of the plan. It just happened. Maybe it was my subconscious at work, demanding payback for earlier affronts. One day as I read another book in the garden while she weeded, she asked me where I had learned Chinese. It was a polite gesture. In return I let her have it: "There is no language called 'Chinese.' People living in China speak two hundred ninety-two languages, most of them mutually incomprehensible. Characters signify different words in different languages. There is also one dead language, Jurchen, that only scholars understand. The language I am reading is Mandarin." Absorbing this spurt of bile, Magdalena was transformed. The change was startling. She looked stricken—in danger of tears, even. She darted away. I was not exactly amazed by her reaction. In my experience, people who dish it out seldom can take it. Magdalena came nowhere near me for the remainder of the day. But supper was especially tasty that night: bouillabaisse, no less. She drove all the way to Great Barrington, to Mother's favorite store across the Massachusetts line, to buy the fish. She spoke no word while serving at table. She wore a skirt and a scoop-neck blouse. Her eyes looked bigger. Mascara? Possibly.

As I ate my chocolate mousse I heard the clatter of china being put into the dishwasher, and also a new sound. Magdalena was humming a tune. Amazed, I rose from the table and went into the kitchen. Her back was turned to me. Even though she could see my reflection in the window above the sink, she went on humming in a pretty but muted soprano voice that sounded trained. She was humming an aria from

Madame Butterfly. I couldn't have been more astonished. Magdalena didn't sing the whole of it, but she sang enough to let me know she could have sung louder and longer if she chose. When she was done, I stifled an urge to applaud, knowing that she would take it for what it was, sarcasm.

Instead, I said, "Where did you train?"

No reply. After a long moment of silence, however, she spoke. With her back still turned to me, she said, "You're straight, right?"

Ah. I said, "Right. You, too?"

She said, "In case you're wondering because of my past, I have no STDs. Not now, not ever."

I said, "What does that mean, you don't sleep with Republicans?"

"It means I have no sexually transmitted diseases. Given my background you've got a right to ask."

"Me either."

"I don't like condoms."

"Neither do I."

What a romantic turn this conversation was taking. Clearly the seduction scenario I'd been putting together in my mind had been a waste of time and imagination. All of a sudden Magdalena turned around, skirt swirling. She could dance, too. She had a little color in her face. She smiled a fleeting little smile. She was a different woman altogether. A certain nervousness—how after all could she know what she was getting herself into?—added to the appeal.

After a small silence and a moment of eye contact, I said, "Where?"

"What about right here?" Magdalena said.

"On the floor, on the center island, up against the sink?"

"Not until we're married. Go upstairs. I'll join you."

I did as I was told, wondering if she would actually follow or if she had sent me to wait upstairs while she slipped out the back door. For long minutes, she did not follow. I took a shower to kill time. When I emerged, Magdalena lay on the bed. With her clothes on she may have looked a bit stringy. Naked, on her back, in this light, she made a different impression. I turned off the bedside lamp, thinking again about infrared images. I really wanted the watchers to watch this, but on my terms. She turned the lamp back on. Expertly she took hold of me. In bed as in kitchen or garden, Magdalena was a no-nonsense woman. She knew everything, and as far as I could tell, she liked everything. In her enthusiasm she reminded me a little of Mei, but only a little, and I shooed the comparison from my head because it didn't seem proper to my inner puritan to think of Mei while copulating with another woman. Or, strangely enough, vice versa. There was a difference—Magdalena was satiable, whereas Mei was not. Immediately after the third orgasm, she got up and left without saying good-bye or anything else for that matter. She came back the next night and several consecutive nights after that. The routine was the same. She wasn't impolite about it, but when she had achieved what she wanted to achieve she departed—brusquely, as if she didn't want to miss her favorite sitcom.

As experience teaches us, all good things come to an end. One night after Magdalena had taken her leave, I lay in bed thinking of a touchdown run the Hessian had made in the mud in the last century. It was the last play of the game. The six points he scored clinched the league championship for our school. Everyone else on the bench rushed onto the field to hug the Hessian. I walked away. The coach kicked me off the team for unsportsmanlike conduct.

In this place and time it was midnight, the weather was warm. The windows were wide open. The curtains stirred. I heard a telephone ringing—not the one in the front hall, but a phone outside the house. It had a novelty ring, like the horn of a Jazz Age car: Ah-*OO*-ga! Ah-*OO*-ga! I had left the special cell phone Burbank had given me in Mother's Mercedes, which was parked in the driveway and had never before heard it ring. In bare feet and pants and a T-shirt I walked to the car, started it up, and drove about five miles north—out of range of the gizmos in the walls. I parked, got out of the car, and dialed the number of the missed call. Naturally Burbank didn't answer. After the fifth ring I switched off.

Burbank replied almost instantly with a text message composed entirely of wild cards that translated as: "Report to Washington immediately. Do not repeat do not go back to the house or the apartment. Make contact when you get here."

It is a greater bother than you might think to travel in bare feet. For one thing, your feet get very dirty very quickly. For another you keep stubbing your toes and stepping on sharp or unclean things (it's no fun to pump gas or enter a public restroom). For yet another, going barefoot in public is frowned upon in bourgeois America. It is no easy matter for the unshod to buy shoes. Most stores post signs forbidding the barefoot to enter. Stores don't open until ten in the morning. When I got Burbank's message it was about half past midnight. You cannot get on a train or a bus, let alone an airplane, without shoes. I stopped at the first rest area on the New Jersey Turnpike. The convenience shop didn't even carry flip-flops. I bought a roll of paper towels and a bottle of soap and washed my feet in the restroom. This drew disgusted glances, but by then I didn't care.

The Mercedes's top speed was about fifty miles an hour, so I heard lots of horns on the turnpike. I regarded this as an advantage, because I figured that few drivers, whether under Guoanbu discipline or not, would be so foolhardy as to drive slow enough to tail me in this bat-out-of-hell traffic. To my surprise the car made it all the way to the Metro station in Vienna, Virginia. I parked it in the lot, wiped it for fingerprints, and abandoned it. Whoever towed it away would trace it to my late mother, whose last name was different from mine. I sent an encrypted text message to Burbank. Rigmarole intervened, but at last Burbank himself picked me up in his Hyundai at the third Metro station to which he directed me. How like the movies was the world I had wandered into.

I hadn't stopped to eat. I was very hungry. This time Burbank had brought no sandwiches. I was tired. Driving a clunker for four hundred miles, thinking every minute that the wheels were going to fall off, had been a fatiguing business. Even with all the windows and the roof open, I had inhaled enough carbon monoxide to euthanize a horse.

I said, "I can't stay awake. Let me know when we get there."

Later—how much later I don't know because I had left my father's Rolex on the bedside table in Connecticut—I was awakened by Burbank pinching my lower lip. We were in the countryside, at the same converted barn we had visited before. Crickets chirped. We went inside, me limping slightly more than usual. The god-awful paintings were still there. The caretaker-painter was still absent, so Burbank must have had the same housekeeper. I tried to picture her, but the woman I saw in my mind's eye was Magdalena. I wondered what she would make of my sudden departure—$20,000 watch left on the table, shoes on the floor, socks and underwear strewn on the rag rug made by my grandmother and her sisters, razor and toothbrush in the bathroom.

Burbank brewed tea. He said, "You're quite informally dressed tonight."

"Your fault," I said.

He said, "Meaning what?"

I told him. I told him about the break-in and the bugs. I told him about Magdalena in her many guises mean and mellow. I described the seduction scene. Taken together, this made her sound like a suspicious character—a simple accomplishment, as any character assassin knows. Burbank listened impatiently, obviously controlling his face with an effort.

He cleared his throat and said, "You do seem to have a way with the ladies."

"With a little help from my friends."

"Well, let's hope this Magdalena is still a friend."

"She's not the type."

"Oh?" Burbank said. "What type would you say she is?"

"Hard to tell," I said.

"She's good at what she does? Apart from the sex."

"No end to her skills. Terrific cook, frugal housekeeper, world-class gardener, very smart. I wouldn't be surprised if she can make pottery or fly a helicopter or read Sanskrit. She was very observant, almost like a trained investigator, in picking up clues about the break-in. I told her she was a born detective, and meant it."

"That also fits."

"Fits what?"

"Our files," Burbank said. "But you left something out. Magdalena, as she told you to call her, is a professional assassin."

Oh, was *that* all? I had to suppress a laugh. At the same time I felt a little sick. I was supposed to believe this? I said, "Are you serious?"

He said, "She has seven kills we know about. Just as you say, she cooks like Escoffier, she leaps from scorn to lust, she screws the target regardless of gender, she crawls on her belly like a snake. She does her thing. The target dies. She disappears. We don't even have a picture of her."

"What's her method?' "

"Poison. Untraceable poison. That's why she's never been caught. That and her all-around talent."

"Which talent?"

"What better profession for a poisoner than chef? What better way to build trust than sex?"

Now I was the one who meditated. Burbank wouldn't kid around about something like this—unless he had an operational reason—or, most unlikely, a personal one—in which case he might very well make up whatever fairy story suited the purpose. I made room in my mind for doubt even though I was under oath to believe anything he might say.

This didn't fool Burbank. He said, "You're skeptical. Good. I wouldn't think much of you if you weren't. But you'd better believe what I'm saying to you. Magdalena always gets her man. Others have tried to escape. In the end she always made the kill."

I said, "Who does she work for?"

"If you've got the money, she's got the poison."

"You think she's been paid to do me in?"

"In the context, it's not such a wild surmise."

"The next line in the script is, 'Who put out the contract?'"

"If we knew that," Burbank said, "we'd know who wants you dead, wouldn't we?"

He seemed to savor his words.

22

By the time federal agents got to the house in Connecticut the following morning, Magdalena was long gone. There was nothing Burbank or
anyone else at Headquarters could do about this. Bogeyman fantasies
notwithstanding, the U.S. intelligence service has no power of arrest or
police authority of any kind, and it is prohibited by law from running
operations on American soil against American citizens. It has to rely
on other feds who carry guns and badges, like the FBI, to apprehend
people like Magdalena. I could imagine her springing into action on
finding me gone when she arrived at break of day. She would have seen
the signs that I had got wind of her—the abandoned heirloom Rolex
on the bedside table, the dirty clothes and all the other telltale signs of
a sudden departure. She would immediately have done the professional
thing and dematerialized. Sooner or later, somewhere else on the planet,
she would pull her molecules together again and continue the hunt. If
Burbank could be believed, she took her work seriously. She was under
contract. Her reputation, her future, her business prospects, even her
sex life, depended on fulfilling the contract. I would see her again—or

more likely, *not* see her again. One evening I would come home from the office, microwave a leftover, swallow a mouthful of it and suddenly the world would go dark, this time for real. Or maybe I'd feel a pinprick through the seat of my pants while standing at a urinal at the movies, and then in the mirror see the last thing I would ever see—Magdalena's face over her shoulder as she walked out, disguised as an undersized male. As I drew my last breath would she wink and smile that decimal of a Magdalena smile?

These thoughts were in my mind as Burbank, having dealt with the question of my likely assassination, moved on to the next issue, the one that really interested him—namely how to handle Lin Ming by leading him to believe he was handling me. Burbank did not like to wing it—better to be ready in our minds before we acted, to have a plan, to avoid improvisation, to shun impulse. For Burbank, if something did not take years it wasn't real. If it moved too swiftly, it wasn't an operation. As he explained all this yet again, I fought the urge to fall asleep.

Burbank said, "Are you awake?"

I twitched. "Not really," I said. "Can we continue this in the morning?"

"Unfortunately, no. I'm catching a plane early tomorrow. You've got to stay awake."

He went to the refrigerator, drew a glass of ice water, and carried it back to me. I held it in a nerveless hand. He took a pill bottle out of his coat pocket and shook a tablet into my other hand. "Take this," he said.

I said, "What is it?"

"A wake-up pill."

I saw and heard Burbank as if through a gauze bandage. I had never been so sleepy in my life. But why? This had been a day like any other. Had Magdalena poisoned me after all? Slow-working poisons, Burbank had said. Suspicion moved within me. *The hell with it,* I thought. Anything was better than this. I took the pill.

"Drink the whole glass of water," Burbank said. "It'll take a couple of minutes to kick in." He watched me as if counting the passing seconds on a mental stopwatch. Immediately I began to wake up. Burbank brought me a mug of instant espresso, black. I drank it down. All of a sudden, I was wide-awake, as if adrenaline had been injected into my heart.

I said, "Wow. What is that stuff?"

"I don't know exactly," Burbank said. "But it works."

It sure did. I was even hungry again and said so. Burbank got a supermarket pizza out of the freezer and put it in the microwave.

As we ate the pizza we mapped out the Lin Ming operation. Thanks to the pill, my mind was clear, my spirit tranquil. This was the sequence of the plan: very soon I would move back inside Headquarters and work closely with Burbank. I'd be given a title and Burbank's enthusiastic trust. This would put noses out of joint at Headquarters, but it was necessary cover. I would give Lin Ming information—real but not vital information. Over time I would give him more information. And then, when the dirty trick had been done and the key had been turned in Lin Ming's mind, I would give him the false information that would blow Guoanbu to smithereens. It was a brilliant plan. It was a game of surround. It would change the balance of espionage. We would be the aggressors, the pranksters, the ruthless ones. The winners. Both Burbank and I felt wonderful—in his case, presumably, without a chemical stimulant.

"The key element—always remember the key element—is that nobody, *nobody* can know what we are doing until it's over except you and me," Burbank said yet again. "Just the two of us. No one else."

I was not insensible to the risks of this operation. To begin with, it was crazy, but then so were all really good operations. This one had the potential to put an end to me. If Burbank was killed in a plane crash or developed early Alzheimer's or turned out to be a bastard or a traitor, I was lost and gone forever. No one would believe that Burbank, one of the most trusted and steady figures in the apparatus, had ordered me to do the things I was going to do. My own country would be my nemesis. I would be crushed, locked up, delivered to Magdalena or her equivalent. Even while still feeling the exhilarating effects of Burbank's pill, I didn't in my heart want to do this. Burbank, studying my face, saw this.

"You'll be in danger, no question," Burbank said. "But you've been in danger before and come out the other side. The payback will be that for the rest of your life you will live in a state of satisfaction for having done what you will have done for this country that we love."

This meeting was all but over. Formalities remained. Burbank had yet another new contract for me to sign. I signed it. Just like that I was a staff agent again—but no promotion this time. At dawn, Burbank departed. He left a spare car, an environmentally correct electric one, for my use. I could stay in the house until he got back. No one would bother me. Burbank and I and the caretaker and no one else knew this house existed. The caretaker was on vacation in the Seychelles. After Burbank returned I'd move into something more suitable, more secure, and report for duty at Headquarters.

By midafternoon the pill wore off. I was exhausted again. Burbank had shown me my room. When I put my head on the pillow I felt something beneath it. I slid my hand under the pillow and pulled out a fully automatic ten-millimeter pistol with one of those extra-long gun-nut magazines sticking out of the butt. If nobody knew this barn existed why did I need this thing? I fell asleep before I could answer my own question.

THREE

23

I realized after a day or two as Burbank's house guest that I could live no longer with the caretaker's psychotic paintings. When I was awake they depressed me—angered me. In dreams I came downstairs in the dishwater light of early day and found mammoth portraits of Chen Qi or Steve or the tenor or sometimes the Hessian in his muddy football suit, silent and still, waiting for me. The house itself was so isolated, so surrounded by forest, so empty of life—not even an insect lived in it with me—that I became pathologically watchful. I half expected to wake up some night and see Magdalena at the foot of the bed, syringe in hand, having just injected the venom of the Dahomey viper between my toes. I moved to a cheap motel in Manassas, and on the next nights to other motels in other towns. I went to the movies. I ate junk food, so I nearly always tasted scorched grease at the back of my throat. On the fourth morning, while I was having a superheated breakfast at a McDonald's, Burbank texted me. We would meet at the barn at ten that evening.

I got there a little early. I did not turn on the lights in the room where the paintings were. Though surely he knew about it, Burbank didn't mention my absence from the house.

He handed me the ID card suspended on a chain that would get me through the gates at Headquarters and into the building in the morning. It was a lot like the one I wore around my neck in Shanghai when I worked in the tower for Chen Qi.

"The daily meeting is at seven-thirty," Burbank said. "Be there at seven on Monday. Use the main entrance. Sally will be there to greet you."

He told me the number of my parking space and gave me a parking sticker. He asked if I had any questions. I didn't. He was brusque. He said, "Let's go. Do you have a credit card or a checkbook on you?"

Both, I said. He dropped me off at an all-night car dealership that sold used and new cars at low but nonnegotiable prices. "Nothing fancy," he said, never one to eschew the obvious. "No bright colors." Using my debit card I bought a gray Honda Civic with eighteen thousand miles on the odometer and not a scratch on it and drove it away. There was some difficulty about the registration because I had no local address, so I had to rent the car for a week to give me time to find a place to live. One of the first things I was told when I joined Headquarters was that espionage was a capital crime in every country in the world, so it was vital to be up-to-date in all your papers, for everything to be strictly legal, even in the United States, so as not to give the cops a pretext to mess with you.

The next morning I rolled through the gates as if the guards had known my Civic and my face since childhood. As promised, Sally was waiting for me in the lobby. She led me through the color-coded labyrinth of doors to a blue one that was new to me. At seven o'clock exactly, Burbank joined us. Sally awaited orders but received none. He left her standing there and pushed open the door. A big room. About a dozen people in suits sat at a polished conference table. Heads turned. All but two chairs were occupied—Burbank's, which was a sort of high-backed throne at the center of the table, and an ordinary one just beside it. He gestured me into the ordinary one. Those attending had an air of entitlement about them—gray heads and bald ones, and in the case of the women, mostly dyed ones. Everybody except me wore reading glasses perched on the bulbs of their noses. I recognized none of these people, but why would I? The silent question they seemed to be asking in unison was, What is this unwashed person doing in this holy of holies?

Burbank explained. "For some time I have felt I needed a younger mind closer to me, and I have decided that this young man is the person I have been looking for," he said. He told them my true name. "He will be my right hand," Burbank said. "He will sit in the office next to mine, which has been unoccupied since Suzie Kane left us. He has my confidence. He reports to me, takes his orders from me and no one else, and is to be regarded as a full and equal member of this group. He has done good work in the field and has just completed an exemplary three-year tour under deep cover in denied territory. He will do more good work in Headquarters."

The others listened with blank faces. I detected no enthusiasm for discussing in my hearing the profound, the unutterable secrets known only to this exalted committee. But they spoke freely, and I learned some things I quite possibly might never have known if Luther Burbank had not come into my life. Most of these family jewels seemed trivial to me, as the deepest and darkest secrets often do. I listened, not too intently, and kept my mouth shut. When the meeting broke up, after an interminable hour, nobody shook my hand and bid me welcome. No one smiled. Nobody paid any attention to me at all. I might as well have been an inflatable doll that Burbank had placed in the seat beside him to make the highway patrol think he wasn't alone in his car as he drove in the HOV lane. Burbank gestured for me to follow him into his office, the one with all the safes, where we could talk. He said, "What did you think of the Gang of Thirteen?"

"Is that what it's called?"

"Not by you, if you're wise," Burbank said. He paused, waiting for me to answer his question. When I didn't answer he said, "Well?"

I said, "I sensed no great enthusiasm for your new assistant."

"Nothing surprising about that," Burbank said. "I sprang you on them. They didn't see it coming. They believe they have a right to see things coming. They can't fit you into the picture. They'll freeze you out, isolate you, put you in Coventry."

"Coventry?"

"Old schoolboy word for the silent treatment. Shunning. Be a man and you'll be fine."

"Yes, sir."

"'Luther' when we're alone, but that's the spirit," said Burbank.

I nodded.

"Sometime tomorrow you will be provided with a computer password," Burbank said. "It will give you access to all CI files. Or almost all. Only myself and the people you met this morning have that level of access." He pointed a finger. "Your office is through the door behind my desk. Come through it only when I buzz."

The tiny windowless office was a far cry from the glass stage set I had occupied when working for Chen Qi. It was about the size of a walk-in closet, a cubbyhole into which were crowded a desk and chair, a computer, a see-through burn basket, a safe. Had I been an inch taller or ten pounds heavier I would not have been able to squeeze my body into the remaining space. Burbank buzzed at four o'clock that afternoon. My day had been idle. I had been given no work to do, so I surfed the Web on my cell phone to pass the time. I read the *Times* and the *Wall Street Journal* and the Chinese newspapers and looked up facts at random, establishing among other things that Luther Burbank, the great nineteenth- and twentieth-century American horticulturist who created some eight hundred hybrid plants, had had no children and so could not possibly be a direct ancestor of the Luther Burbank I knew. A century and a world apart, the two Luthers used similar techniques to tweak nature—grafting, crossbreeding, happy accidents. Plums (113 new varieties) and most other kinds of plants and Shasta daisies in the case of the original Luther, spies and traitors for my man.

The end of the day, a very long one, was near. The promised password had not been issued. Evidently it had been a frustrating day for Burbank, too. His voice was hoarse, his eyes red-rimmed. He slumped. He sipped green tea and held it in his throat for an instant before swallowing. I was standing up. He pointed at the chair. I hesitated because it looked just like the one with the sawed-off front legs. He said, "Different chair. Trust me. Sit down."

Burbank said, "There was some resistance to opening the files to a newcomer. Tomorrow you will have full access. This is a turf thing. Nothing of great importance is in the computer. If that were otherwise it would be a great folly, given the ability of geeks in Nigeria and Nepal, let alone our more dangerous adversaries, to hack into any known system and read the mail. But we've covered that ground already."

Burbank looked at me expectantly, as if he knew I was bursting with curiosity. The higher-ups were talking about me. Why wasn't I asking what they were saying? It wasn't difficult to guess. But I did have one unaskable question, namely why was Burbank antagonizing these people and turning them against me if he wanted me to be useful to him? I could just as well have been another Sally, no threat to anyone. Even if you're dealing with a Burbank, a master of evasion, you learn more by letting the other guy fill the silences. I waited for whatever was coming next.

"What I want you to do for the next few days is go through some of this computerized stuff at random and cut and paste whatever interests you into your brain," Burbank said. "A lot of the data is iffy—*all* unprocessed information is iffy and so is a lot that has been processed—but I want you to find something that intrigues the mind, a lure that a fish named Lin Ming would take, maybe something from a friendly intelligence service that can be attributed to that service, and then I want you to find a second and a third such piece of plausible junk. Include at least one item about Taiwan. And discuss this with me next time I buzz."

I said, "May I ask how much time that gives me?"

"I don't know. And stop saying 'may I ask.' The whole point of this arrangement is that yes, you may ask. So just fucking ask."

Burbank was not usually given to such language. He really must have had a bad day. He finished his tea and got to his feet. He said, "That's all."

As Burbank had warned, the files were a hard slog. The content was mostly gossip, unsubstantiated and nine times out of ten hardly worth substantiating. Many, even most files are like that. On opening them you ask yourself, *What's so secret about this?* But every now and then something catches the eye. The natural reaction to such a find is not to cry hallelujah, but to be twice as skeptical as usual. If it's plausible, it probably isn't true. One of Burbank's famously demented predecessors was so controlled by this idea that he could never bring himself to believe that any defector from an enemy service could possibly be genuine. He refused to listen to them, refused to give them shelter. In his youth he had been badly burned by a turncoat, a secret Communist, whom he had trusted absolutely, whom he admired and emulated, even loved, and when the man turned out to be a Soviet agent, he never got over it. Thereafter he slammed the door in the faces of all defectors from the other side. If he was overruled, as sometimes happened, he would do his best to destroy the defector and discredit his sponsors. In the end he thought everyone in Headquarters was a potential turncoat if not an actual traitor and had the delusions to prove it. In the opinion of some, this made him better at his job. His crotchety spirit still stalked these hallways. I felt him at my back as I read.

The next afternoon, Burbank buzzed on the stroke of four. He seemed to be more like himself today. I waited thirty seconds for him to say something. He remained silent, so I spoke.

"It's no picnic to find something in these files that fits the requirement you laid out for me yesterday," I said. "But I have two or three possibilities for you."

I was still on my feet. Burbank said, "Sit down, you're giving me a stiff neck."

While combing the files I had borne in mind that what he wanted was something that would pique Lin Ming's interest. The first two items I mentioned would not necessarily have had that effect. They certainly did not interest Burbank. I slid over them quickly. Then I described a report about a meeting between a man whom Headquarters knew to be an officer of a Taiwan intelligence service and a second person the source said he knew to be an official of the Chinese embassy in Cairo.

To my astonishment, this was news to Burbank. The perplexed look on his face could not be read in any other way. He said, "Names."

We didn't yet know who the person from the Chinese embassy was. I named the Taiwanese. Burbank nodded, as if he knew the fellow.

"How fresh is this?" he asked

"The report, twelve days. The sighting, not specified."

"I'll ask Cairo to take an interest."

I was dismissed.

Cairo took Burbank's request to watch the Taiwanese case officer seriously. Soon he was never alone. Relays of sidewalk men were with him wherever he went. Either he did not notice them or did not care. He was a trawler who caught what he could when he could. He made his rounds as if he hadn't an enemy in the world. He met other foolhardy people from the Chinese embassy. He loaded and unloaded dead drops.

In photographs taken at diplomatic receptions he was a tall handsome Manchu with a tall beautiful Manchu wife. Besides several of China's languages they spoke the polished East Coast American English that was standard for their class. The wife had been overheard speaking fluent French at a dinner party. The situation was somewhat embarrassing for us because the Manchu had liaised with our stations in several different countries. He was by no means an asset of ours, but over the years he had traded scraps of information with us. He had given us good stuff and we had kept him posted on matters of interest to him. He was regarded as a reliable source, a friend.

As reports from the Cairo station dribbled in I made their contents known to Burbank. His interest in the case, strong from the start, grew stronger. But he took a wait-and-see line. This was something we could work with, but we would bide our time. He explained his decision. We didn't want to compromise our old friend the Manchu. Who knew what he might lead us to? We had to be careful not to step on Cairo's toes or the toes of our own Middle East people. At least not right now, not until we knew more, not until the time was right. There was no deadline. We were learning things it was good to know. That was an end in itself. Locking the product in a safe would be a good enough outcome. Maybe it was the impetuosity of inexperience, but I didn't agree.

Friday came at last.

24

Over the weekend I rented a town house a few miles from Headquarters. It was a clone of hundreds of others in the neighborhood, but it had its surprises. At dawn and twilight herds of white-tailed deer, dozens of animals, grazed outside my window as if the fringe of saplings that separated my "community" from the one behind it was a pre-Columbian wilderness. The cul-de-sac on which I lived showed few other signs of life. With one picture window in the front wall and three small ones at the back, the house was dark, but because I went to work at six in the morning and came home late at night, the murky atmosphere didn't matter. The deer were mute, no birds sang when the sun came up, so all in all there were few noises from outdoors except the distant murmur of traffic, no signs of life except the occasional sound of a car motor starting or someone shooting baskets in a driveway. I liked the silence. I didn't miss the uproar of Shanghai or the sirens of Manhattan. Living in this suburb was like living in a science fiction movie in which telepathic aliens have taken over the bodies of human beings. Even the kids made no noise, coming home as silent as manikins in their soccer uniforms, leaving just as wordlessly in the morning with bulging book bags on their backs.

On Monday morning when I got to my computer, I found that a breakthrough of sorts had occurred. The Cairo station had identified the man from the Chinese embassy who was meeting with the Manchu as a Guoanbu officer who used the pseudonym Xu Anguo. *Anguo* means "protect the country." He was a counselor to the embassy, big game. He and the Manchu met more frequently than is usual in clandestine relationships, always at night at an odd time like 4:27 A.M., always in a poor out-of-the-way neighborhood, always very, very briefly. The station tried picking up their conversations with a listening device and caught a few words. They spoke to each other in Hokkien, the language used in Taiwan. I reported this to Burbank.

"So what do they talk about?"

I handed over a transcript of the disjointed exchanges our techs in Cairo had managed to record. Burbank ran his eye over the Chinese characters. "Not much here," he said.

"But it's interesting in its way," I said. "The guy from the embassy has been telling the Manchu that everything has to be word of mouth only. Every paper is guarded. No one is ever alone with an embassy document. The Manchu says he has a camera that can be concealed in a ring. The other guy says he'd be shot if he showed up wearing a new ring."

"We don't want that to happen," Burbank said. "Draft a cable for my signature telling Cairo to tread softly and keep up the good work."

As the weeks passed, the case file fattened. We learned nothing much that was new and had no idea what secrets Xu Anguo was handing over to the Manchu, but the mere fact that we were aware of something that was none of our business justified the trouble and expense.

One morning after the daily meeting I walked down the hall as usual with Burbank, but instead of leaving him at the door of his office and continuing on to my cubbyhole, I followed him, uninvited, into the room of safes. He sensed that I was right behind him. His shoulders hunched slightly, he walked a little faster—but made no comment. When he got to his desk he sat down and went right on ignoring me. I waited, standing. It would have been presumptuous to sit down, and I didn't want to give him an advantage beyond the ones he already had.

Finally he said, "Yes?"

I said, "I have a proposal."

"Make it."

"I think I should go to New York, wait for Lin Ming to stumble over me in the street, and give him a hint about the Cairo stuff—without mentioning Cairo or the target's name or any of the details."

"Why?"

"First, because it's sensational material and he'd soon confirm that, and that would plant the seed of curiosity."

Burbank looked at his watch. "Go faster," he said.

"It would give us the initiative."

"Why?"

"Because we'd only give him a sniff," I said. "He'd have to give something back before he got the rest of it."

"Why would he do that?"

"Because if there's one traitor in one of their embassies there might be others in the same place or in other embassies. Just like you hoped."

Burbank said, "You realize this might blow our whole primary operation before it gets started?"

"That's one possibility," I said. "Another is that it would jump-start it."

"Why do you think that?

"Because sometimes taking a chance is worth it."

"A thrill seeker," Burbank said. "Just what we need."

He said it nicely, giving no sign that he was displeased. He had been given something to think about and he was thinking about it. I let him think.

After a while he said, "You realize that if you take this to its logical conclusion you're pronouncing a death sentence on that fellow in Cairo?"

"Yes."

A flicker of something—pride in a protégé?—came and went in Burbank's eyes. "Also that you're messing with the Manchu, who has been such a help to us in the past."

"That I regret. But what the Manchu is doing is just a diversion."

Burbank relaxed. This was a visible thing, his muscles unknotted, his eyes focused in a new way. He said, "You're coming along. Remember, keep this between the two of us. Keep thinking."

I said, "What about New York?"

Burbank held up a hand in case I was going to say more. He had no more time to spend on me. He said, "Okay, give it a go. But don't go too far."

25

I traveled to New York like an honest man—the shuttle to LaGuardia, a taxi to the apartment, a chat with the doorman. I found nothing of interest in the mailbox. After taking a nap and showering I walked downtown, thought about looking for a woman in a singles bar but decided against it because I didn't know of any singles bars. I had never been inside one. What were the rules? How many drinks did you have to buy for a lady before making your move? I didn't really know Lin Ming's rules, either. Surely he had noticed that I was no longer roaming the streets. Maybe he wasn't roaming the streets, either. I decided to show myself and see what happened.

In the Sichuan Delight the cashier on duty was the same young man who had shown me upstairs the last time I was here. He glanced at me, registered nothing, and said, "Any table, sir." I chose one in a corner and sat with my back to the wall. The food was good, but not in the same class as the feast Lin Ming had ordered the last time I dined from this kitchen. Another familiar face appeared—the waiter was the same wiry man who had carried the laden tray upstairs to Lin's safe room.

If he recognized me he gave no more sign than the cashier had done. However, the latter had vanished. When he came back half an hour later, entering through the kitchen door, I was working on my chili hot pot. He stopped for a moment to ask me how everything was. When I said it was just fine, he complimented me for having ordered the specialty of the house. With a broader smile he said, as if offering me some exotic delicacy reserved for the restaurant's most sophisticated customers, "Fortune cookies very nice tonight."

Normally I am too conscious of my image to crush fortune cookies, let alone eat them, but on this occasion I slipped them into my shirt pocket. On the subway I cracked them open. The first told me I would have true friends, the second that Confucius say a traveling man and his girlfriend are soon parted. A Manhattan phone number was written on the back of that one. I waited until I got home to call because I wanted Lin Ming to know where I was and the GPS on my cell phone would give him that information. A female voice answered. Without preamble, in Mandarin, the speaker said, "Basketball at the same gym as usual, same time, day after tomorrow."

I arrived at the gym five minutes late. I was not followed, but as I approached the door, a man loitering on the opposite side of the street made a phone call. Lin Ming was waiting for me inside. He was not his usual smiling self.

"You're late," he said, as if I were already under discipline.

"Am I? Then we'll have to play fast."

We did. This time I beat him. Badly. I had different purposes than I had had in our first encounter. He was pretty good, but he had few moves and only two shots, a pretty good hook and a wobbly jumper. He was smaller, slower, older, and he had learned the game as a grown-up, which meant he relied too much on his intellect instead of letting his body do the thinking. I got a little physical—not to the point of bullying, but enough to make him look behind him for another me. The scores were lopsided. At the end he was drenched in sweat, breathing hard. He had lost face. He didn't like it. However, we were in America, so Lin Ming shook my hand like a good sport and said, "Nice game." I couldn't really read him—probably few people could—but I had wanted to make him wonder why I did what I did. By the look of him, I had succeeded. Lately I had made an enemy of everyone I met except Burbank, and who could tell what exactly was going on with him?

After we showered, Lin Ming said, "Shall we go for a walk?"

"Why not?"

We found a park—"found" in quotes because clearly Lin Ming knew exactly where we were going—and sat down on an empty bench. In English he said, "You played much better today."

I shrugged. "Bad days and good days."

He said, "So you are back inside Headquarters as we discussed."

As we discussed? When was that? I said, "Well, I'm back inside, anyway."

"Are you still being completely truthful with Mr. Burbank?"

"Invariably."

"So what does he think of our friendship?"

"Maybe you should judge that for yourself, Mr. Lin."

"No names, please," he said in Mandarin. "Names are bad luck."

"Whatever you say."

Lin Ming smiled at last. The smile was tighter now. Possibly this was just the humiliation of losing at basketball. Maybe, though, it was the particle of doubt about where we stood that I was hoping to plant.

He said, "It is now time for me to ask you if you have considered the offer we discussed the last time we met."

"I considered it when you made it." I said. "I gave you my answer."

"You were serious?"

"Of course I was. So were you, I thought."

"Then why are we meeting today?"

"Because I have a counteroffer."

"A counteroffer? You think we can bargain?"

"Do you want to hear what I have to say?"

Lin Ming absorbed this affront. He said, "I am a listener by profession, my friend."

I told him that a man from one of their embassies was meeting regularly and secretly with a man we knew to be a senior officer of the National Security Bureau, the intelligence service of Taiwan. That we had recorded conversations between the two. That we had photographs. Then I stopped talking. He listened with such an absence of reaction that I knew he was shaken. Heavy silence. No eye contact.

Finally Lin Ming said, "And?"

"And we will give you the details if you will give us something in return."

"This is outrageous," Lin Ming said.

"Just business."

A long pause, then Lin Ming said, "What do you want?"

I told him: the complete Guoanbu file on Chen Qi's only son, Jianyu.

Lin Ming was shocked. His face reddened, his mask slipped—not much, but enough. He truly was outraged—a good sign, I thought. Two men I recognized as sidewalk people who used to follow me around were playing cards a few steps away. A gym bag rested on the table. I didn't doubt that it contained a camera, pointed at us, that recorded sound as well as video.

Abruptly, Lin Ming got to his feet and started to walk away. I stood up with my back to the card players, blocking their view with my bulk. I handed Lin Ming a fortune cookie. He resisted what I saw as the temptation to throw it on the ground and step on it.

"In case you want to shoot a few baskets," I said in a whisper, in English. No wink. Then I walked away. If he opened the fortune cookie he'd have my throwaway phone number. In the dusty trees starlings landed, squawked, and took off.

Thereafter, to make things as easy as possible for Lin's sidewalk crew in case they should come back into my life, I adopted a predictable schedule, going out for a morning run at seven, shopping always at the same grocery on the way home, going to the same gym at the same hour every other day, buying the same sandwich at the same shop at the same hour. It was a metronomic existence, and if Lin Ming was truly annoyed because I had put him on the spot, a chancy one. I did remember the tenor and the acrobats, and watched for them. What they had done in Shanghai, they could do in New York, where they had two rivers to choose from.

The possibility of something worse than a dunking happening was remote. Hollywood and Magdalena notwithstanding, assassination is not routine among spooks. There is no point in killing an agent of the opposition because the opposition will merely replace the dead operative with a new agent you don't know, and then there you are, back at the beginning, trying to identify the new man. Totalitarian types, like the Chinese and the Cubans and the Nazis and the Soviets in the good old days, mainly kill their own people—usually the ones they suspect of treason or even more dangerous crimes such as questioning revolutionary scripture. That was why Lin Ming was annoyed with me. I had put him in a position in which his home office might think it a good idea to reassess him. No doubt he had enemies within Guoanbu. So did I, apparently, though it was early in my career for this to be so.

I felt the need of a refuge, somewhere I could go and not be followed —someplace where I was inaccessible if not protected. There were such places. My university had a club in New York. In theory, if you didn't belong, you could not enter unless you came as the guest of a member. Up to now I hadn't been tempted to join, but I decided it might be a good idea to do so. After supplying the necessary credentials and paying the initiation and membership fees, I was admitted.

On the day I received my membership card I dropped in during happy hour and went immediately to the bar. I had been there years before as the guest of a faculty member. The bar itself was a magnificent mahogany thing, as massive as the poop of a whaling ship. Behind it hung a mirror that was installed when there were a lot of penniless immigrants available to polish it. Apparently there still were, because the thick glass sparkled. Alumni of all ages bellied up to the bar and nearly all of the tables were taken. This was a world I did not know. I had gone straight from graduation to the army and straight from training to Helmand province—and then, as you know, to hospitals, to spookdom, to China, to where I was now—one hermit's cave after another. I was no longer used to good fellowship, but I found a space between two brokers or lawyers or bankers and ordered a single malt whisky, spring water on the side. I studied the crowd—good fellows having a good time together. I imagined that they had all kept in touch from college days, as almost certainly they had, because most people soon discover that the chief benefit of going to a good college is that it provides you with a cohort for life—people you can make money with, people who talk your language, people who know the secret handshakes, people who sound alike. People who will usually help you out even if they don't particularly like you.

A good many women were present, mostly in twos, mostly at tables, mostly attractive, all of them pictures of chic. I reimagined them as kids just out of high school. Freshman year had been a sexual circus, and even though my ROTC connection repelled the more political women, who were usually the ones most interested in mindless sex, I found partners. I looked from face to face hoping to recognize someone about my age, someone perhaps I had known, as the Bible puts it. No luck. Lately I had been thinking a lot about women. There had been no one after Magdalena, and no one for quite awhile before her, so I was in the market for companionship. I was not such an optimist as to think that I would find it here. But it seemed possible that I might. It would be nice for a change to sleep with a woman who was not just doing her job.

I smelled perfume. A woman, almost as tall as I was, stood beside me. She was Chinese. She was striking. The bartender hurried to her without being summoned, a glass of white wine in his hand. With a smile that must have made the poor fellow weak at the knees, she signed the chit in an undecipherable scrawl and said, "Thanks, Guillermo."

Clutching her chardonnay, she started to go, then met my eyes in the mirror, then turned and looked at me. Bright obsidian eyes, thick brows, arched nose. She spoke my name followed by a question mark. I didn't remember her, but I nodded.

She said, "The student soldier. The athlete. The Mandarin major. I used to watch you play tennis. Great backhand. Terrific serve. Incredible match against that guy from Dartmouth."

True, I had been on the tennis team. Searching for her name, I said, "Freddy something. Ponytail. Very good player."

A nice, not quite eager smile. "Yeah, that's the one."

I said, "I didn't know anyone came to the matches."

"What power of concentration. The stands were always full." She had amazing diction, each syllable, each letter perfectly audible. She lifted her glass to me. No rings on her fingers. We drank.

She said, "You don't have a clue who I am, do you?"

"I should be ashamed." I meant it. How could I have forgotten this goddess? Before I could ask her name, she gave it.

"Alice Song. We were in some of the same classes, but I was a couple of years and a couple of rows behind you."

Now I remembered. Hair in braids wound round her head, no makeup. Shy. Silent in class. Aced every exam. A little gawky. Slumped to hide her breasts inside her baggy shirt. All that had changed except the brain.

"Now I remember," I said. "Are you meeting someone?"

She hesitated. Who could blame her? I said, "Well, maybe another . . ."

But she said, "Come on. My friend is a one-drink girl. Then she hurries home to the kids."

Following her to a table where a thin blonde awaited, smiling happily until she saw me. She didn't stay long. After she left, Alice Song asked me a question in Mandarin—something about one of our old professors. I answered in the same language. She said, "My God, listen to you!" We went on in Mandarin during dinner in the club dining room. She spoke it like a native, but with a very slight Queens intonation. She ate with appetite, an excellent thing in a woman, and drank sparingly. Wanting my wits about me, so did I. Like an old-fashioned girl who took her dating advice from *Cosmo,* she got me talking about myself. I told her about my time in Shanghai—not all about it, but enough. She asked why I wasn't still in the army. I told her. She was a lawyer, a litigator. She named the firm. Even I had heard of it. She was single. She had a young daughter from a failed marriage. She hadn't visited the club for more than a year. So talk about coincidences.

The conversation was the standard getting-to-know-you stuff—old times, books, movies, stories, did I remember so-and-so. We spoke English now, so the banter had different dimensions. Alice was a brilliant talker even when she was being careful what she said. I was drawn to her. I thought it conceivable that the evening might not end with the signing of the check and that what happened after that might not be the end of things. It was Friday. Her daughter was spending the weekend with her father, she said. On our way to the front door we switched back to Mandarin. "It's amazing how well you speak the language," Alice said. "If you were Chinese my mother would be crazy about you."

Visions of sugarplums danced in my head. And then I woke up and realized I couldn't possibly accompany her outside and let her, a Chinese woman unsuspecting and alone, walk into Lin Ming 's surveillance. So I shook hands and said how nice it had been to run into her after all these years, and moving swiftly, went out the door ahead of her and still walking fast, drew my watchers away. It was late, the street was almost empty, I could see them move, hear one of them cough.

26

At one o'clock the next morning, using maximum tradecraft for a change, I took a bus to Washington, then the Metro, then shank's mare to my town house. Nobody was behind me at any point in the journey, but then why should anybody be? Only in New York was I under surveillance. Whoever was watching me already knew what I did when I was in Virginia, or thought somebody in the government must be keeping an eye on me and didn't want to walk into somebody else's surveillance and find themselves being watched as they watched me. After a shower and a shave and a change of clothes, I went to work.

At Headquarters I intercepted Burbank on his way upstairs—he always used the fire stairs, not the elevator, and ran up the steps. I ran along beside him. He barely gave me a glance. At the top, to my surprise, Burbank steered me into my office instead of his own. With two people in it, my cell seemed even smaller. It had no chair for a visitor, so Burbank sat in my chair. I stood before him in front of my own desk. There was barely enough room for my shoes between the desk and the wall.

Burbank said, "Fill me in." I had sent him bare-bones letters about each development, but now I gave him the details. He listened, asking no questions until I finished.

"How do you read this?" Burbank said. "What's your gut feeling?"

"That it's going to take a long time for this grain of sand to become a pearl."

"Maybe not," Burbank said. "They know they've got a problem with one of their people but they don't know which one. That's a motivator."

Hadn't I mentioned that when last we talked? I said, "True, but they might just investigate everybody, everywhere. They've got plenty of manpower."

"You're discouraged?"

"Impatient. Bored. Idle. Everything takes forever. You've said so yourself."

Burbank lifted his eyebrows. Evidently he thought I needed encouragement. "You're questioning your own idea. You're frustrated by a lack of progress after two weeks?"

"I think Lin Ming is going to have trouble selling this in Beijing. Guoanbu is a bureaucracy. Bureaucracy exists to prevent things from happening."

"Is that what you think?" Burbank said. He walked out of the room. Was the conversation over, had I taxed his patience once too often? But a couple of minutes later he came back carrying a bowl of green tea and sat down again in my chair.

"Forget about how long it takes," he said, as if there had been no interruption. "List the possibilities."

"We can wait forever. We can back off and let the Manchu run his asset in peace and hope he'll share the product," I said.

"What else?"

"We can fold the operation."

"Forget that. It's barely begun."

"We could grab the Manchu's friend and talk to him in private. He may know other malcontents."

"They'd put everybody the suspect knows on a watch list the minute he disappeared," Burbank said. "Besides, it would really piss off the Manchu and his service, neither of whom we want to piss off."

Burbank said, "Let me ask you something. Who does your exgirlfriend know?"

"You mean Mei?"

"Who else?"

"In Shanghai, pretty much everybody."

"Inside the corporation, in the tower?"

Why was he always asking for information he already possessed? I said, "I ran into people she had introduced me to in the tower's elevators."

"What kind of people?"

"Wild by night, spoiled brats of the Party hierarchy."

"Wild in what way?"

"Alcohol, marijuana, loud music, punk clothes, outspoken disdain for the Party leadership. Sex, I suppose, but I wasn't an eyewitness to that."

"They trusted each other?"

"They grew up together, for whatever that's worth. At bottom they were just playing games. By day, they were very serious junior functionaries, and they seemed to take the work seriously."

"Strange," Burbank said. "It makes you wonder."

"About what?"

"Everything. For example, this Mei of yours. If she's who she seems to be, the child of someone who counts in the Party, why would Guoanbu use her as they do."

"Maybe she's not Guoanbu."

"You think she *loved* you?"

I didn't answer.

Burbank said, "Did she over time?"

I said, "She was always herself."

"No change at all? Mood, behavior, habits?"

"Toward the end she was less ebullient."

Burbank meditated, but very briefly. He said, "And you never knew who her father was, never asked?"

"No. I've never put that particular question to anybody."

"Is it possible she has something to resent at home? Something serious?"

"Anything is possible."

Burbank finished his tea. He looked at his watch. He stood up and sidled by me on his way out. For an instant we were breathing on each other.

I said, "Why do you ask me these questions?"

"Because resentment has been a factor, usually the key factor, in ninety percent of the defections of foreign assets in the history of this organization," Burbank said. "Somebody doesn't get promoted or doesn't get the respect he thinks he deserves or can't forgive an insult. Or hates his daddy because the old man did him so many kindnesses or has the wrong expectations. He decides to get revenge. Resentment is the open sesame of our business. It's also the demon when it comes to our own people. It hides, it evades, it smiles at you as if nothing is wrong."

Was he talking about Mei? Or was he talking about me, putting me on edge? Certainly I had my resentments. So probably did Mei. Who didn't? I said, "So?"

Burbank said, "So be aware of the possibilities."

27

It was midwinter before the phone call came, early on a Sunday morning. The familiar female voice told me that I was invited to dinner at six o'clock the following evening at Zorba's Café near Dupont Circle, not far from the Chinese restaurant where Lin Ming and I had met for the first time. I accepted. Around three, snow began to fall. I called the Hilton on Connecticut Avenue and booked a room for the night. By the time I parked in the hotel garage and checked in, two or three inches of snow had accumulated, and it was falling even more heavily than before. It didn't take a weather prophet to know this was going to continue. Washington, whose snow removal capabilities are next to nil, would be paralyzed by midnight. It also meant that the U.S. government, including Headquarters, would shut down for at least a day.

I had just enough time to walk to Zorba's. Inside, I saw myself in a wall mirror. I looked like a snowman, my parka whitened by the stuff. Usually at this hour the place was thronged, but tonight even neighborhood people were staying home, so it was all but deserted. Lin Ming, wearing a puffy, down-filled, made-in-China winter coat with a fur collar, waited at one of the half-dozen occupied tables. He waved. He smiled. He leapt to his feet. No gestures could have been more unexpected. He threaded his way among the tables, shook my hand with yet another smile, and said, "It's good to see you again, my friend."

We ordered at the counter, a Greek salad with chicken for Lin, a yero and oily Greek fries for me, two beers. He paid both tabs, holding up a warning hand to prevent me from even thinking about reaching for my wallet. When our number was called over the loudspeaker, Lin Ming fetched the tray, as if all of a sudden he was the lesser person. We ate in a businesslike way, making almost no conversation. About halfway through the meal Lin Ming remarked that the lamb in my yero had a funny smell. Very greasy. Did it taste the way it smelled?

"Pretty much," I said. "You've never eaten lamb?"

"Never," Lin Ming said with feeling.

Just as we finished, the lights went out. A female voice screeched in the darkness. Lin Ming said, "Let's go for a walk."

I didn't like this situation at all. The streetlights, the traffic lights, the shop windows were dark. I hadn't experienced such pitch darkness since Afghanistan. You could half-see snowflakes falling and hear the snow squeak when you stepped on it. By now it was ankle deep. We walked—slogged—for what seemed to be about half an hour. Lin Ming must have been sweating inside his coat. Because the falling snow stuck to its fur collar, he was faintly visible in the darkness. This was not a particularly dangerous neighborhood, but what a laugh it would be if we were mugged—two blind desperadoes handing over their valuables with knives at their throats. Even a master of martial arts—I didn't doubt that Lin Ming was just such a master—would have difficulty taking a blade away from an assailant if he could see neither the knife nor the assailant.

Lin Ming cleared his throat loudly and spat into the snow. A few steps afterward, he did it again—the aftereffect of smelling the lamb, maybe. Or, who knew, a signal to the assassin who awaited us in the blackness that had descended on the city. This was the most aimless clandestine meeting I had ever had. All the usual stuff—the signals, the double-talk, the solemnity, the darting eyes—was missing. We walked on, neither of us speaking a word although we could have chattered in Mandarin to our hearts' content and the odds were ten thousand to one that no lurker would have understood a word. Lin Ming was mute for reasons unguessable. I kept my mouth shut because I wasn't going to be the first to break the silence. My feet were wet. I was edgy for other reasons. I should have used the urinal before leaving the restaurant, but it was just as dark inside Zorba's as it was outside.

By now my eyes had adjusted. I could see Lin Ming quite plainly—not just as a shape in the darkness, but the man himself, his face inside the hood, his gleaming teeth. Apparently he could see me, too, because he put a hand on my arm and said, "Stop. I think we're here."

He turned on a flashlight, a blindingly bright one, and swept the building before us. He read the number on a door and said, "We've passed it."

We turned around. After fifty steps or so, Lin Ming again switched on his flashlight and this time found the number he was looking for. He lighted our way into a doorway. The door was ajar. No elevators were in operation, of course, so we used the fire stairs. Through the darkness Lin Ming moved upward almost as fast as Burbank. On the fifth landing he switched on the flashlight again, located the door, and shone us through it. This on-and-off business with the flashlight destroyed my night vision, so I practically had to hold on to Lin's belt to find my way down the corridor.

At last we came to a door that showed a thread of yellowish light around its edges. Lin Ming pushed it open—it was unlocked—and stood back to let me go first. An inner door stood open, and through it I could see candles burning—many candles. Lin Ming was behind me, almost pressed against me, like one of the acrobats.

I walked through the door, and there in a puddle of buttery candle-light sat Chen Qi with a glass in his hand. I smelled scotch. I was not surprised. Of course it was Chen Qi, the most unlikely man in the world to be here all by himself. Who else would it be? He stood up, he smiled, he extended a hand and shook mine firmly. He spoke my name. I looked around to see if anybody else was lurking in the shadows, if there were other doors, other ways out. The answer to all these questions was no.

I said, "Good evening, CEO Chen. What a pleasure."

"I agree," Chen Qi said. "Sit down, please. We have things to talk about."

As of old, I did as I was told. Chen Qi did not quite snap his fingers at Lin Ming. But without turning his head he said, "Single malt." To me he said, as if he had some reason to be nice to me, "I think you'll like this whisky. Eighteen years old. Very smoky." Lin Ming, obsequious as a waiter, brought my whisky—two ounces, one ice cube.

Chen Qi was in affable mode, as on the night we dined together in Shanghai and he offered me a job. He hoped that I had been well. He brought me greetings from my former colleagues in the tower. My good work, my American humor were missed.

He said, "I hope you're enjoying your new posting."

"It has its moments."

"It must be stimulating, working so closely with your new chief. So famous for being infamous," Chen Qi said. "You have a way of finding your way to the top. I think you will have a very interesting life. I have always thought so."

"Not nearly so interesting as your own life," I said.

"You shouldn't be so sure about that. You should be on the lookout. Opportunities hide, then leap at a man," Chen Qi said. "I'm sure you remember the young woman you knew in Shanghai."

"Zhang Jia?"

"Zhang Jia has married and is pregnant. A boy, according to the sonogram, so she's a fortunate person."

"I'm glad for her," I said. I was.

"I wasn't asking about Zhang Jia," Chen said. "I meant the earlier one, the first woman you had. What did you call her?"

"Mei."

"Yes, Mei. Now I remember."

"She's well and happy, I hope."

"As far as I know she's well," Chen said. "But happy? Probably not."

"I'm sorry to hear that," I said. I took hold of myself and said, calmly I thought, "What's the problem?"

Chen Qi said, "You've finished your whisky. Did you enjoy it?"

"Very much."

"Then you shall have another."

He gave no order, not even a gesture, but his words were enough to bring Lin Ming and a tray at the trot. He poured one finger of the amber fluid into each of our glasses, and deftly handling silver tongs, added an ice cube.

Chen Qi said, "There's something about your friend Mei—several things in fact—that you may not know."

"There is an infinity of things I don't know about Mei," I said. "She never supplied a single fact about herself. Not even her true name."

"Really? And you never asked for facts? Why not?"

"I thought she was entitled to her privacy."

"How sensitive. Especially for an officer of U.S. intelligence."

His voice roughened. His eyes hardened. That much showed, if only for an instant. Had he been a softer man, his face might have been flushed. I put down my whisky glass. The moment was not right for a friendly drink. Chen Qi noted the gesture and put his glass on the table as well.

"Why were you so incurious?" he asked.

"In her case, at the time in question, who she was was irrelevant. I thought I understood what she was."

"And what was that?"

"A woman who lived her own life as she wanted to live it."

"Like an American woman. Do you know what Chairman Mao said about that? 'Never trust an American girl.'"

I said, "He knew American girls?"

Chen Qi brushed away my words with a gesture. It was Mei he wanted to talk about. "Consorting with an American spy is never irrelevant to the people who may now have this Mei of yours in their hands," he said. "They insist on facts. Believe me, she will supply them. Anyone who is her friend would urge her to supply them."

"In this case, what I was, or was suspected of being, *is* beside the point," I said. "I thought it was possible that Mei was an agent whose job was to observe what I did and report. I also thought any woman in China would do the same—would have no choice."

Chen Qi blinked—actually blinked. I had crossed the line. I was guilty of disrespect. His affability evaporated. I was not dismayed by this mood swing, though a saner man might have been.

I said, "So how long has Mei been in the hands of Guoanbu?"

"Guoanbu?" Chen Qi said, as if the term were new to him. "She was placed under protection shortly after you and Lin Ming, here, had your most recent conversation."

"Do you know where she's being held?"

"If I did why would I tell you? What can you do for her?"

The answer was "nothing." To Chen Qi I said, "Let me ask you a question."

A gesture—*go ahead if you must.*

"What's your interest in Mei?"

Chen Qi said, "I have her interests sincerely at heart."

"I don't doubt it. But why? Is she related to you?"

No flicker of a reaction from Chen Qi. No sound. Lin Ming, somewhere behind me, moved—twitched. I could feel it.

At this moment the power came back on, fluorescent tubes flickering and buzzing. Chen Qi paid no attention. The bluish electric glare was less flattering to him than the candlelight had been. With no shadows to conceal the reality, he looked just like the heartless bastard he was. I hoped that I didn't look as sick to my stomach, as strangled by anxiety, as I actually was—Mei in prison, confined, silent, learning, session by session, the *Kama Sutra* of pain and fear that was secret interrogation.

I made the feeling worse with my next guess about her identity. "Your mistress?"

"Don't be ridiculous," Chen Qi said.

But Chen Qi, the invulnerable man, looked caught. He looked as if he wished Mei's mother had drowned the girl in a bucket on the day she was born. How else would he feel? If she actually was his relative, however close or distant, and she was under investigation for sleeping with an American spy, he would be under suspicion himself, because how could she commit such crimes without his approval? Chen Qi got to his feet. Lin Ming rushed to help him into his overcoat.

"Our time together is over," Chen Qi said. "You and Lin Ming will have a chat after I go. But before I leave I have a suggestion to make to you."

Chen Qi looked me in the eyes. "You must do what's best for yourself," he said. "But if you are concerned about this girl—Mei? Is that what you call her?"

"Yes."

"The situation may not be hopeless. Obviously she is in difficulty," Chen Qi said. "But if you were to create an opportunity, so to speak, by reconsidering the offer of employment Lin Ming has made to you, then that might give this Mei an opportunity of her own to make amends, to improve her situation."

His eyes were still locked on mine. I said, "How would she do that, and what would it have to do with me?"

"She is said to be willing, even eager, to return to you, to marry you, even," Chen Qi said. "If you were with us and she were with you, she could be a help to you and you to her. It is an opportunity, a rare opportunity, to have what you want by doing a good thing. In my opinion, it is not impossible that a similar thought might occur to the people who are now deciding what should happen to her. She could come to America, become a citizen, live as an American. Make her own life as you say she wants to do. I see no other way this, or anything like it, could happen."

Lin Ming opened the door. Chen Qi walked through it.

28

Burbank went straight to the obvious question.

"What do they gain from this?" he asked.

"Who knows?" I said.

"Come on!" he said. "*Think,* then answer the question."

I had already thought—all night long in my overheated hotel room, all the next day and another night while I waited for thirty inches of wet snow to be scraped off the streets and highways, and all during the inchworm drive along the one plowed lane of the George Washington Parkway. I arrived at Headquarters at 6:00 A.M. on Tuesday. Burbank was already at his desk—showered, shaved, wide-awake, crisp clean shirt. He had slept in the office. His folding cot and rolled-up sleeping bag stood between the rows of safes. He asked about the weather, unable to check it out himself because his office, like mine, was windowless. I told him it was snowing again. Government workers do not drive in the snow. Before the last straggler arrived we'd probably be alone for hours, maybe all day, maybe longer.

I really didn't want to rephrase my answer to Burbank's question. "Who knows?" *was* the answer. Nobody ever knew Chen Qi's purposes for certain. To Burbank's mind, however, the answer I had just given him had merely obscured the real answer, which was, of course, the hidden answer.

I said, "Try this. Chen Qi has enemies he wants to get rid of. Or wants us to think so."

"And he wants us to get rid of them for him."

"Meaning he knows or guesses what we want to do, namely set up a fictitious network inside Guoanbu, and wants to make sure his enemies are on the list of traitors."

"Or wants us to walk into a trap."

"What makes him think we'd be dumb enough to do that?"

"Because he has a low opinion of us," I said. "Because he wants us to think we're counting on a coup. Because he thinks we'd calculate that doing his dirty work will rid the world of certain people who are enemies of the United States and are stealing its secrets. Because we'd think it would make our organization look good to the White House. Because it would help on the Hill at budget time."

Well, yeah. The usual drawn-out Burbankian pause followed. I waited in silence for it to end.

Finally he spoke. "So should we refuse or accept?"

"Refuse."

This was not the answer he had been looking for. "Explain," he said.

I said, "I don't want to be the go-between in this business."

"Really? Why the sudden change of heart?"

"It's dirty," I said.

"We're paid to be dirty so that the virtuous may be immaculate," Burbank said. "What else?"

"I'm personally involved. Emotionally involved."

"You're talking about the woman?"

"Yes, and the fact that I used to work for Chen Qi and the whole world knows that."

"Start with the woman," Burbank said. "You have feelings for her?"

"You might think that. We had sex every day for two and a half years."

"Every day?"

"No. We took five days a month off."

"Why did the two of you split?"

"She disappeared."

"Because she had carried out her mission and was moving on?"

"That's one possibility. She could have been kidnapped or drowned or locked up by Guoanbu just as Chen Qi told me. For whatever reason, she vanished. I went to work in the tower. Another woman was supplied. You knew all this."

"Not about the annual sixty days of abstinence."

Burbank was amused, an interesting thing to see.

I said, "I'm going to ask you a question about Mei."

He waited.

I said, "I've searched the files. I found nothing to suggest that anyone in this building or in any of the stations knows Mei's true name. Do you know it?"

Burbank hesitated. He gestured at his safes. "Somewhere I have a name for her that isn't a funny name," he said. "The person named fits her description, more or less. Whether or not it's her true name is another matter."

"What is the name?"

"I don't remember," Burbank said. "But I'll find it for you."

Maybe he would. That didn't mean that I'd find Mei among the multitude of Chinese women who had the same name. Burbank was right about that. She was gone, lost, probably in a labor camp in Inner Mongolia. They would never let her out.

Burbank showed no sign of wanting to end our chat. I would have been more than glad to do so. But we did have a lot more to talk about, and thanks to Mother Nature, he had no one else to talk to. The prospect of being snowbound and alone with my chief in this airless, sterile building for two days and nights made the heart sink. It was impossible to know what line of action Burbank might decide on, if any. It might even, for once, end with Burbank doing the rational thing, like refusing to fly into Chen Qi's butterfly net.

Burbank was meditating again. I used the time to look back on the events that had led me to this day. My upbringing. Football. Sex. My show-off decision to take an ROTC scholarship rather than accept my stepfather's generosity. That patrol in Afghanistan when my men— bunched up because I had not done my job and kept them spread out as I was supposed to do—had taken the force of the blast and saved my life because I happened to be crouching behind them when the bomb went off. And everything since. I had been scouted, spotted, selected, trained and conditioned and screwed and tattooed by two intelligence services for the suicidal job they were both offering me, as if they had cooked my fate by mutual agreement. And maybe they had. Both Burbank and Chen Qi had drawn certain conclusions about me, probably the same ones. They thought that I cared so little for myself, cared so little for life, for consequences, for shame, for my ancestors, that I would accept this poisonous offer. Did they have me dead to rights? I wasn't sure.

More quickly than usual, Burbank regained his focus. He said, "Are your reservations about carrying out this mission written in stone?"

Anyone with a brain in his head would have said yes in a loud voice. I said, "Why do you ask?"

"Because there's something in this for us. I've always thought so. You've always thought so."

"Have I?"

"Does memory deceive or were you the one who came up with the idea?"

"A fellow can change his mind."

"Can he now?" Burbank said. "Even if what Chen Qi is offering us almost exactly what we wanted?"

"Especially because that's true."

"You have a peculiar mind," Burbank said.

No argument.

Burbank said, "You think what just happened changes things?"

"Profoundly."

"It's a rare operation in which anomaly doesn't show its face. It's the law of the craft."

How Kiplingesque, that choice of words. But then, if Burbank hadn't been a Kipling character at heart he wouldn't now be the man of mystery and power that he was. Nor would I be sitting across a desk from him, not quite in full possession of my senses, while he offered me the chance of a lifetime to become the king of Kafiristan.

There was no place left to go with Burbank except in circles. For the next couple of hours, around and around we went. By then we began to hear voices outside the door as people began to arrive.

Burbank picked out a safe, opened it, went unerringly to the correct folder, and pulled it out. He had known exactly where this particular file was, exactly what it contained, exactly what the combination of this particular safe was. He handed me the file. It was not a very thick file. "The female in question," he said. "Your eyes only. Bring it back the next time I buzz." Burbank's clockwork day had begun. Every fifteen minutes, from now until closing time, he would have something pressing to do, someone to see, some gnarled issue to decide. There was no way of guessing when he might have time to buzz me again.

The file was labeled WILDCHILD. There was no mention of a true name. I began to read, fast, even before I sat down. Most of the file on

WILDCHILD was rank speculation—and so was my conviction that the woman therein described was the Mei I had known and no other. Like Mei, WILDCHILD had gone to high school in Concord, Massachusetts, and later attended Shanghai University. She spoke fluent English. She dressed like an American, acted like an American, had acquired the bad habits of Americans. Her father, true name redacted, called KQ/RUFFIAN in our files, was said to be a figure of consequence in the Party. As a kid of eighteen he had been an activist during the Cultural Revolution and established the reputation for ruthlessness that had carried him upward. WILDCHILD had become sexually active in her later teens, while in America. She had been withdrawn from her American high school and sent back to China when the family with which she lived complained that she and their teenage son had been discovered in bed together in his room, naked, joined, after the household was awakened in the wee hours of the morning by WILDCHILD's "ecstatic outcries."

After this summary introduction, several pages in the file were missing. These were followed by my own e-mail reporting the bicycle accident to Tom Simpson. Attached was an outraged footnote from admin about the cost of the bike I bought for Mei. Admin wanted to deduct the money from my salary. Burbank had ordered it reimbursed as an operational expense. I was surprised that this exchange hadn't been redacted because it confirmed that Mei and WILDCHILD were the same person, and that Burbank had seen an opportunity in our getting to know each other, and that he had encouraged our relationship from the first. And that I had been left in the dark like an unwitting asset. As the relationship ripened, Headquarters's interest in WILDCHILD—that is to say, Burbank's interest in her—intensified. He ordered the officer in charge of CI operations in Shanghai—his man, not Shanghai's—home for consultations. They met in private. No account was given of what was said, but shortly after the man from Shanghai got back to Shanghai, the file began to be enlivened by reports on WILDCHILD's movements.

These were paper documents, mostly written in Mandarin in several different hands, none of them in Mei's dashing calligraphy. They had been sent by pouch for Burbank's eyes only. Burbank's man in Shanghai was an industrious fellow. His sidewalk people were always with WILDCHILD. One or another of them, apparently, had been stationed at all times outside my door to log the times on her comings and goings. They photographed her, listened in on her cell phone, listened in on our sex life through bugs and cameras they planted in my rooms—just as I had suspected, although I had suspected the wrong suspects. Naturally the file did not reveal who these sidewalk people were or where Burbank's man got them or how they got away with what they did under the all-seeing eye of Chinese counterintelligence. Obviously they were Chinese. But were they Chinese Chinese or Chinese-Americans or Taiwanese or one of half a dozen other types favored by our own China people? Whoever they were, they were always there. Just like the ones who shadowed me in New York, just like the acrobats.

There were no reports on WILDCHILD's activities except when she was with me. If, as I had suspected, she had another lover, if she reported to a Guoanbu case officer, if she had any kind of life at all when we were apart, if she slept in her coffin, Burbank had not been interested. He cared only about Romeo and Juliet. How strange that would have seemed in anyone but him.

29

There were two possibilities. Either someone had slipped something into my scotch and I was hallucinating, or I was truly paranoid. Make that three possibilities. The third was that Chen Qi and Burbank knew each other and were working together, had been doing so all along on some perverse operation and needed an unwitting go-between who could be the fall guy in case things went wrong. If so, I was the designated fall guy. That thought tipped the scales toward paranoia. I knew this. I did my best to dismiss suspicion from my mind. Those who have learned what they think they know about the craft from deluded zealots are convinced that it is a world of deception and distrust in which no positive human emotion or sense of decency is involved. In reality the opposite is true. The entire basis of espionage is trust. Spying could not exist without it. If such trust is imperfect or not quite complete, then it is like all other varieties of trust. Ask yourself—do you, does anyone trust absolutely his spouse, his doctor, his lawyer, his best friend, his employee, his mother? Trust is selective. In practice, the agent trusts his case officer to protect him, to keep secrets that are a threat to his life and the lives of his entire family, to make the promised payments in full, in cash, and on time. In return the case officer trusts the agent not to set him up for capture, torture, imprisonment, and perhaps death at every clandestine meeting, and to provide reliable information or perform certain acts when called upon to do so. Within an intelligence service, colleagues may dislike one another and often do, but they trust one another absolutely. It is part of the contract, part of the mystique. It is the indispensable element. Its perversion makes treason possible and all but undetectable among professional spies, but when uncorrupted it is the code that drives the system. Everyone inside an intelligence service has been investigated to a fare-thee-well and is polygraphed on a regular basis. By these means doubt has been caged, even though every professional knows exactly how unlikely are most investigations, and especially the polygraph, to discover the truth, the whole truth—and most unlikely of all, nothing but the truth.

The idea that our side or their side might kill me never crossed my mind. If I became a problem, Burbank and Chen Qi (I had gone so far as to begin thinking of the two of them as a unit before I buried the thought) would just cut me loose. I could do them no harm. Fox News or the *New York Times* would hang up on me if I called and babbled the truth. A psychiatrist would put me on drugs. I'd live in a virtual world—or in the real one in case I had already been living in a virtual one. No one in Headquarters or Chen Qi's corporation or Guoanbu or any other intelligence service in the world would have anything to do with me. Hardly anyone at Headquarters even knew me. Those who did (remember the Gang of Thirteen) did not wish me well. They would be the Greek chorus: "There was always something funny about the guy. We all saw it even if the shrinks and the box missed it." I certainly couldn't count on the brave support of my few remaining friends on the outside. And wait a minute. "No fear of sudden death?" Did I not remember Magdalena? Oh, yes, I remembered her. But if she had been under instructions to kill me, she had already had a hundred opportunities. Had I been the target, I would not now be alive and trying to figure out what she was up to and whom she worked for. She got next to Mother, then next to me because she wanted access to someone I could get next to. But who? And why?

I told myself a lot of things. The fact was, when it came right down to it, I would go on doing the job no matter what, simply because I didn't want to walk out before this movie was over, no matter how bad it was. Not that there weren't worrisome signs I was loath to discuss with myself. For example, resentment was taking up more and more space in my mind. And you know what Burbank had to say about that.

Most of the above were night thoughts fueled by single malt whisky. In daylight I controlled my fantasies and waited for instructions. These were not long in coming. Late on a Friday afternoon, as everyone else headed for the parking lots, Burbank buzzed. It was the first time he had done so since we had our discussion about my meeting with Chen Qi and Lin Ming two weeks before. When I entered his office to return Mei's file, I found him bent over a small refrigerator. He extracted two frosty bottles of beer. He gave me one. "Cheers," he said. We clinked bottles and drank.

After a medium-long pause Burbank said, "You still have a phone number for your friend the basketball player?"

"If it still works, yes."

"Call him up on your way home and set up a meeting for this weekend. In New York."

I said, "What about Chen Qi?"

"He's in Cairo."

Chen Qi was in Cairo? Burbank read my thought, not that there was anything difficult about that.

"It's probably just a coincidence," Burbank said. "Business. But if it isn't, he'll walk into our surveillance and we'll know something new."

I asked what I was supposed to tell Lin Ming.

Burbank said, "What do you think you should tell him?"

"'No, thanks.'"

"Why should we do that?"

"Because what they offer is of no use to us."

Burbank lifted his beer bottle in another toast. "Right," he said. "Isn't it interesting how seeing the obvious makes things so much simpler?"

I said, "So now what?"

"So now you go to New York, meet Lin Ming, change the climate of your relationship with him."

"How? In what way?"

"You say Chen Qi treated Lin Ming like a servant on the night of the blizzard, humiliating him. You saw that Lin Ming resented it."

"And?"

"Remember what I told you. Resentment makes things happen."

Burbank's lip lifted ever so slightly. He pointed a forefinger at me and clucked his tongue. I took this as positive reinforcement, as a reward for good thinking, as a sign of camaraderie. Or condescension.

I said, "You really think it's possible to turn Lin Ming?"

"Didn't you just suggest that it was?" Burbank said. "Maybe not this weekend but if you play him right, you can get the process started. As I hope you're beginning to realize, these things take time. You know how to do it. Would you say that you and Lin Ming have the embryo of a relationship?"

"Maybe."

"Are you sure? Will it grow, will its heart begin to beat, will it create its own brain and liver and arms and legs? Will it in time create others like itself?"

His face was a mask of earnestness. What was he up to? I laughed.

He said, "What's so funny?"

"Nothing," I said. "I just didn't know you had a metaphorical side."

"Everyone has a metaphorical side. The question is, can you rattle his bones with a single question? Are you two friendly enough for that?"

He was grinning—a sight I had never seen before—and watching my reaction.

I said, "Maybe."

"That's the right answer," Burbank said. And then, as if granting me permission to do something I absolutely longed to do, he said, "Okay, go. Go to it. Don't fly. Take the next train. It will give you time to think."

30

By the time the Metroliner pulled into Penn Station I knew everybody in my car by sight. Walking out of the gate, I scanned the crowd: a buck-toothed girl hopping up and down in excitement, a Hasid who greeted another Hasid who had been sitting in the fifth-row window seat, a very short man with gym-rat biceps and a boxer's flattened face. And at the back of the crowd, Lin Ming. Our eyes met. He turned around and walked fast across the waiting room. I followed him up the escalators and into the street, then uptown on Seventh Avenue to the Forties. He kept track of my reflection in store windows. I saw no one worth worrying about behind us or across the avenue or ahead of us, and no sign of the sidewalk crew. I wondered if we were headed for the Algonquin, but before we got there Lin Ming for some unfathomable reason walked into an all-night sporting goods store. He headed straight for a rack of warm-up jackets at the back of the store and got behind it. From there he had a good view of the door. The display window was a sheet of light. A stalker could look in, but Lin Ming could not look out. This made him nervous, very nervous. This person was not the relaxed Lin Ming I knew. How pleased Burbank would have been at this sudden change in behavior. I stationed myself on the other side of the clothes rack, facing Lin, my back to the door, as if screening him from a defender while he took his shot at the basket. I took a cheap Mets jacket off the rack, held it against my chest, and raised my eyebrows in inquiry. How do I look? Lin Ming paid no attention. He said, "Take the uptown local to Seventy-second Street and walk down to the river." Then he left. I looked at two more jackets and tried on a Giants cap, then did as I had been instructed.

Forty minutes later, when I sighted Lin Ming, he was still on edge. You could sense a churning within him. A light breeze came off the Hudson. I could smell the river, glimpse New Jersey's polluted sky, faintly hear its clamor over the monotonous hum of the West Side of Manhattan and the counterpoint of its many sirens. After a couple of blocks, Lin Ming turned into the park and found an empty bench. I sat down beside him. He didn't flee.

In a voice I could barely hear he said, "Why are you here?"

"Because we have something to talk about," I said.

"This is not good."

"How do you know? We haven't talked yet."

"It's impromptu."

Inasmuch as Lin Ming himself was nothing if not a devotee of the impromptu, this should have made the contact more interesting to him, but what did I know? No matter how good my Mandarin might be, I wasn't Han and could not think like a Han no matter how hard I tried. We simply had different ways of thinking about thinking.

I said, "If you don't want to do this, I can leave."

"Too late," Lin Ming said. "Say what you came to say."

I did as he asked. Beside me in the half-dark, Lin Ming flinched. In the wash of the streetlamp he looked pale. He grew even more ashen as he listened to my words. Afterward he fell into a stillness. I waited for him to speak, to make a gesture, to leap to his feet and stalk away in anger, to pull out a stiletto and attempt to bury it in my heart or brain. Instead he remained as he was—speechless, inert. He leaned forward and rested his forearms on his thighs. His hands dangled between his knees. This pose of despair was as much out of character as the rest of his behavior. Was he acting, playing a scene? Making a joke of the whole thing? And if all this was genuine, how could Lin Ming of all people have believed that I had come to give him an answer different from the last one I had given him?

He muttered something. I said, "What? I didn't hear you." I spoke a little louder, a little more peremptorily than was absolutely necessary. This was method, one infinitesimal move in the reconfiguration of our relationship. He had to know this. It was a humiliation, however tiny. I felt a flicker of regret. I liked this man. I didn't like what I was doing to him. He had had enough humiliation lately.

Lin Ming gave me a sidelong look. After a minute he leaped to his feet and walked, fast, toward the next streetlight. I caught up to him. Another empty bench came in sight. I took his arm, thinking that he would shake off my hand, but he let himself be steered to the bench. He sat down and turned his head to stare at me.

"Speak," he said.

I told him what we wanted. Names, résumés, assessments of six high-quality targets within China, within the elite—perhaps within Guoanbu, though neither one of us would know about that. These people were so exalted that nobody less trustworthy than the ghost of Zhou Enlai would be cleared to possess such knowledge. Lin Ming did not flinch. What I had asked was too outrageous to register while my words still hung in the air.

Lin Ming laughed. In English he said, "You've got balls, I'll give you that. Just as a matter of curiosity, what do you propose to give us in return?"

"The same valuable goods already on offer."

"You're crazy. You know who these people are—who their fathers are. They are untouchable."

True. I didn't even nod but waited for Lin Ming to go on.

He said, "What you're offering us is chicken feed. One man in one embassy in return for the Party jewels? Be serious."

"How do you know the man we are offering to you is the only one like him?" I asked. "How do you know it's just one embassy? How do you know it's not a network? How do you know what we know and you don't know?"

"How do we know you know what you say you know?"

"You don't. You won't, either, unless you start playing ball."

He smiled—you might have called it a twisted smile, but even so it made Lin Ming look more like himself. "I have already played basketball with you," he said.

Without thinking I said, "Meaning what?"

"Meaning I know you are better than you pretend, that you can fake it when you feel like it," Lin Ming said.

I had thought he might just walk away. He made no such move. He seemed to be waiting for something else. But I wasn't going to request anything more and spoil things. I reached into my jacket pocket and showed him the brand-new cheapo cell phone I had bought for him.

I told him the number of my own brand-new phone. He committed it to memory, I could see him doing this. I said, "Give me a call when you've had time to think this over more carefully and realize just how much to your advantage it could be."

Lin Ming knew exactly what was happening. If he took the phone he would take the first step toward life as a turncoat, because there was no conceivable way he could give me what I was asking for with the permission of his masters. He made no move to take the phone. I continued to offer it. He looked at the ground, he looked over my shoulder at the empty park. On the count of twenty he took the phone from my hand and hurried off into the darkness.

31

It was only eight o'clock. I was hungry. I wanted to be with my own kind. I decided to drop in at the club. It was Friday again and I was dressed down like everyone else in this city and every other city in North America. Human beings cannot even go without a necktie unless they do it in unison. All mammals are the same—happiest when they all look alike, think alike, travel on well-trampled ground. Consider the wildebeests of the Serengeti, walking in their thousands around in the exact same semicircle season after season, all headed in the same direction, all eating the same grass, all watching placidly as reckless young nonconformists reject the blood wisdom of the herd and dash outside it to be killed and eaten by carnivores. I myself felt the pull of the herd. I hoped that Lin Ming would not feel it too strongly. Meanwhile, who knew, maybe I'd run into someone at the club who'd keep me company. On my first visit I had run into Alice Song, hadn't I?

This time the street outside the club was deserted. Inside, the cocktail hour was over, so there were many fewer people in the bar than last time. Not a single woman was among them. There was no babble, no laughter. I recognized a face or two—half-drunk white-haired men with raddled cheeks and whiskey noses. Guillermo the barman was on duty. Clearly he had not memorized my face on our single meeting. I ordered a Belgian wheat beer and drank it and because I had come here in hope, waited for Alice to show up. She did not appear. If she did appear I was sure she would cut me cold. But that might not last. I could break the ice by telling her the truth and making her laugh: I was being followed on the night in question by sinister foreign agents who were always with me and my disappearance was my way of saving her from such evil company. Meanwhile I was still hungry. I asked Guillermo if the dining room was still open. He looked at his watch, nodded, and said, "Better hurry. It closes in ten minutes."

The greeter was not happy to see me. No one was happy to see me today, almost certainly not even the phantasm I called Alice. Half a dozen tables were still occupied. White tablecloths, nice old silver cutlery engraved with the university crest. I ordered fettuccine Putanesca and a glass of a wine that the card on the table identified as Montepulciano d'Abruzzo. The pasta wasn't bad. I bolted it because I had had no other food that day and signed the chit. No one bothered me, but I had company of a kind in the pensioners across the room. We shared memories—the look and scent of the campus on the first warm day of spring and the delusion that the weather had always been like that, the drone of a lecturer, the sweet misery of hangovers. After only two visits I was beginning to like being a club member. It provided a sort of chaperoned aloneness that was new to me.

I heard female voices and went out into the foyer. A group of women, chattering and laughing, was descending the main staircase. There were fewer of them than the decibel level had led me to expect. One of them especially had a bell-like voice—Alice Song, of course. She was in the middle of the pack and some of the women at the front turned around and looked upward at her, as if they wanted to absorb the whole glamorous experience of her—voice, face, mind, the aura of her brilliant career, smashing clothes even if it was dress-down Friday. Certainly that's what I wanted. She was tall. She was striking, with a beautiful face that was not quite a woman's face, as if it were a female duplicate of the face of a handsome father. She spotted me immediately but went on with her story.

At the bottom of the stairs most of the women headed for the exit. Three of them including Alice disappeared into the lavatory. The other two emerged after a long interval and left. Five minutes after that Alice appeared. She walked up to me as if she knew I had been loitering. She looked neither happy nor unhappy—bemused, I thought, by the sight of me. She said, "So, someone paid the ransom?"

"I escaped my kidnappers," I said. "Who are your friends?"

"The house committee. Did you have dinner here?"

"The pasta."

"How was it?" she asked.

"It was okay. The service was a little grumpy, but I came late. There are no male members of the house committee?"

"There used to be," Alice said. "That's why the food was so bad. Men just show up at the mess hall. Women bitch."

"Let me guess," I said. "You're the chairperson."

No response but a level stare—what else would she be? All this was a way of avoiding a discussion of the mystery of the disappearing schmuck. She didn't want to suggest that she gave a damn about my running away by asking for an explanation. I couldn't apologize, couldn't explain. Alice wasn't exactly overjoyed to see me, but at least she was talking to me.

I said, "Can we have a drink together?"

"Not here," Alice said. "The bar closes at ten."

The club's grandfather clock whirred and struck the three-quarter hour. We went to a place down the street. Alice was a cautious drinker but voluble nonetheless. We spoke Mandarin—she started it. We talked about China. She had never been there, though she had lived in a replica of it while growing up in her parents' house in a Chinese neighborhood. Facts were her thing, though she knew as only a lawyer can know there is no such thing as immutable truth. She had been in court all week defending a company that had poisoned an entire river in Massachusetts with chemicals from its paper mills that turned the water green or magenta or yellow, killing everything that lived in it and making people who lived on its banks sick. In her heart she hoped her clients would be impoverished by the jury's verdict, but she was trying hard to keep that from happening because such an outcome would cost her firm money. The practice of law, she said, was morally exhausting. She said she would never say that in English. Neither would I regarding my own profession, or in Mandarin either. Alice asked what I did for a living. I told her I worked for the government.

"In which part of it, doing what?" she asked.

I said, "I'm not a civil servant. I consult under a contract." All of which, technically speaking, was the truth.

"Consult about what?" Alice asked.

"The mysterious East."

"Poor darling."

She let it go at that. I guess she thought she already knew all she needed to know about me from the classroom, the tennis court, the hallowed halls of yesteryear even though we had barely known each other in college. As a sexual possibility she became more intriguing by the moment. My girlfriends had always been on the small side. I had never known a woman who looked anything like Alice, who was so tall, who had so much voice, such a brain, who got so much more likeable as the evening wore on. She reminded me of no one.

We exchanged cell phone numbers. I put her in a taxi at 2:00 A.M. She had a dinner party the next night. We made plans to spend Sunday together, maybe drive up to Connecticut or somewhere and have lunch, then go for a walk in the fresh air. She had to be home by five, when her ex-husband would bring their child back. She had only the one kid. She liked it that way. Her daughter, whose outside name was Caitlin (in Mandarin, at home, Liling) was a nice person for a six-year-old, but Alice felt like a slacker because the child did not have a sibling. She said she might be better off living in China, where she would have no choice in the matter.

32

Next morning I listened to Mandopop while I ate breakfast and read the newspapers. The music activated a mental slide show—Mei in daylight, Mei in the dark. To pass the time I played solitaire on the laptop. By setting the level of difficulty at "beginner" I managed to win 8 percent of my games. The computer refuses to be cheated, and that takes away a lot of the fun of the game, but even so solitaire opens the mind. That was the problem—more Mei, more Chen Qi, more Yangtze. After an hour or so I surfed the Web and found one of those ads that invites you to track high school classmates. I clicked on it and typed in the name of Mei's high school. She had told me she played volleyball, so I tried "girls volleyball team." No luck. I tried different class years, and on the third try, there in the team photograph was sweet seventeen-year-old Mei in gym shorts, kneeling first row center. She was identified as Susan Peng. I typed this name into the search box and found her graduation picture—apparently the book had gone to print before she was thrown out of America on a morals charge. The caption said: "She is full of vim and vigor and is always on the go." Her nickname was "SuSu." She was a member of the National Honor Society and had participated in volley-ball, skating, debating team, Shakespeare Society, math club, waltz club, class play, school newspaper, and more. She was president of the math club. She was a princess of the homecoming queen's court. She was elected class brain and class madcap. I couldn't believe my luck. Never had a Headquarters file told me so much about her. Had she stuck to rules and lied to me about where she went to high school, I would never have tracked her down. The information was useless, of course, because the name she used as a student could not be a true name. Had Burbank recruited her when she was in high school and sent her back to China to lie in wait for the sucker who would give him entrée into the shadow land that was Guoanbu headquarters? This was an old question. There were no new answers.

With half a day and an evening to kill and a lot to think about, I lunched at the meatball sandwich place and went to a popcorn movie at the theater around the corner. Emerging from the theater at dusk I half expected to see Lin Ming in the crowd with his gym bag, but he wasn't there and neither was anyone else I had ever seen before. A light rain fell. Headlights bounced off the shiny pavement. I walked back to my building. The rain intensified. Although it's easier to follow some-one in the rain because the target's mind is on not getting wet, there were no signs of surveillance, just lots of people hurrying through the downpour.

The doorman stood under the awning with his big black umbrella. As he opened the door for me he said, "You got a delivery." He unlocked a drawer in his desk and withdrew a padded envelope and the ledger in which he recorded deliveries. "Came in at three fifty-seven," he said as I signed the book. "By messenger," he added.

"What did the messenger look like?"

"Guy on a bicycle. Skinny."

"American?"

"How can anybody tell anymore?" he asked. He thought, then shook his head. "Just a guy," he said.

Inside the apartment, I examined the envelope—my name and address typed on a plain label, no return address. I slit the sealed end with a kitchen knife and shook the contents onto the kitchen counter. A thumb drive fell out. There was nothing else in the package. I inserted the drive in my laptop. A photograph of Da Ge, Mei's favorite princeling, popped up. His real name was Chen Jianyu and he was, as I already knew, the son of Chen Qi. There followed a narrative of many pages, with references to other semiprincelings, including Mei as an unnamed subject. In some of the pictures she was with Chen Jianyu, in others with me. In the ones with Chen Jianyu she was radiantly happy. I had always supposed and now I was certain that there was something between the two of them.

I read for hours. It was a workout. Mandarin bureaucratese is no less convoluted than the same kind of gibberish in any other language, and I sometimes had to use the dictionary, so it was slow going. Toward dawn I made some tea and ate some cereal. As I chewed the Raisin Bran I tried to think. When at last I was done reading, I felt a great unease. Was this file a document or a forgery? Why the indecent haste to put it into my hands, mere hours after I had horrified Lin Ming by asking for this material?

Someone was trying to tell us that we had set the hook in Lin Ming's lip. Maybe we had—anything was possible. *The wise man does not believe in triumph,* I thought, inventing a Laozi proverb. I was tired, eyesore, completely sober. My stomach was sour. My eyes hurt. I turned everything off—Mei first, then the rest. I flopped on the unmade bed without bothering to undress. What a busy day I had had, what dark dreams I had to look forward to if I could talk myself into falling asleep.

When I woke at midmorning my mind was on Lin Ming, as though continuing a thought that had begun while I was asleep. Still abed, I called the number of the cell phone I had given him in Riverside Park. He did not pick up.

"Hey buddy," I said in English to his voice mail. "I've got an extra ticket to the game right here in my hand. Good seats. Gimme a ring before twelve if you're interested."

This message had hidden meanings, wild cards on which I had briefed Lin Ming when I gave him the phone. "Extra ticket" meant I wanted to meet, "right here in my hand" meant urgent. "Good seats" meant the Museum of Natural History at the entrance to the Planetarium. "Gimme a ring" meant cough twice if the coast is clear. "Twelve" meant three o'clock because its two digits added up to three. "If you're interested" meant *really* urgent. Could Tom and Huck, swearing a blood oath in McDougal's cave, have been more devious?

It was ten-forty now. After showering and shaving for the first time in two days, I poached two eggs in the microwave, remembering to prick the yolks with a needle. I made some toast and heated milk for instant hot chocolate. I tried to read the *Times* but failed because yesterday's ideograms still fluttered in my head like moths.

At two-thirty I headed for the Planetarium, the thumb drive containing Chen Jianyu's file in the watch pocket of my jeans. According to my maternal grandfather, who in 1943 parachuted into Lombardy for the OSS, the Gestapo never looked for the watch pocket when frisking a captured American agent because Old World pants did not have watch pockets. That's where the men of the OSS hid their suicide pills, said Gramps.

The museum was mobbed, just as it had been on Sundays when I was a kid. Shrill adolescent voices bounced off the walls. Inside this clamor, quiet and still, stood Lin Ming. The hood of his Knicks sweatshirt was up, making him hard to recognize or even to tell that he was Chinese. He saw me and coughed twice, his all-clear signal. I saw but did not hear the cough.

And then, with a twist of the bowels, I remembered Alice Song and our date for lunch. I looked at my own watch—not a signal to Lin Ming that the coast was clear, though maybe he took it for that, but a spasm of embarrassment and guilt and panic. I was an hour and forty minutes late: strike three. I walked into the crowd, trying to escape from my own stupidity. Lin Ming followed. *Asshole!* I called myself. *Idiot!* Because of the noise it was impossible to call Alice, and anyway how could I make amends and why would she pick up after she saw my name on caller ID? I paused in front of a glassed-in display of American birds. The skylarking crowd surged beyond us, reflected in the big backlit pane. All the kids seemed to be wearing baseball caps and costly sneakers. Lin Ming obviously thought this was no place for a clandestine meeting. Actually, it would have been perfect had we continued on into the darkened Star Theater. When the stars and planets and galaxies were out and everyone else's eyes were fixed upon the ceiling, it was an ideal place to pass documents and money. Plus, the microphone that could filter our voices in this bedlam had not, as far as I knew, yet been invented.

In a loud voice I asked Lin Ming a question. He could not hear me. I asked it again, even louder. He still could not hear me. I pulled the thumb drive out of my watch pocket and showed it to him.

"Put that away," Lin Ming said, genuinely shocked by this breach of security. "Are you crazy?"

"Please answer the question." I was still bellowing.

Lin Ming said, "Let's get out of here."

"Not yet. *Did* you send me this?"

"I'm going. You can follow me if you wish."

He walked away. I followed. Lin Ming threaded his way through the screeching, rowdy, chaotic mob, never slowing down but never bumping into anyone either. Outside, he led me into Central Park, then slowed his steps until I caught up and was walking beside him.

He said, "So what was it you wanted to know?"

"The provenance of the material I received yesterday."

"Ultimate or immediate? How was it delivered?"

"By bicycle messenger."

"At what time yesterday?"

"Three fifty-seven."

"In the afternoon?"

Lin, who had been so depressed only two days before, was now making fun of me. This is not the way humble assets are supposed to behave, but Lin Ming was no garden-variety asset. He was used to being the case officer. In his mind he had been born to be the case officer and that was what he still was and always would be. He was certain that he was a lot smarter than I was. Such hubris was supposed to give me the advantage, but I wasn't so sure about that. Chances are he was right. He started to say something.

I interrupted. "It's a simple question," I said. "What's the answer?"

"I was about to tell you," Lin Ming said. "The package came from me. The guy on the bicycle is a man I sometimes use for errands. He's a recovering addict, he's not Chinese, he's unwitting, he has no curiosity, he rides fast. He charges twenty dollars a delivery, anywhere in Manhattan."

Just like the psycho who, a while ago, was handing out flyers at the right time and place in Greenwich Village.

I said, "Name?"

"The guy on the bicycle. Have you read the material?"

"Yes."

"The whole thing?"

"Yes."

"You know that many ideograms?"

"I have a dictionary," I said. "I also have a question."

"Ask it."

"I only asked for the information day before yesterday. It arrived yesterday."

"True. What's that got to do with anything?"

"A lot," I said. "How did you produce it so fast?"

"It already existed."

"So all you had to do was copy it?"

Lin Ming shrugged. What business of mine were these trivial details?

I said, "I've been told that in your service no one is allowed to be alone with a classified document, that only one copy of any document exists in any one place, that they are never taken outside of the safe room where they are stored, and that making photocopies is regarded as prima facie evidence of treason. So how did you happen to have an extra copy on hand?"

"My, my," said Lin Ming. "If those really are the rules, you're a lucky man to have that thumb drive in your watch pocket."

He was smiling—smirking. The subdued Lin Ming I had bullied in Riverside Park had turned himself into a different Lin Ming. Now he was turning into a third version, this one a comedian.

I said, "You expect us to believe that this file was created in a matter of hours?"

"No," Lin Ming said. "As I've already said, the file already existed."

"Why?"

"Because it was obvious that you would ask for it sooner or later. You Americans are a very strange people. You're always in a hurry and then when something happens fast you get suspicious. Do you imagine you're the only quick people in the world?"

"So how many more of these files already exist?"

"To find that out, you must give me something," Lin Ming said. "Like you, I must give my superiors reasons to trust me."

"I'll be in touch," I said.

"Make it soon."

"I'll call when the time comes."

"No more Planetarium, if you don't mind," Lin Ming said.

He strode away to the east. I went in the opposite direction, seething. Around Seventy-fifth Street my everyday cell phone rang. It was Alice Song. Apologies welled up in me. I spoke her name. Before I could say more she cut me off and said, "How much ransom are they demanding this time?" Her voice was cheery but extra loud, as if she were waking up a dozing juror. I could have heard her perfectly well in the Planetarium. She said, "Listen. There's a nice snooty little California cuisine restaurant." She named it. "Look it up on your iPhone," she said. "If you're not seated at the table by seven o'clock, it's all over between us."

I said, "Will I need a jacket?"

"They probably wouldn't let you in if you showed up in one," Alice said.

33

Dinner at the snooty restaurant consisted of microportions of organic stuff arranged on oversize square plates by some Zen abstractionist in the kitchen and haughty service by a meager young man who clearly thought I didn't deserve and couldn't possibly appreciate the extraordinary creations he placed before me. The courses, four of them, were mere specks of color on the bone-white crockery. The food had no odor, little taste. Decidedly, The Quail, as the restaurant was called after its specialty (two tiny birds, disjointed and garnished with what looked and tasted like steamed leaves of the gingko tree), was in the front line in the battle against morbid obesity.

However, the company was good. Alice, watching me as I ate the two forkfuls that comprised tonight's special, grinned and said, "Do you eat like this every night?"

"Usually it takes a little longer to finish."

"What's your favorite food, just so I'll know next time?"

"There's going to be a next time?"

"Why wouldn't there be?" Alice asked.

"Well, I stood you up twice. Usually that's grounds for an unhappy ending."

"Being kidnapped is always a defense," she said. "So what's your favorite food?"

I told her. She looked amused. She looked as if she had been prepared to be amused.

Because the wait between courses was long in order to provide time for meditation, the meal lasted a couple of hours. Afterward we sipped herbal tea, of which The Quail offered a great variety. The check came. Alice grabbed it. I was not surprised, because I had been given the menu that did not show the prices. She paid it in cash—three hundred dollars and change.

"Next time, me," I said.

"Great!" Alice said. "I love Subway."

It was raining again. Just as we walked out the door a taxi pulled up. "Our lucky night," Alice said. A couple got out of the cab and dashed toward The Quail. Alice got in. I leaned over and gave her a little wave good-bye through the cab's open door. She said, "What's that for?"

"Thanks for dinner. I enjoyed the company a lot."

"So you've had enough enjoyment for one night?"

She was not smiling. A car splashed by in the other direction, its headlights lighting up her face. Her almost-black eyes were filling up with scorn, as in an animated film. What was the matter with this guy? It was nine o'clock. I had planned to take the next train to Washington so as to brief Burbank bright and early the next morning. Instead, I got into the backseat with Alice.

"Sorry about that," I said. "I thought I was still on probation."

"You are," Alice said. "But there's such a thing as time off for good behavior."

She gave the driver an address on Park Avenue. I didn't get a look at her apartment, which felt large and smelled of books, because she did not turn on the lights, but holding my hand, led me to the bedroom. In the next few hours I learned a lot about being in bed with a six-foot woman. Like Mei, though less acrobatic, Alice was an originator. She didn't talk or make any sounds at all while things were happening, but in between she liked to chat. She did not murmur and cuddle as did nearly every other female I had ever slept with, but propped herself up on one elbow and conversed in her customary half shout. For the first hour or so this was disconcerting, but as the night wore on I grew used to it. It was a treat, in its way, to hear every word she spoke instead of the usual muffled commentary into the pillow. Although Alice had had no small talk when fully clothed, she now expressed her opinion about just about everything except Kierkegaard. Things like, "In college I had a professor—Wendell Pitt, do you remember him?"

"No. I was warned."

"You were lucky to have such thoughtful friends," Alice said. "Wendell Pitt said that *Finnegan's Wake* had to be read as if it were music. What do you suppose he meant by that?"

"He didn't tell the class?"

"No, he just read aloud from the thing. Every day. It was torture. The music sounded like a truckload of pots and pans falling off a truck. Listen." She quoted Joyce from memory, her gem-cut diction almost proving Professor Pitt right by turning Joyce's Dadaesque gibberish into a vaudeville routine. "I hope I haven't bored you," she said.

"Don't worry," I said. "Have you read the book since you took the course?"

"Are you kidding?"

"I've never heard of anyone memorizing that stuff. How did you do it?"

"I have positive reinforcement to thank. Regurgitate and you get an A. Come here."

There was a fast train to Washington at 6:00 A.M. At four-thirty I slipped out of bed. Alice lay on her side in a wash of feeble streetlight, a living Velázquez—curved hip and spine, glorious legs, luminous skin, fan of silken hair on the pillow, as if it had been combed instead of just falling naturally into place. I wanted a shower but did not want to wake her up. Then I realized it would be a bad idea to leave without saying good-bye, so I took the shower. When I returned, Alice was wide-awake. She had turned over. Naked and supine, one knee raised, she had become a different woman. Her face was softer, her eyes, filled with sleep, had changed from umber to chocolate, her movements were languid. She had made love with languor, the opposite of Mei's ride-'im-cowboy style. This was the first thought I'd had of Mei since Alice took off her clothes.

Once again Alice said, "Come here."

I thought I was going to miss my train, but all she wanted to do was to sniff me. She said, "You smelled better before you took the shower."

"Sorry about that," I said.

"You've got nothing to be sorry about." She turned on the bedside lamp. "I didn't realize you were so furry," she said, stroking my chest hair.

I started to tell her she had been a surprise to me, too, but thought better of it. I told her I was going to take the train to Washington. Early appointments.

Her demeanor changed. Suddenly she was all-business. She said, "You'll never get a cab at this hour. Get dressed and I'll be right with you."

Still naked, she walked out into the apartment. Seconds later she called to me. I found her in the hall. She was wearing a trench coat and Keds. In the elevator she gathered her hair into a ponytail and bound it with an elastic ring she pulled out of the pocket of the raincoat. In the basement garage we got into an Audi convertible—spoils of the divorce, she said. She drove fast to Penn Station, and as if under an enchantment found a parking space a block away from the entrance. She went inside with me. We had half an hour to spare. At the gate Alice said, "Wait here." She vanished and in minutes came back with a fast-food bag. I could smell the meatball sandwich inside.

"Breakfast," she said. "You must be famished."

We were standing quite close together. I could smell the bed on her skin. It was ten till six. The announcer called my train.

Alice said, "I don't think we know each other well enough yet to kiss good-bye."

This made me smile. She smiled back, as if we had a secret. I felt the greatest goodwill for this woman. Words, I thought again, would spoil the mood. Alice had no such inhibitions.

She said, "Let me ask you this. If I invite you to a dinner party next Saturday, the twenty-third day of the month, will you show up?"

"That would certainly be my intention."

"Not good enough. You have to say 'no' now or show up then. Eight o'clock. My place. I'm not going to remind you."

"What's the address?"

She handed me her business card, street address and apartment number already written on the back in a dashing hand. Then she walked away, wiggling her fingers over her shoulder. As she went I glimpsed her legs winking through the vent in her Burberry, bare under the raincoat like the rest of her body.

34

The train was only twenty minutes late, so it was not yet eleven o'clock when I got to Headquarters. Burbank buzzed before I could sit down. Later I stood in front of him. He didn't tell me to sit down but, without looking up, continued to work on a paper he was annotating in red ink. No wonder he ignored me. I was unshaved and, thanks to Lin Ming and Alice Song, bleary-eyed after two more or less sleepless nights. The jeans I had worn in New York were wrinkled and stained, my shirt was smelly. Everybody in CI was supposed to dress like a banker. I had missed the Gang of Thirteen meeting. I had not called in to say I was running late. However, when at last Burbank dropped his document into his out basket and looked up at me, his expression was neutral.

He said, "Speak."

I described my meeting with Lin Ming. Burbank listened with his eyes closed. When I got to the thumb drive and its contents, the deep-set pale blue eyes snapped open.

"This is Chen Qi's son you're talking about?"

"Supposedly."

"You know him." No question mark.

"We met several times in Shanghai," I said. "He was, I suppose he still is, a friend of Mei's."

"How close a friend?"

It cost me something to answer this question. "Quite close," I said, "if you believe the pictures in the file."

"Do you believe them?

"They tend to confirm old suppositions."

A look, half amused, half contemptuous, crossed Burbank's face. If I was a cuckold, that fit right in with my being late and unshaven. He held out his hand. I dug the thumb drive out of my watch pocket and handed it over. Burbank rolled back his chair and fiddled with something on the back of his desk. I was still standing up, so I could see him punching an access code into a keypad on a bottom drawer—evidently even his desk was a safe. He took a laptop out of the drawer, switched it on to battery power—no wires for Burbank—inserted the thumb drive, and scrolled through the file until he got to the photographs of Chen Jianyu. He looked at the rest of the pictures, lingering over some, then switched off. He made no attempt to read the text.

"Have you read this?" he asked.

"Yes."

"All of it?"

I nodded.

"Did you understand all of it?"

"The surface, yes."

"Have you analyzed it?"

"If you mean have I gone through it with a fine-tooth comb and an all-seeing eye and cross-checked it with other sources, the answer is no," I said. "It took me all night just to read through the thing."

"Who originated the file?"

"No identifying marks. It's sterile."

"So what does it say about this young man?" Burbank asked.

"He was rebellious, defied his father. As a child he wet the bed. He started fires. He killed a cat. . . ."

"How?"

"Beheaded it with a cleaver."

"At what age?"

"Seven. He was rebellious, disrespectful to his father—who is never named in the file even by a pseudonym, by the way. He had a quick mind—did well in school, transcripts of marks and teachers' reports appended. As a teenager, lots of drugs and girls and rock music. He was arrested at seventeen for possession of LSD but the cops let him go after a scare and a lecture. He was a good boy for a while after that, or at least didn't get caught. Kept up his marks, kept his nose clean. After graduating from Shanghai University with an engineering degree, he went to Purdue for an MBA."

"Skip that stuff," Burbank said.

"Are you sure you want me to do that?"

Beneath his unruffled surface Burbank was annoyed. He made an impatient gesture: spit it out.

"Whoever in Guoanbu assembled this file thinks it's possible that he was recruited by us while he was in Indiana."

"Do they believe that actually happened?"

"It's the theme of the file. Everything—his childhood, his look-at-me behavior, his rebellious nature, his disrespect for his father, the wild life he led at Purdue, is treated as part of a pattern."

"What kind of wild life?" Burbank asked.

"The usual grad school kind—alcohol, cocaine, weed, girls, girls, girls, loud music. He paid for two abortions in a single semester. The girls are named."

"All of them?"

"The file does not say otherwise."

"How would anyone know them all?"

"I wonder," I said. "But Chen Jianyu wasn't the only Chinese at Purdue."

"Tell me more."

"Chen Jianyu made friends with a professor the Chinese regard as a spotter for U.S. intelligence."

"Name?"

"Milo D. Fletcher, East Asian studies."

"Background?"

"Not specified, except that he has fluent Mandarin and has published what the file calls 'reactionary capitalist-imperialist anti-PRC propaganda.'"

"Why do the Chinese think he was a spotter?"

"Because two other students reported that Fletcher had introduced them to a stranger who took them out for dinner and made a pitch."

"Did they say yes?"

"The file doesn't say. Nor does it name them. But if Beijing knew about the attempted recruitment, it follows that the students might have said yes on instructions from Beijing."

"Or no for reasons of their own."

"Not if they wanted to serve the motherland by penetrating this Headquarters, or were ordered to do so."

"Thanks for the tutorial," Burbank said. "So why did Chen Jianyu let himself be cultivated?"

"According to the file, because that's the way Chen Jianyu is," I said. "Anything that might outrage or embarrass his father is the thing he wants to do."

"Why?"

"Resentment?"

Burbank broke wind, a string of little detonations, a shocking sound coming from him, and leapt to his feet. "Stay put," he said and hustled from the room. He was gone for a while, and when he came back he unlocked another desk drawer, shook a couple of pills from a drugstore bottle, and swallowed them.

"So how did the professor go about cultivating this fellow?"

"The usual—invitations to parties, introductions to girls and eminent professors, a sympathetic ear, a willingness to treat the target as an intellectual equal. Fletcher cultivates an erudite manner, which the file says made a great impression on Chen Jianyu. The one thing he reveres, apparently, is learning. To him, Fletcher was a figure out of Henry James—a gentleman and scholar, a living contradiction of everything he had ever been told about Americans."

"Speculation."

"No," I said. "Two of the informers at Purdue reported Chen Jianyu had said this in so many words, and not just once but several times."

"So what do you make of this?" Burbank asked. "Don't cover your ass, just answer the question."

I said, "I don't know what to make of it."

Burbank sat forward, as if to interrupt. I held up a palm. He looked displeased. I was telling him when he could speak? Who did I think I was? I raised my voice slightly.

"There are two ways to go," I said. "If you believe the file is genuine. . . ."

"Do you believe that?" Burbank said.

"It smells genuine, but if it's a forgery that's the way it would smell," I said. "The little I know of Chen Jianyu confirms the file. Unless he was playing a role when we met."

"Unless, unless, unless, the almighty *unless*," Burbank said. "Did you study Latin in school?"

"I showed up for class. I remember very little."

"How about the word for *unless*?

"Sorry."

"*Nisi*," Burbank said. "That should be the motto of our craft. *Nisi, nisi, nisi.*"

He pulled the thumb drive out of his laptop and handed it back to me. "Take good care of this," he said. "You know the drill. Mention it to no one. Share it with no one. Do not leave it in your safe. Carry it with you. Make no copy. Go through it again, this time with that fine-tooth comb. Keep an eye out for lice. Research it. Think upon it. Come to a conclusion. Do you have anything else?"

The answer was yes, but I had had enough of this, so I didn't say so. I had already told Burbank in passing about the unbelievable speed with which Lin Ming had delivered this file. I had told him about Lin's mood swing. There was no need to tell him again, but I thought the least he could do was show some curiosity, ask a question or two. This did not happen.

We were done. Burbank took a paper out of his in-basket and said, "Work at home for the rest of the day. You look like you've been sleeping under a bridge in a cardboard box."

FOUR

35

Somehow I did not forget to call Alice Song before I fell asleep that afternoon. When she heard my voice she said, "It's you? How come you didn't say 'surprise!' instead of 'hello?'" I was too tired to think of a comeback. Alice went on with the kidding. I held the receiver well away from my ear. Two tin cans connected by a string would probably have done as well as our smart phones in transmitting her speech from New York to Virginia. I told her with only a touch of insincerity that I was looking forward to her dinner party.

"Good," Alice said, "because you're the guest of honor."

I laughed.

"Don't laugh. A guy who works in my law firm is dying to meet you."

"Why? Is somebody suing me?"

"He worked in Shanghai, too, at about the same time you did. He's heard a lot about you."

"That sounds ominous."

"Maybe it is," Alice said. "Ole says he's got something to tell you."

"Ole?" I said.

"That's his name, Ole Olsen."

"What does he want to tell me?"

"He didn't say," Alice said. "I think it's a secret."

"Why do you think that?"

"His manner suggests it. Got to run. See you at dinner."

I said, "Wait."

"Can't." Tomorrow, in court, she had an expert witness to dismantle and she needed her sleep. The next sound I heard was the dial tone.

I had other things to think about than somebody named Ole Olsen. He was out of mind almost as soon as Alice hung up on me. For the rest of the week I was glued to the computer, checking out every possible reference in Chen Jianyu's file. Nearly every detail of the material he gave me was confirmed, including the decapitated cat. How Lin Ming had obtained such intimate, detailed information on his early life I could not imagine. The files did not assign a pseudonym to the source or sources. That could mean that we had an investment in this juvenile delinquent, that he was someone we valued and wanted to protect even from ourselves. It could mean nothing or anything. Reading the rows and rows of tiny Mandarin characters under the jumpy light of the fluorescent ceiling fixtures irritated my eyes. I was lying behind my desk on the floor, putting drops into them, when Burbank opened the door between our offices, looked in, and said to himself, "Where the hell is he?" Before I could decide whether to sit up and answer the question, he retreated and slammed the door. I got to my feet and knocked. Burbank replied by buzzing me. Feeling like Pavlov's dog, as Burbank probably intended, I opened the door and walked through it.

"Where did you come from?" Burbank said.

I pointed over my shoulder with a thumb.

"You weren't there ten seconds ago."

I said, "Well, here I am now."

Burbank pointed at the visitor's chair. "Tell me something new," he said.

I sat down and said, "On the whole, it checks out."

"What parts don't check out?"

"Practically none," I said. "In fact we already have almost all of the information Lin Ming gave us in our own files."

Burbank blinked. This was like watching a statue scratch its nose. The expression on his face, which is to say the lack of expression on his face, did not change. But his eyes did, ever so slightly. Or maybe I imagined this.

Burbank said, "We do? What, for example?"

I told him, in brief.

"So what don't we have?"

"The identity of the source or sources of this information. No indication that it was ever sent over to the analysts or shared internally in any way."

"What does that suggest to you?"

I said, "What it suggests, Luther, is that something funny is going on."

"Define 'something funny,'" Burbank said.

"I just did."

Burbank took a deep breath. He shifted to sarcastic mode. "You're the designated thinker on this one," he said. "You've read the files. You run the asset who gave you this document. You've found something suspicious. For the fun of it, let's say that you've come to some sort of conclusion, or to the starting point for a conclusion—let's call it a hunch. I haven't read the files. I can't read Mandarin well enough to decipher them. Therefore I must rely on you to brief me. I *am* relying on you. I'm cleared to know everything. So tell me about your hunch. Please."

I said, "I think the answer is obvious. This file is phony. It doesn't suggest the man I know. Lin Ming is trying to sell us junk from our own files and at the same time trying to write a death sentence for Chen

Jianyu. Either somebody inside our Headquarters furnished Lin Ming with this information, which may very well be fabricated, or the Chinese have hacked into our files."

"What do you mean, 'fabricated?'"

"Fed by a Guoanbu agent to a credulous case officer, or just hacked into our files by some computer virtuoso in Beijing."

"Are you serious?"

"You asked me to describe my hunch," I said. "That's what I've done."

Burbank faded away into his secret garden of thought. The meditation lasted quite a long while. Was this habit real or did he just hide out when he didn't know where to go next in the conversation? Had I told him something he already knew but did not want to hear? I told my inner paranoiac, who never listened, to back off.

Burbank's eyes came back into focus. He moved—lifted a hand, swiveled his head. He said, "What did you think of Chen Jianyu when you knew him in Shanghai?"

"I didn't know him all that well."

"Granted. But you knew him. It's possible you and he were sleeping with the same woman. What did you think of him?"

"I thought he was a run-of-the-mill B-list princeling," I said. "A little less ridiculous than some of the others. Smarter than most. He seemed actually to think, to have convictions."

Burbank said, "Nothing more?"

"About Chen Jianyu? What more is there?"

"You do know that bed wetting, playing with fire, and torturing animals in childhood are almost invariably the warning sign of a potential serial killer?"

"I think I read that somewhere," I said. "But as I understand it, not everyone who does those things grows up to be a serial killer."

Burbank looked at his watch. So did I. By now it must be dark outside. We had been talking for longer than I realized. Quitting time had come and gone. I listened to the building. Headquarters was hushed, emptied out, closed for the weekend.

Burbank said, "Why don't you come to my place for dinner around seven? The caretaker is there. She's a good cook—better than good. I'll give her a call, ask her to leave dinner in the oven, then disappear. Can you find the way?"

It was dark by the time I reached the hidden drive that ran through the woods to the converted barn. It was little more than a footpath. Tonight it was choked with rutted snow that was axle deep. About a hundred yards in, my headlights bounced off a black Range Rover coming from the opposite direction, headlights flashing, horn blasting. I put my car in reverse and stuck my head out the window. When I reached the paved road, I caught through tinted windows a blurry glimpse of the other driver, possibly a female, maybe the mysterious caretaker. The Range Rover, scattering gravel, roared onto the slippery macadam, tires spinning, vehicle fishtailing as it made a ninety-degree turn and sped away. The driver did not switch on the lights until the vehicle was far enough down the road that the license tags could not be read. Who was this idiot?

Burbank had told me to just walk in when I got to the house, so that's what I did. I found him standing in front of the dining room fireplace, in which a roaring fire burned, and drinking red wine from a large Burgundy glass. He had changed into a cardigan and slippers. He poured me a glass of the wine from a bottle on the table, which was set for two with nice china and silverware. Mother would have approved. An appetizer, unrecognizable from where I stood, had been placed at either end of the table. Candles burned.

"Sit ye down," said Burbank. "You're a bit early. Hence the heavy traffic in the driveway." He shook his head, laughed as if something amusing—endearing—had occurred.

The dinner was excellent. It ended with key lime pie with billows of whipped cream on top. Burbank cut the pie in fourths. He watched my face intently as I took my first bite. He asked me how I liked it. I said it was terrific. He grinned. "Best in the world. The caretaker may not be the new Rembrandt or much of a driver, but in the kitchen she's matchless. Matchless." He gave himself another piece of pie.

Throughout the meal Burbank did all the talking but said not a word about business. He was so animated I wondered if he had taken a pill. He talked about himself. When as a young officer he had been posted to Paris, he and a fellow spy and a couple of *filles de joie,* always one natural blonde and one brunette, went on an annual gastronomic tour of France. Each August in a different region of France, they hit all the Michelin three-star restaurants, having made reservations two years in advance. Like the regions, the girls changed every year, and after the first week he and his buddy swapped partners. They ate *croques monsieur* and drank beer for lunch at cafés and gorged on haute cuisine at night. The men had a budget—so much for the *chatte,* so much for the girls' suitable new clothes, so much for dinners. To pay for all this, each man deposited a certain monthly amount into a joint account in the embassy's credit union. "Like your grandmother's Christmas club, but hush-hush," Burbank said. They stayed at modest hotels so they could afford better wines. Burbank fairly glowed as he rattled on, menu by menu, *poule* by *poule.* This Proustian tour of old happy moments was touching in its way. Burbank was a good storyteller, which was not surprising considering his eye for detail. He actually made me laugh, the last thing I had expected ever to happen while in his company.

Finally, when it was quite late, we moved into the living room and got down to business. Burbank seemed reluctant to do so. I expected a long inquisitorial session, but he was not eager to start. He stretched, yawned, sipped the last of the wine.

"So tell me," he said. "Where does this thing go next?"

He expected me to do the talking yet again? My spirits sank. At this point I would have been glad to be given instructions. I had hoped for instructions. I was tired of doing all the thinking, making all the meetings, taking all the responsibility, setting myself up for all the blame if things fell apart.

I said, "You tell me."

Burbank said, "Sorry, I can't do that. This is your baby. It's up to you to get the stroller across the street."

My instinct, almost irresistible, was to rise to my feet, thank Burbank and the absent caretaker for a lovely dinner and an enjoyable evening, quit my job, and walk out. Just go. Find another way of earning a living, start over again in some honest low-stress occupation like foreclosing mortgages on poor widows while writing poetry by night in an idyllic small town. Marry a sweet local girl without too many smarts, get laid every third night. Have kids. Shoot baskets with them in the backyard, sing in the choir, drink beer and eat pizza while watching football on TV with the idyllic village's other bachelors of arts. Every spy's daydream. But instead of acting on my impulse, I answered Burbank's question.

"Apart from more of the same," I said, "I haven't got a clue what's next."

"You asked that fellow in New York for six case histories," Burbank said. "He delivered the first one the next business day. You should be encouraged. Motivated."

Really?

"Are you not curious about the fact that Lin Ming acted so fast?" I said. "That he gave us information that was already in our files? Don't you want to know who gave it to *him*?"

"That's the entire purpose of this meeting. But do you think that what we already know will lead us to the culprit?"

"No. It will lead us around the mulberry bush."

"So get more information. Get the other five files from your guy. Plod. Dig. Make comparisons."

"And if I fail?"

"So far you've succeeded beyond any reasonable expectation," Burbank said. "Beyond my expectations, which I admit were and are anything but reasonable."

I said, "Suppose information is not enough?"

"Then do what you have to do."

"Meaning what?"

"Just do it."

"Are you telling me to use my own judgment?"

"Up to now that's worked out pretty well."

"Up to what limits do I use my own judgment?"

"Short of treason, premeditated homicide, or grand theft of government funds, there are no limits."

"I can go where I want, see whoever I want to see, do as I see fit?"

"You're as free as a bird," Burbank said. "You know the mission. Accomplish it."

He smiled like a fond father sending his boy off to school after stuffing him with good advice. He all but patted me on the head.

36

On Saturday evening I was the first to arrive at Alice's place. She opened the door and said, "You! Early! What next?" A firm dry hand-shake, a whiff of the same perfume I had smelled on the night we met in the bar of the club. The light in the hall was low. In her black dress against this dark background she looked like one of those half-smiling rich women in a Sargent portrait—dark, tall, aloof, hair dressed, face painted, beautifully gowned, and richly bejeweled, the favorite wife of the King of Qin. She gave me a drink and disappeared. I heard her talking to someone, another woman, in the kitchen.

I wasn't the only punctual one. Soon the other guests began to arrive, two by two. All the rest except one blonde wife were Chinese. Everyone was better dressed than me. My best Shanghai suit and a good shirt were shoddy in comparison to the Armani suits and designer dresses on display, not to mention the jewelry. Since abandoning my father's Rolex I wore a Timex.

No one went quite so far as to look me over and make a face. This was a well-mannered crowd. The conversation was in Mandarin. Everyone except the blonde seemed to assume that I knew the language. She took pity on me and spoke to me in English. Her name was Fiona Wang. She and her husband, a neurosurgeon at Mount Sinai, were just back from a medical conference in Hong Kong. Caitlin was an endocrinologist. The couple had met in medical school—Harvard, actually. She had chosen her specialty because it gave her time to be a mother, and her beeper rarely went off during the night. Wesley, on the other hand, was forever leaping out of bed to repair some motorcyclist's damaged brain. The Wangs had a girl and a boy aged five and seven. Did I have children?

Before I could answer her question the last couple arrived. Alice brought them directly to me and introduced them in Mandarin—Ole and Martha Olsen. The husband's unwavering eyes were blue. This created an odd Siamese cat effect in what was otherwise a standard Han face. Clearly his Norse father had passed along very particular genes. Ole Olsen seemed uptight, condescending. He looked me over and didn't like what he saw.

In Mandarin Olsen said, "Are you the person of the same name who used to work for Chen Qi?"

How did he know that? I hadn't mentioned it to Alice. "I was one of many who worked for CEO Chen, yes," I said. "Do you know him?"

"Does anyone?" Ole asked. "I spent some time in the tower just after you left, but in the bowels of the ship, not upstairs like you."

"Doing what?"

"Legal matters."

I barely registered his words. My mind was absent, pondering how he knew about me and what he knew and why he wanted to tell me what he knew. Now that I had met Olsen I was uneasy. My time with Chen Qi was no secret, but it was infected by other secrets.

Olsen said, "What did you do for CEO Chen?"

"I often wondered," I said. "Do you work with Alice, Mr. Olsen?"

"Ole, please," he said. "Alice and I are at the same law firm. She's a litigator, I'm a backroom type. I handle the boring stuff. I heard quite a lot about you in Shanghai. When I arrived your name was on everybody's lips."

"Why was that?"

"Topic One at the watercooler was that you had been sleeping with Chen's niece or maybe his daughter and he'd rescued her from disgrace or worse by hiring you and fixing you up with a different woman to channel your animal instincts."

"No kidding."

"Some were surprised he hadn't drowned you in the Yangtze," Olsen said. "Apparently that was more his style."

As he spoke these words, he watched my face closely. I tried to look amused. I said, "Obviously the conversation was more interesting downstairs than upstairs."

"It could get pretty interesting."

I said, "What was this daughter's or niece's name?"

"You tell me."

There was no lightness in Olsen's tone. He wasn't bantering. On the contrary, judging by the look of moral distaste on his face, he looked as if he was annoyed with me for religious reasons.

I started to turn away. Olsen took hold of my arm. "The story was that when the maiden came to her senses and was out of danger he sent you to the States and then fired you," he said. "The substitute comfort woman, Zhang Jia—is that name correct?—was given a bonus, a promotion, and a suitable husband. Also a transfer. The rumor was that she was a professional, hired for this one particular job."

He was enjoying this. I thought it was unlawyerlike. Maybe Martha, Olsen's wife thought so, too. She touched his hand, a little warning, but he paid her no attention.

Out of the corner of my eye I saw someone in an apron, a female, peek out the kitchen door. She wore a white Nehru-type chef's cap, her hair concealed beneath it. Her hand, which held a napkin—she was touching her nose with her thumb—concealed the lower portion of her face. I had seen that gesture before. Catching the signal, Alice announced that dinner was served.

To me Olsen said, "Anything you want to say to all that?"

Alice had been listening. She answered for me. "I think the answer to that question is no," she said. "But I have a question for you, Ole."

"Ask it."

"Are you drunk or is this your idea of small talk?"

"Small talk," Olsen said. "The white man's name for avoiding the truth. So the answer to that question is also no. This isn't small talk."

Apparently he had more to say. He pointed a forefinger at me and started to speak, but Martha took his hand, smiled brightly, bent Ole's finger back into place, and said, "Dinnertime, dear." She led him into the dining room.

Alice took my arm and walked me to the table, as if we were dining in a country house on *Masterpiece Theater*. She sat at one end of the table, a gleaming expanse of inlay and veneer, and I sat at the other end, as far away from either Olsen as she could put me. The woman on my right immediately began talking about a new Broadway play. Apart from the conversation there was nothing Chinese about the dinner, but it was very good indeed. A waiter in a tuxedo served, assisted by a short plump woman who also wore a tuxedo. He was Chinese. Although he wasn't the same man, he reminded me of the waiter who had balanced that enormous tray on the night that Lin Ming and I dined together in the safe room upstairs from the Sichuan Delight. Everybody in the world, except maybe Ole Olsen, looked a little like someone else. The figure in the apron, the one who had materialized in the kitchen door, found her way back into my mind. I knew her, but how? With the help of my imagination, this mental image became a little more detailed than the one I had actually seen. Now I put my finger on a clue. She had touched her nose with her thumb. In that small way she resembled Magdalena, who when Mother was alive used the same gesture to signal when dinner was ready. Maybe it was something all chefs did. Chewing sliced duck breast as these thoughts passed through my mind, I wondered if I would die before morning with the lingering taste of this food on my tongue. The woman next to me—I hadn't caught her name—was telling me more about the Broadway play. It was called *The Death of Gershwin*. Gershwin was an unhappy woman, not the composer, and death was what she called her marriage to a banker because it had taken the music out of her life.

As the evening wore on the conversation got livelier, more gossipy. Alice made sure I talked to everyone except Ole Olsen. This was the first time since I left Shanghai I had been in a roomful of people who were all speaking Mandarin. I felt contentment, as if I had escaped back into some idyllic parallel existence, as if talk was making sense for a change.

Around ten-thirty, as everyone said their good-byes in the front hall, Olsen smoldered. Martha Olsen held tightly to his arm. I thought he might have something more to say to me—after all, he had never told me whatever it was he wanted to tell me, so I walked over and said good night to Martha.

When I held out a hand to Olsen himself, he ignored it and said, "I'd like a word alone with you before I go."

He walked back into the empty living room, and placing himself where he could see the door and the people milling about and kissing one another in the hall, he put a hand on my shoulder. He seemed to be a little drunk. His eyes blinked, his speech was slurred, he was having trouble with his balance.

He said, "Sorry the conversation went wrong a little while ago, but this is awkward for me. There's something I feel I need to tell you."

"Why? You don't even know me."

"I know Alice. I think I know what you really are and that bothers me. . . ." He lost his balance. I grabbed him. Over his shoulder I saw Martha hurrying toward us. ". . . but I have to break a professional confidence to tell you the facts. That's hard for me to do."

"Then maybe you shouldn't tell me. Maybe you should take it to the FBI."

"You think I haven't thought of that? You think they'd listen?" He wobbled, took hold of my forearm to steady himself. He said, "You think I'm drunk. I'm not. I don't know what the fuck is wrong with me, but listen to me, I'm trying to give you a chance to—what? I can't think of the fucking word."

I said, "I hear what you're saying to me, Ole, but maybe you should sleep on this. We could get together another time for a drink or something."

"No, Listen to me. The Yangtze was nothing compared to what's coming. These people are going to destroy you. You've got to get away."

Olsen's wife took him by elbow. "Time to go, Ole," she said in loud English.

"Not yet," Olsen said. "There's more."

"That's enough, Ole," Martha said.

Olsen really looked sick—addled, as if he didn't know where he was or who this woman was. Martha dragged him out of the room, Ole loose as a rag doll, Martha saying not a word to me. I followed them into the hall. All the others had left, though voices could be heard in the corridor outside the apartment door. Martha, keeping her grip on Ole, placing herself between him and me, thanked Alice for a lovely evening. Alice patted her on the cheek, then air-kissed both Olsens good night and walked them the five steps to the door.

Alice and I went straight to bed. We were too well mannered to talk about Ole Olsen. I told myself he was drunk, that he had been playing a sick prank. But he knew something, and even if what he knew was a useless crumb of gossip, I'd run him down tomorrow and get it out of him while he was still hungover and vulnerable.

At four in the morning Alice's phone rang. She felt for her reading glasses (I could hear her doing this in the dark), found them, picked up the phone, read the caller ID, grunted, and answered it.

"Martha," she said. "*What?*"

She switched on the lamp, and wearing nothing but her reading glasses, leaped out of bed. She fired the questions into the phone, then said, "I'm on my way to you."

I knew what she was going to tell me before she uttered the words.

"Ole Olsen died an hour ago," she said. "He collapsed on the way home in the car. The Wangs were with them. They worked on him on the way to the hospital, but he's gone. An aneurysm, they think, but they're not sure."

As she spoke she pulled clothes out of a closet—underwear, jeans, a sweater, shoes, her Burberry. She was dressed and on her way out before I could get out of bed. "Be sure the door is locked when you leave," she said, and left. A moment later she was back. "What was Ole trying to tell you?" she said.

"I don't know," I said. "He didn't finish."

All I could think about was that female chef, standing in the kitchen door, touching her nose with her thumb.

37

Standing in the mouth of an alley off the Bowery, Lin Ming coughed twice, then once again. Half a dozen derelicts lay on the pavement behind him, sleeping or drunk or both—or maybe the tenor and his acrobats or their equivalent. I asked Lin Ming why he had given the all-clear signal despite the presence of all these unknown people strewn on the pavement. "They're just bums," Lin Ming said. "Relax. Capitalism's victims are everywhere." We walked away and found an empty doorway. Lin Ming stepped into it, hiding himself, as the asset is supposed to do. I stood outside and kept a sharp lookout, as the case officer is trained to do.

Lin Ming immediately switched roles. "I assume you have something for me," he said. He spoke in tones of authority, as if I were working for him.

"What would that be?" I said.

"The name you promised. My friends are anxious to talk to the person in question."

"Our arrangement was based on the expectation of a swap of things of equal value," I said. "You gave us nothing that was remotely equal in value."

For a long moment Lin Ming was silent. His face was masked by the darkness, not that I had ever been able to read it anyway.

He said, "I am puzzled. Confused."

"I don't see why you should be. What you gave us was boilerplate. We might as well have Googled it." I was not at liberty to tell Lin Ming that we knew that his information had been cribbed from our own files. *Never tell the asset what he should not know even if he already knows it.*

Lin Ming said, "There seems to be a misunderstanding. You are acting like the case officer and treating me like an agent. You did this the last time, but I thought it was my imagination. I wasn't feeling well that day."

"So?"

"So why do you have this delusion?"

"In what way is it a delusion?"

"We made an agreement," Lin Ming said. "In this city, on a certain day in a certain park."

Which was recorded by a chess-playing cameraman and soundman. I assumed that Lin Ming was recording this conversation, too. Therefore he was choosing his words carefully. So was I, because I, too, was making a record for the file. In fact there was no particular reason to be careful. There was a good chance that the chip on which our conversation was being recorded would get lost in Guoanbu's archives. Even the Chinese did not have enough manpower to sort out, in time to do anyone any good, the tens of thousands of aimless conversations in a Babel of languages—any nuggets well buried—between their horde of case officers and their multitude of informants. As for my own recordings, only Burbank knew about them, and even he did not know about all of them. They didn't exist as far as the rest of Headquarters was concerned. I kept them in a safe place in case I ever needed them.

Breaking the silence, Lin Ming said, "You do remember that day in the park, and other days and nights as well, do you not?"

"Vividly," I said. "But I remember nothing about agreeing to become the property of whoever or whatever you work for."

"Then you should reremember. Think carefully. Go carefully."

"What I remember, Lin Ming, is that we agreed on an exchange of information."

"That was later," Lin Ming said. "On the day in question, and on other days, we talked of you as someone who would work for world peace and friendship between our two countries from inside Headquarters, who would receive certain benefits in return for certain information. You even spoke enthusiastically of the importance of winning the confidence of your targets inside your Headquarters. How could all that slip your mind?"

"It seems you have misinterpreted my words, whatever you think they were."

"And so you renounce our agreement?"

"There is no agreement to renounce. The deal was, you'd give me something that is equal in worth to what I was, and still am, prepared to give you."

"Why? So you can win and keep the confidence of the reactionary gangsters you work for?"

We weren't going to be polite? Fine. I said, "You sound like a Maoist, my friend. That's out of style. You should be careful."

"And you should be careful who you betray."

His voice quivered with anger. The usual question arose: was this real or was he just playing a part? More likely the latter, not impossibly the former. After all, his backside was on the line. He remained deep in the doorway, wrapped in shadow. I still could not see his face or for that matter his body. I would not have been able to detect a sudden move. I was surprised by a little involuntary shiver. I was exposed. If Lin Ming was truly angry, if he was convinced that I was of no further use to him, if he was the murderous type, he could easily spray cyanide into my face or shoot me dead with a silenced pistol or even stab me in the heart. Or cough and bring another team of acrobats on the run. I told myself to cool it. Lin Ming wasn't the murderous type, at least not on foreign soil.

"Betray," I said. "That's a strong word."

"In this case, not too strong," said Lin. "Believe me when I say that. You're playing with fire."

I had never before heard anyone speak that cliché aloud, and certainly not in the language we were speaking. I laughed. While I was still chuckling, Lin Ming said something I did not catch. Between one breath and the next, his voice had regained most of its normal agreeable timbre. What had just gone on between us was out of character for this typecast smoothie. He *was* playing a role. He was always playing a role, of course. That was his job: shake the foreign devil up.

"All I ask," Lin Ming said, "is that you acknowledge reality."

I said, "Same here. I'll tell you what. Forget the nonsense about my being your creature or ever becoming your creature. I don't give a rat's ass"—this, too, was a nice translation problem—"how you describe your relationship to me."

"I have just described it, exactly as it is," Lin Ming said.

"If you think that," I said, "you need therapy. If you keep your end of the bargain, we'll keep ours. If not, we'll use the information we have, the information you want and must have, in our own way."

Lin Ming stepped out into what little light there was on this backstreet of a great city that was too broke to turn on all of its streetlamps.

He said, "Is that your last word?"

"Yes."

Lin Ming smiled. He had remarkably straight teeth for a Chinese who had been a poor kid during the Cultural Revolution. He put a hand on my sleeve.

"If that's the way you want it, fine," he said. "But a word of advice. Have your horoscope updated."

He turned away and walked into the murk in his usual half-stagger, half-quickstep style, as if carrying a load on a pole with the help of the ghost of an ancestor at the other end of it. Despite what had just passed between us, it was difficult not to like him, difficult to take him seriously as a tough customer who would not hesitate to do whatever was necessary to get the job done, even though I knew that was exactly what he was. He made his exit, heading downtown. When he was a block or so away he stopped, turned his back to the light wind that was tumbling papers west to east, and lit a cigarette. I could see his face quite plainly in the flare of his lighter. He was looking at me, too—eyes lifted, hands steady. The flame went out. He faded into the darkness.

Less than a minute afterward I heard men walking in step with me. There were maybe half a dozen of them, marching in quick time, as if stepping off to fast music. When they were right behind me, almost touching me, they stopped moving forward and marched in place for a couple of moments, soles slapping, leather boot heels punching the concrete. Then they split into four groups, two men close behind me, one at each elbow, two close in front, just as the tenor and his acrobats had done in Shanghai. They wore matching black sweats, black caps, black shoes. The two in the lead carried baseball bats at shoulder arms. All were Han. They marched on for a full block with me wedged in among them, then they halted in front of a store window and marched in place again. Two of them broke formation, and batting righty and lefty and on command from the leader, swung at the display window.

The plate glass rang, quivered and turned into huge shards that hung for an instant as if held in place by some giant thumb and finger, then fell like blades. The gang broke formation and scattered, shouting. Had all this meant anything? Were they a Chinatown gang, rented by Min Ling for an hour, or just a bunch of wild and crazy guys out on a lark? They had done me no harm, so what did it matter? Nevertheless— someone could be watching—it seemed important to act as if nothing had happened. I walked on as coolly as I could, though with nothing like the nonchalance with which Harold Lloyd might have played the scene before the introduction of sound.

38

So far it hadn't been a very pleasant weekend, apart from the abbreviated night with Alice. If what Olsen said to me about the connection between Mei and Chen Qi was true, if she was Chen's niece or his daughter, then we were not dealing with Guoanbu at all. We were in ancient China. Whatever was about to happen to me was personal revenge. Chen Qi's plan was to destroy me in the most humiliating way possible. I knew this. To murder me after torturing me was not enough. He wanted me alive and in his power, so that he could remove my bones from my flesh one at a time. That was the message Ole Olsen had delivered.

In the swaying, trash-strewn, all-but-empty club car of the train to Washington I remembered my way back to the beginning—not just the weekend but the complete phantasmagoria right back to the day Mei crashed her bike into mine—and tried to convince myself I was imagining things. When the train pulled into Union Station and squealed to a shuddering stop, I woke from my reverie as if from a long sleep. Had I in fact been asleep all the while without knowing it? As my brain began to function normally again I feared that by waking up when I did, I had just missed discovering something important. When I picked up my car from the parking garage it was 5:30 A.M., the city was still dark and so hushed that I could hear the Civic's tires humming on the pavement. Would Alice be awake in Manhattan? Probably. I knew she rose early to get her child ready for school, do her exercises, eat her organic granola, rehearse the questions she was going to ask in court that day. My car had a hands-free telephone that worked through the sound system. I pushed the button and spoke Alice's number in the voice of an anchorman, or as close as I could come to it. The device understood me for once and placed the call. Alice picked up on the last ring before the answering machine kicked in.

"What?" she said.

"It's me."

"I know. Why is it you?"

I really didn't know. There was nothing more to be said about Ole Olsen. I had my own theory about his death, but Alice was the last person with whom I wanted to share it—or next to last, counting Burbank. I said, "What are you doing?"

"Shivering," Alice said. "I'm all wet from the shower."

"I'm calling on an impulse," I said. "In my imagination you are now drying off."

Alice said, "Phone sex before dawn? Have you been a pervert all along, or did you just think this was a good moment to let me in on your secret?"

I said, "I am now going to change the subject."

"Good. You've got thirty seconds to grow up before I hang up."

I said, "I have a question about the woman in your kitchen the other night."

"You do?" Alice said. "What, is the chef an old flame?"

"I just glimpsed her but she looked familiar. Have you used her before?"

"No. She was part of the caterer's package. Very efficient, not a talker. She did what she came to do and left."

"What did she look like?"

"Skinny but shapely. Thirtysomething. Big ears with her hair tucked under her hat. Maybe five six, not a lot more than a hundred pounds. Light blue eyes. Very capable. Intelligent face, not a beauty but not plain. With makeup, the right hairdresser and the right clothes she'd be quite sexy."

"Voice?"

"Slightly hoarse. Why are you asking all these questions?"

I said, "Name?"

"Name, name, name," Alice said. "Started with a consonant, three or four syllables long. I can't remember more than that. Anyway it was probably an alias. Those people do that, you know, in case a customer doesn't like them and warns all her friends not to hire her."

"Who was the caterer?"

"Stella's Moveable Feast. There's a Web page. Did you sleep with this woman in the past or what?"

"Good luck in court today," I said.

"Same to you if your day ever comes."

Suddenly I knew what came next. I pulled over to the curb and booked a flight to China.

39

It was almost as hot and sticky in Shanghai as in Washington, which is to say that Kinshasa could not compete. The immigration and customs inspectors at the airport paid no particular attention to me. My papers were in order—one more entry and exit remained on my visa. They didn't even ask if I was still a student before stamping my passport. Demonstrative suspicion had long since gone out of style here. If Guoanbu was interested in you it preferred that you remain as relaxed as possible. Long before you landed it would just arrange for you to be put into a bugged hotel room with watchers in the lobby buzzing around you like gnats. I stayed in a cheap hotel in a bad neighborhood because I was paying for this trip out of my own pocket and because the staff here might be a bit less used to keeping tabs on people who interested the security services. I was not difficult to follow, being white and four or five inches taller than almost everyone else, and as usual not really caring whether or not I was followed.

After a long afternoon nap and a lukewarm shower I got dressed and went into the street. My objective was to find Chen Jianyu. Finding him was possible, I thought, despite the vigilant father and the teeming crowds that screened him from me. However, I was by no means confident I would succeed. I had only two weeks to do what I had to do in a culture that had a very long history of confounding its enemies by wasting their time. However, the situation was not hopeless. "*If you wait by the river long enough, the bodies of your enemies will float by,*" says Laozi. I had no idea where Chen Jianyu lived and no way of finding out. I would never get through the door if I did find out. But I knew he worked in the tower, where punctuality was an ironclad law. Therefore he would have to get to work on time in the morning and leave at quitting time in the afternoon. I also knew his hangouts and the hours he was likely to be there. I knew the hours he was likely to be at one or another of them—his cohort of princelings might live in what it thought was anarchy, but for all its make-believe their gang ran on a tight schedule. If I visited all the hangouts for fourteen nights I had a reasonable chance of finding him. Interception was my whole plan, catching him on the fly. After that, everything depended on his turning out to be what I hoped he was, and what his social life suggested he was—a secret American. The world was full of them.

It was about three miles to the tower. No taxis cruised in this part of town. If I walked the whole distance I would be very sweaty by the time I got there. I needed change for a bus so I bought a fried egg embedded in a pancake from a vendor, who held up four fingers for bus No. 4 when I asked him which one went east. I should have known better than to take a bus. I did know better. Passengers, with more getting aboard at every stop, were packed in like, well, sardines. The temperature was well above body temperature. I had an advantage because my head stuck up above the crowd and I had a little more air to breathe than anyone else. Within seconds, however, I was drenched in sweat, my own and that of many strangers. I kept my right hand on my wallet and my left fist balled so that slipping off my WalMart wristwatch would be more difficult. The

Chinese eat a lot of cabbage. Gas escaped from the intestines of many passengers and mingled with untold amounts of recycled bad breath. By the time I got off, a block from the tower, no bloodhound could have detected my original scent beneath the rank odors my clothes and skin had absorbed from the many bodies that had been crushed against mine for the last half hour.

The building, magnificent and vulgar, stood not far from the harbor. A weak breeze from the sea wafted over the crowd, and I cooled off somewhat while I waited for Chen Jianyu to make an appearance. It was rush hour and I was a rock in a flowing stream of humanity, so it was difficult to stand still. Every third person, it seemed, tried to push me out of the way, but I had a weight advantage on most of them, so I was able to hold my ground. After about twenty minutes I spotted Chen Jianyu inside a midnight blue 7 Series BMW sedan that emerged from the tower's underground garage. The crowd ignored it. Chen Jianyu did not bother to blow the horn or flash the lights. Instead, he inched into the throng. Mostly people got out of his way when nudged by the car's bumper, but most refused to yield the right-of-way. The car pulsed with rock music playing at very high volume. I pushed my own way to the passenger-side front window. Inside the BMW, Chen Jianyu was smoking a cigarette and seemingly talking to himself as he chatted on the hands-free telephone. I rapped on the window. He paid no attention. Probably he could not hear me over the music, but even if he could, he probably knew no one who traveled on foot, so he just wasn't curious. I tried the door handle. He saw who I was and unlocked the door. I got in. A woman's voice came over the speakers. I overheard just a syllable or two before Chen Jianyu disconnected.

He looked me up and down, betraying no surprise. He turned down the music and said in English, "Nice aftershave."

"Can I hitch a ride?"

"Where to?"

"Where are you headed?"

"Quite a long way as soon as I run over all these people."

Now he blew the horn, he flashed the headlights. Pedestrians shouted, banged on the hood and the roof. Chen Jianyu paid no attention. He sounded, he looked, he dressed—in designer suit and necktie—as if showing up for a photo op.

I said, "Can I ride along?"

"Suit yourself," he said. "I can't promise you a ride back. Where are you staying?"

"You wouldn't know the hotel."

"Ah, traveling incognito." He turned up the sound system—the Foo Fighters' greatest hits. "Let's observe silence while I'm driving," he said, putting a finger on his lips.

It took us two hours on a six-lane superhighway that looked like a mock-up of the Interstate—same signage, same tollbooths, same everything—to drive to Suzhou, a city about sixty miles from Shanghai. Not a word passed between us the entire way. We parked by a large lake. By now the sun, hanging behind the city's perpetual scrim of pollution, was a red blister in the west.

Once we were out of the car, Chen Jianyu spoke, this time in Mandarin. "Have you been here before?" he said.

"No. This is Suzhou?"

"'Heaven on earth,' they call it because of its gardens," Chen Jianyu said. "Birthplace of the Wu culture. The Yangtze flows through the city. But you know all that."

"There are a lot of things I don't know," I said.

"A common complaint," he said, switching back to English. "What specifically do you want to know that you don't now know?"

I told him, straight out. All of a sudden he was no longer a lounge lizard. He listened to my questions with what seemed to be keen interest, as if he were learning something interesting—which of course he was.

When I had finished—I didn't have all that many questions and they were all short and to the point—he said, switching back to English, "The answer to all your questions except one is, 'Be patient.'"

"What about the one you can answer?"

"Okay," he said. "Yes, I was approached by some spook who thought he spoke Shanghainese when I was at Purdue. One of my professors set up the meeting. I told the spook to get lost. I'm not crazy, even if hanging out with you would suggest otherwise."

"What about the others that professor approached?"

"How would I know? But they're not crazy, either."

He looked at the sun, which was sinking rapidly, lighting a path across the lake. It would be dark in a matter of minutes. Chen Jianyu said, "Let's go for a walk."

We strolled along the lake—Taihu Lake, the signs said—and into a park. Thousands of others were taking the evening air, half of them watching the sunset with oohs and ahs and the other half taking pictures of it with their cell phones. One slim woman stood apart with her back to the spectacle and watched us approach. The light was behind her, so it took a moment before I made out her face.

Mei.

40

The sunset had everyone else's attention, so had that been my impulse I could have swept the love of my life into my arms and kissed her hungrily. It was not my impulse. This had nothing to do with confused emotions. I knew exactly what I felt—astonishment and relief that Mei was alive and free, rage but no surprise that Chen Qi had lied to me about her fate, certainty that Mei had never loved me, resentment that I had never been more to her than a target and possibly, if she hadn't been faking it, a sexual toy. The facts that I had not loved her until I lost her, that I would have deserted her and never looked back if so ordered by Headquarters, that I had used her with a cold heart as a cheap teacher and a convenient lay, that I was worse than she was, didn't count. I stood where I was, five steps away from her, rooted to the ground, unsmiling, seething, staring. It was, in short, a very human moment. What right did she have to ambush me like this? What right, what motive did Chen Jianyu, who had her to himself now, have to taunt me in this way? Mei, up to her old tricks, locked eyes with me. I looked away, searching for Chen Jianyu. He was nowhere to be seen.

With a jerk of her head, Mei beckoned me closer. I took four steps in her direction but remained out of reach. She did not stir. "You've got a problem," she said, "or are you just surprised to see me?"

I had not heard her speak English since I forbade her to do so on the day we met. She still had the Boston accent. In Mandarin I said, "You're looking like yourself."

This was the truth. She hadn't aged a day or gained or lost an ounce, her hair was done in the same way as before and was just as lustrous, she had the same belle of Shanghai face and manner. True, some of the mischief had gone out of her eyes, or so it seemed to me in the failing light. She wore trousers, loose white ones, so I had to reimagine her legs. What my brain produced was the image of Mei sprawled in Zhongshan Road, her miniskirt awry, her sweet bottom in its good-girl underwear, her honey-colored thighs and calves. My mind and body responded now as they had responded then.

"Speak English," she said. "If we talk in Mandarin we'll attract even more attention."

The sun dropped below the horizon. Show over, everyone turned around. About half the crowd spotted me at once. You could read their questions in their faces. They were all the same. What was this foreigner, this *laowai,* doing here all alone and not in a tamed group of other foreigners as a *laowai* was supposed to be? Why was that pretty Chinese girl talking to him? What was the matter with her? The light was fleeing. They squinted in unison. It got darker, then it got dark. Weak lamps switched on along the paths.

"Walk with me," Mei said. "I have things for you to hear."

Walking away from the already curious, we awakened curiosity in almost everyone else we encountered. Someone would certainly go for a policeman. Within minutes, Mei would have questions to answer in addition to the ones I meant to ask her.

I said, "Let's start with this. How come Chen Jianyu brought me to you?"

"Out of the goodness of his heart," Mei said. "He phoned me from the car as soon as he saw you knocking on the window."

"Why?"

"Maybe he thought that the hope of finding me was why you were in Shanghai. He asked if I wanted to see you. I said yes."

"So he wanted to help. That seems like a strange motive in his case."

"Why?"

"Isn't he the lover you left me for?"

She laughed explosively, arms hanging helplessly, as if the joke had stolen their strength. She stopped walking. So did I. People behind us bumped into us and into one another.

She said, "My lover? Is that what you think?"

"You two were lovey-dovey enough."

"He's my brother, you nitwit."

The crowd was flowing around us now, rubbernecking, asking one another what ghost-people language this ill-matched couple was speaking, why they were together.

I said, "Chen Qi is your father?"

"Jianyu's, too. Different mothers."

"So you're half siblings?"

"We never made the distinction," Mei said. "There were just the two of us, we thought, but who can be sure? Chen Jianyu is two years older than I am. His mother was the official wife. My mother was somebody my father kidnapped. We all lived together in the same house, wives as best friends, sisters in misery, like in the Xia dynasty."

"What do you mean, 'kidnapped?'"

"Kidnapped. He saw, he lusted, he confiscated. It was the Cultural Revolution. To make things easier, her father and mother were sent to a commune in Yunnan for reeducation. My father was the Red Guard leader who made the arrest, the one who put a dunce cap on my grandfather's head. In his mind he saved my mother from sharing her father's humiliation. She was fifteen."

"Wasn't that against the rules?"

"'Rules?' The whole idea of the Cultural Revolution was that there were no rules."

"Just days ago someone told me you were Chen Qi's niece," I said. "Chen Qi himself said you two were related—distantly, he implied."

"He said that to you?" Mei said. "For him that's the same thing as a full confession."

"Why would he tell me, of all people?"

"He has his reasons. He always does. But he never speaks the whole truth. Ask my mother. He told her that her parents would be well treated on the commune and she would be reunited with them when their reeducation was complete. They both died of hunger and exhaustion. She never saw them again, never had a letter."

"You sound like you hate your father," I said.

"That's why this is your lucky night," Mei said, "so listen to me."

I did as she asked. Her English was far better than I had imagined. She sounded like she had been born and brought up in Concord, Massachusetts. After a moment I stopped being impressed by her fluency, started listening, and realized she was telling me things I desperately wanted to know. As if reading from a checklist, she informed me of matters I realized might save my life—and might very well cost her hers, no matter who her father was, or more likely, because he was who and what he was.

I didn't like listening to these revelations in the presence of ten thousand eavesdroppers.

"Old Chinese proverb," Mei said when I complained. "There's safety in numbers. We're lost in the crowd instead of being in plain sight."

But how did we know that one or more of the myriad who were using their cell phone cameras were not taking our pictures in support of their local police? How did we know that the little old lady sitting on a bench, wrinkled and hunched and so short that her feet didn't touch the ground, wasn't a Guoanbu informer? I spoke these thoughts aloud.

"You should remember to take your medication," Mei said. "Listen, in the right circumstances, everybody in China is an informer, a spy, a danger to everyone else. In the U.S.A., too, except in that country they usually sell their story to the *National Enquirer* instead of going to the secret police. It's the same everywhere—the Eskimos, the Khoikhoi of the Kalahari Desert. Remember the Russians, the East Germans. Everyone informed on everyone else—husbands, wives, lovers, best friends, Party comrades. Especially Party comrades or fellow Christians. Or lovers. It's in our DNA. Get over it."

Her upturned face was deadly serious, an expression new to me. God, but she was a beauty. She must look like her mother. She certainly didn't resemble Chen Qi. Mei resumed talking—more softly, so it was difficult to hear her voice above the babble. I mimed turning up the volume. She shook her head. I slouched, so as to put my ear closer to her mouth. Still, I had to listen so hard that I could think of nothing else. No doubt that was the idea.

"About a month before I went away I missed a period," Mei said. "This didn't seem possible because I had always taken two kinds of precautions. Like an idiot I hoped for the best instead of doing something right away. Then I missed another period."

I started to speak. Mei stopped me. "Don't ask," she said. "You were the only suspect. That was the problem. I saw a doctor, someone I didn't know and who didn't know me, and had the thing done. But I had to show identification."

Chen Qi found out about the abortion in a matter of days.

"He already knew about you," Mei said. "Why he didn't kidnap me but just let us happen, I don't know. He knew what and who you were. He knew that the baby was an abomination, half me, half *laowai*. The worst of it was, now others knew, too—people high in the Party, people who could do him harm, who were already doing him harm by making a joke of his name. These people were being overheard by the lowest people in their offices. Whisperers everywhere. He knew this. He had lost face—lost it as if a chimpanzee had attacked him and chewed it off."

Apt choice of words.

For a weekend, Mei was left in peace. Then Chen Qi's assistant called. Mei's father wished her to join him for dinner that night. A car would come for her at six-thirty. Dinner would be at seven-thirty, the regulation Shanghai time. The car arrived precisely on time. Chen Qi was in the backseat.

"He was in a rage," Mei said. "He trembled like someone who was totally out of control. His face was bright red, he shouted, spit flew out of his mouth. His eyes were distended, the whites were reddened, as if his anger had ruptured the blood vessels. He was like a crazy talking animal in a cartoon. He told the driver to get out of the car and turn his back to it. As soon as the front door slammed, my father grabbed me—this was the first time he had touched me since I was small—and slapped me, first one cheek then the other very hard, as if he was trying to knock the baby out of me. Probably he would have succeeded if the child had still been inside my body. He's a strong man. My head snapped this way and that. I thought my neck was going to break. I thought he was going to kill me, then drive to the Yangtze Bridge with my corpse beside him on the leather seat and personally throw it into the river."

However, Chen Qi did Mei no more violence. He did what he did next in total silence. He rapped on the car window. The driver got back in, put the car in gear, and without being given an order, drove to Suzhou. When Chen Qi and Mei arrived at the house where she now lived, her mother was there to greet her. She bowed to Chen Qi like a woman whose feet were bound. Three other women and two men, Mei's "chaperones," stood in a row behind her mother. Without a word, Chen

Qi departed. Mei had not seen him since, nor did she expect ever to see him again.

"Suzhou is a place where nothing happens," Mei said. "I know no one in the whole city except my mother and the watchers who live with us. Two of them are always awake. My father has marooned me. My mother, too. We might as well be in Tibet. Mother is happy. I'm back, I'm a big child now, a Barbie with a heartbeat. We live in a nice house, we have good food and several television sets, but no books and no work to do. We play mahjong. We sew. We talk about my childhood. I can never leave. Unless you rape me in front of all these witnesses I will never again have a sex life that involves another person. I am out of sight, out of memory."

"You can come with me," I said.

Mei snorted. "Where to? I have no passport, I have no visa. People watch me."

"We can marry. The consulate can do it. Then you'd have an American passport."

"Ha," said Mei. "I wouldn't be an American for very long."

"Why not?"

"Because I'd be a widow instead of just losing a friend. Face the facts. You've made an enemy who can do what he likes with you, in China or anywhere else in the world. You will never lose him, you will never overcome him, you can't prevent him from doing whatever he plans to do to you. Whatever that turns out to be, death would be a better fate."

"Better than what, specifically?" I said.

"My brother will explain," Mei said. "He's waiting where he left you. Can you find the right gate?"

"I think so," I said. "You won't reconsider?"

Mei didn't answer the question. "I'm out of time," she said. "I have to get on my bike."

Without another word or gesture, she walked away.

I shouted, "Wait."

She stopped but did not turn around. The crowd flowed around her in the watery light like a school of fish eddying around coral.

I said, "Before you go I'd like to know your name. The real one."

She looked over her shoulder.

"Mei," she said.

One breath later she was absorbed by the crowd.

41

The park was emptying. It was almost eleven o'clock when Chen Jianyu's BMW arrived. It stopped some distance away, beyond the edge of the crowd, and I wriggled my way to it. Apparently the rule of silence inside the car was still in force, because Chen Jianyu said nothing to me when I got in and buckled my seat belt. I couldn't have heard him anyway over the deafening music. In the light from the instrument panel I studied his profile. He did resemble Mei—hairline, eyebrows, chin, and when, feeling my gaze, he turned his head and looked at me, his eyes might have been Mei's, large for a Han, smart, bright, lit by mockery.

We headed out of town. After an hour or so, Chen Jianyu exited the highway and threaded his way among the inevitable rows and rows of high-rise apartment buildings. He turned into a gas station. He parked, got out of the car, and walked briskly toward the men's room. As we emptied our bladders into adjoining urinals, Chen Jianyu broke his silence. "Do you have anything at your hotel that you can't afford to leave there?" he asked.

We were still speaking English. "No, not really," I said.

"Then I think you should go directly to the airport," Jianyu said. "There's a flight to Los Angeles in three hours."

I said, "My ticket is nonrefundable."

"So is your life. Go."

My *life*? As if Jianyu had just uttered a perfectly ordinary remark, I said, "I'd never get aboard on such short notice."

"They have one business class seat available, but you have to call them before midnight and pay for it."

I didn't ask how he knew this. People like him knew such things in his country. I looked at my watch—eleven forty-two. I said, "Business class? How much?"

"Five thousand U.S. and change."

"You've got to be kidding."

Chen Jianyu said, "You've got a credit card, haven't you? Call the airline and pay for the ticket now and get on the plane. Get out of China. Tonight."

He was serious. Yet I knew that what happened to me was a matter of indifference to him. He was urging me to leave, scaring me into leaving, in order to protect Mei—or so I was supposed to believe. And did believe. Still at the urinal, I called the airline, paid for the seat, memorized the confirmation number.

I said, "Chen Jianyu, let me ask you this. You've never liked me. Why the sudden concern for my welfare?"

To my surprise, Jianyu answered the question. "Mei asked me to save your skin," Chen Jianyu said. "What other reason could I have?"

"What about your father?"

"What about him?" Chen Jianyu said.

"You think he's going to whack me, send me to a labor camp, what?"

"Not yet," Chen Jianyu said. "But he could be afraid someone else might get to you before he does and deprive him of the pleasure."

"This someone else being who?"

"Use your imagination. And like you said, you're not the most popular *laowai* who ever came to Shanghai."

"So why are you telling me all this?"

"I just told you why. For my sister."

"You're telling me you're saving me because she has feelings for me?"

"She didn't say that, but I think she at least feels responsible for you."

"Why?"

"Wake up. She slept with you for two years and more. She hates her father and he hates you. He's a vengeful person. You humiliated him— or rather, Mei humiliated him with your help, which is a lot worse. So he wants to humiliate you right back. Tear the wings off the fly."

"How, exactly?"

"I have no idea. CEO Chen doesn't share his plans with me. But this much I do know—whatever he decides to do won't be proportional to your offense. Daddy doesn't do proportional." Jianyu looked at his watch. "If we're going, we should go now."

We rode the rest of the way without speaking. The car pulled up in front of the Hongqiao railway station. We got out. Jianyu said, on the sidewalk, "You know how to take the subway to the airport?"

"Yes. All this is very good of you. You have my thanks even if it's all for Mei."

"Some of it, not much, is personal," Jianyu said. "I owe you something for introducing you to my father when he invited you to dinner. I knew he was out to get you. It was a dirty trick."

"No problem," I said.

"'No problem?'" Jianyu looked at me in mild bewilderment. Was I really that stupid?

"Okay," I said. "If you still feel you owe me something, tell me more."

"What exactly? Why should I tell you anything?"

"I can't think of a single reason," I said.

Chen Jianyu hesitated, bit his lower lip. We moved farther away from the car, sidling out of range of the bugs he thought his father had planted in it. I wasn't the only paranoiac in the world.

Finally he said, "What do you know about the Dreyfus affair?"

"The bare details," I said. "What everyone knows."

"You should study his case, take it to heart. Look for parallels."

I must have looked skeptical, though I was merely puzzled.

Chen Jianyu said, "I'm serious. Listen to me." He beckoned me closer and whispered a name in my ear. He stepped away, and still whispering, said, "That man is my father's friend. They're old friends, close friends, like-minded friends who have worked together for years. This American has sinned. He thinks the FBI is on his scent. He fears exposure, ruin. He is what Esterhazy, the real spy, the actual traitor, was to Dreyfus, the fall guy. You're Dreyfus. The *laowai*."

Of course I was. I saw the connections as if a strip of film had just developed in my brain. I wasn't crazy after all.

I said, "Thank you."

"Good luck," Chen Jianyu said. "You're going to need it."

42

When I got back to my town house I checked my balance in the bank I had used when I worked for Chen Qi. In the day and a half I was in China, $250,000 had been deposited to my account. The source of the money was listed as something called Hanyu Consultants Group, otherwise known as Chen Qi. Counting the Chinese money that was already in my account, I now had more than half a million dollars on deposit and I could not account for a penny of it. That meant I could easily afford the five-thousand-dollar business-class ticket I just used. It also meant that I was a dead duck. American banks are required by law to report any single deposit larger than ten thousand dollars to the United States Treasury. Therefore bells were ringing at the IRS, and because Headquarters had a unit embedded in that agency, bells would soon be ringing at Headquarters. And most thought provoking of all, very loud bells would peal at the FBI, which also posted a squad of special agents to the Department of the Treasury.

There is a kind of bullet, jacketed with soft copper, that expands to the size of an eggplant when fired into the entrails. Receiving this windfall was something like being shot with such a bullet. I panicked. The power of this threat overwhelmed thought, reason, breath—everything. My enemy might be a Shanghai tycoon, but thanks to him I was now in the grip of my own country's system, from which few have ever escaped once caught. I knew my life was over even though my heart might keep on beating for the next fifty years. I went into the bathroom, just making it to the toilet bowl, and fell to my knees.

By the time I rinsed my toothbrush I was on the point of falling asleep. You may think this was a strange reaction to the prospect of life in solitary confinement or worse, but with Chen Jianyu as my astrologer I had had my horoscope updated as Lin Ming had recommended and flown twenty hours without sleep. My bones ached, my head throbbed, my throat was sore. My hands trembled. These were blessings in their way because they distracted me from the feeling that an enormous white-hot bullet was pressing against my heart. I took three aspirin and fell into bed. I went to sleep immediately. If I dreamed, as I must have, I didn't remember the details when I woke up ten hours later, wondering what was the matter with me.

I needed someone to talk to. There were no obvious candidates. I didn't have the habit of confession. I had never shared the secrets of my soul with anyone, had never since the onset of puberty asked for advice or another opinion. Would I be able to do so now, when that might well mean throwing away my last and only chance ever to go outdoors again? And if I did suddenly develop the knack for spilling my guts, to whom would I spill them? Everyone I knew by name in the United States or in China was tainted. I was on speaking terms with no one who was clean, no one who could be trusted absolutely to listen to my suspicions—my profound convictions—and keep them secret. Priests had been eliminated. A psychiatrist? No doubt a shrink would find it interesting that I believed I had no friend in the world, but he or she would regard every

word I uttered as a code word for the clinical, the real, the hidden truth.
I had no one to turn to.

Or did I? I picked up the phone and dialed Alice Song's cell phone.
If anyone on the planet might be sane enough to realize that I wasn't as
crazy as I seemed, it was Alice. Chances were that she was clean. That
glimpse of Magdalena (by now I was sure it was Magdalena) in her
kitchen notwithstanding, there was no reason to suspect her of playing
a double game. No one could use Alice, of that I was certain. Our first
meeting in the club bar was clearly pure coincidence. What else could
it be? She could not possibly have known that I was there. I had never
been there before. She had taken me as I was, she had put up with
what she took to be my atrocious manners. She had gone to bed with
me. When I remembered her—anything about her brain, body, that
voice—I entered into a state of delight. She may have regarded me as
a curiosity—who wouldn't?—but she had taken me as I was. She had
never tried to reprogram me. Besides that she was a brilliant lawyer, a
formidable courtroom operative, and everything you told her, if you
were paying for her services, was stamped top secret the instant it fell
from your lips. Just like me, she was under oath to keep her mouth shut
no matter what. How much that would be worth in the long run was
another question.

Alice's voice mail picked up. "Please don't leave a message," her voice
said. "Call me back."

An hour later I tried Alice's number again and was told once more
not to leave a message. Finally I realized there was no point in calling
her again. Sooner or later she would see my number when she checked
for missed calls and get back to me. Or not.

With time to squander, I went for a drive, no destination in mind.
I needed a new line of thought. I didn't need to think any more about
Albert Dreyfus. I understood the parallel. I knew the reason for my
problem, and thanks to Chen Jianyu, I even knew who my Esterhazy

was and who his case officer was, and in rough outline, I knew the fate Chen Qi had in mind for me. But how to act on these apprehensions? My situation was like Fermat's Conjecture—a theorem universally regarded by mathematicians as provable even though its solution eluded them for 358 years. Even if my own conjecture was solved in half that time, assuming that anyone but me was interested in its solution, I would still have ample time to serve the life sentence that was staring me in the face. Who would believe my proof even if I published it? Going to the FBI might make me feel better, it might hatch a conspiracy theory that political loonies could ponder for decades if not centuries, but it would not save me. Or cause justice to be done.

In real time I was alone on a long dark road, no headlights in the mirror. Suddenly I knew where I was going and why. Alice could wait.

Around one in the morning I parked on the shoulder of the road half a mile away from Luther Burbank's barn and sneaked closer to it through swampy woods. As I went, I assumed I was being picked up by motion detectors, even by cameras, but I put my hopes in the possibility that Burbank was meditating and therefore temporarily blind and deaf. After ten minutes or so I came to the last line of trees and the house came into sight. Burbank's Hyundai and the black Range Rover that had chased me out of the driveway on my last visit were parked side by side on the gravel. Inside the house, the lights were on, though dimmed. Through the windows I could see fragments of the awful paintings. Also two human figures moving in a rhythmic way. I heard, just barely, the sound of music and realized that these people were dancing. I couldn't make out their faces, so I moved closer. The man was unmistakably Burbank. He wore tuxedo trousers with a scarlet cummerbund and a white silk shirt. The woman, who was as slim as Burbank, was a brunette. She wore a knee-length skirt of shiny material that ballooned and swung prettily when they turned. Her dark shoulder-length hair, cut straight across, swung in synchrony with the skirt. Her face was hidden in the hollow of Burbank's neck. They were excellent dancers, almost professional—erect as a couple of honor guards, brisk in their movements, attuned to each other. I wondered if Burbank and this woman entered weekend ballroom competitions under assumed names or dreamed of making it on *Dancing with the Stars*. Obviously they had studied and practiced together. Had Burbank been a little younger—it wasn't possible to guess the woman's age because I still couldn't see her face—they could have been an adagio act on a cruise ship. The music changed. They tangoed—thrusting machismo and sultry femininity, legs entwining. The light by which Burbank and his partner were dancing was only slightly brighter than candlelight. Even though the two of them were farther apart now, I still could not make out the lady's face.

It was a typical Virginia summer night, temperature and humidity both in the nineties. Fireflies blinked. Mosquitoes bit. I crushed them when I could reach them instead of slapping them because I feared to make a noise. My mind wandered and when it came back into focus, the lights were off in the house. I heard the front door open. Burbank emerged. He still wore his white shirt, so I could make him out in the darkness. A second, smaller white blur moved beside him. I heard a sound I couldn't quite identify, but then, as Burbank's movement triggered the floodlights, I realized that what I had heard was the inquisitive whine of a dog that smells something it does not recognize. The smaller white blur—not so very small on closer examination—was a pit bull. Where had it come from? No dog had ever before been part of this picture. The pit bull barked—a long string of baritone woofs. It growled deep in its throat, then barked again, louder.

Burbank could see me as plainly as I saw him. He said, "You. Stand up with your hands above your head or I'll turn the dog loose."

At this moment Burbank's dance partner came outside, also still wearing her dancing costume. She carried the gun-nut machine pistol Burbank had put under my pillow on my first visit to this house.

She handed the weapon to Burbank, who handed her the dog's leash in return and pointed the weapon at me. I stood up and put my hands above my head.

"Approach," Burbank said. "Slowly."

I was, say, a hundred feet away. Though I have good eyesight I couldn't quite make out Burbank's face. The floodlights had switched on and were so dazzlingly bright that they hindered vision. After I had taken maybe twenty steps, Burbank and the woman came into focus. At the same moment so did I, apparently, because the woman told the pit bull to lie down, and it obeyed her instantly. I looked at the woman. For a fraction of a second I saw her as if she were captured in a freeze frame. Then she turned her back, whirling as if executing a tango step, and rushed into the house, taking the pit bull with her.

Quick as she was, different as she looked in her dancing clothes and her new hair color, I made her. I knew who she was. There was no mistake. By this time I was beyond surprise, but wasn't it odd, wasn't it intriguing, wasn't it extraordinary, the way I kept on catching glimpses of Magdalena in the strangest places?

43

Burbank led me through the dark house to a tiny study. An antiqued print of *Old Ironsides* under full sail, ensign blowing the wrong way, hung on one wall. A print of the Godolphin Arabian, a foundation sire of the Thoroughbred breed, was displayed on the opposite wall.

"Sit ye down," Burbank said. "I'll be right back." A moment later I heard the pit bull's toenails clicking on the bare floor, then heard the front door open and close and the Range Rover's throaty engine start up and the car drive away. Soon after that Burbank reappeared, now wearing pajamas and carrying two bottles of artisanal beer. He handed one bottle to me and took a long pull from the other.

"Thirsty work, doing the tango," he said. "I thought you were on R and R."

"I am, but I need to talk to you," I said.

"Is that why you're here at this ungodly hour? It's after two."

I said, "This won't take long."

"Then spill it," he said. "Some of us have to get up in the morning."

"I was out of town for a while," I said, "and when I got back yesterday I checked my bank balance." I paused.

"And?" Burbank said.

"And I discovered that something called the Hanyu Consultants Group had deposited two hundred and fifty thousand dollars in my checking account."

Now I had his attention, but he was still Mr. Cool. He sipped his beer, wiped his lips with the back of his hand, and said, "In return for what?"

"Your guess is as good as mine."

"What's the Hanyu Consultants Group?"

It would have been untruthful for me to say that I had no idea, so again I shrugged. I said, "Never heard of them."

"Never consulted for them?"

"No."

"Then why are they dropping a quarter of a million dollars into your checking account?"

"I don't have a clue. I thought you might be able to help me figure it out."

"Why me?"

Burbank was looking at me as if I might be carrying a concealed weapon.

I said, "Because you're my superior officer, my only friend at Headquarters, and I don't know who else to report this to. Because I think the deposit may be an attempt to ruin me."

"'Ruin' you?'" He whistled softly. "How? Why? Who?"

Head cocked, he was smiling in a worried sort of way. Had I lost it altogether?

I went on. "I think the FBI or the IRS or both will investigate as soon as they get word of this. So will CI as a matter of reflex. I think the results of such an investigation could be unfortunate for me and embarrassing for Headquarters and for you as the man I work for."

"Why unfortunate for you if you're innocent of wrongdoing? Have you considered just reporting this to the FBI?"

He actually said this—bluffed on the first card dealt. Now his smile was soothing, his tone of voice infinitely reasonable, as though he might be humoring a wife who was working herself up to accuse him of adultery.

I said, "No. I'm reporting it to you."

"Why not go straight to the Bureau, if you think there's something fishy about it?"

"Because Headquarters wouldn't like that. Because whatever illusions may exist about American justice, nobody is ever considered innocent by the Bureau after being taken into custody. Because very few people arrested by the FBI have ever been proved innocent. Because nobody accused of the kind of crime this payment suggests I committed has ever had a friend in the world."

"Whoa," Burbank said. "Hold on, there. Have you considered the possibility that the deposit is a mistake? Banks make them all the time. What bank are we talking about?"

I told him. He asked how much I had in my account. I told him that. If he thought that half a million dollars was an unusual amount for a GS-13 making $89,023.00 a year before payroll taxes and deductions to have in a checking account, he did not say so. I was certain that he already knew everything I had just told him. Even so, a sign of surprise, however tiny, would have been a seemly gesture. Burbank made no such sign.

He said, "I see your problem. I think you may be giving it a little more weight than it can bear."

"I'm paranoid? Wow, that's a load off my mind."

Burbank was displeased by the sarcasm and he amended his performance to let this show. His reaction—a frown, a sad shake of the head—resembled spontaneity, a quality I had not previously observed in him. I felt I was making progress. He was human after all. It was possible to get to him. I thought I had the key to opening him up, I thought I was in luck. I thought that my latest glimpse of Magdalena was the key. So far tonight nearly everything that had happened was unexpected. I had come here with the intention of penetrating Burbank's shell if I had to waterboard him to do it, but with no plan in mind. I was winging it. I had no idea what I was doing or what might happen next. This was no great change from the life I had been living for months—years, even— and maybe, I thought, the whole dog's breakfast of this operation, the whole inside-out life into which I had stumbled, was a training exercise for the new Afghanistan in which I was now waking up, wondering where I was.

All during this train of thought, Burbank stared over my shoulder, as if there were someone behind me (Magdalena, syringe in hand?) who was going to tell him in sign language what to do about this psychopath who had somehow gotten into the house. He looked a little wan. He looked, yes, unsure of his next move or mine.

I said, "I've been thinking about the obvious."

Burbank swiveled his gaze and looked into my eyes. He was looking wary but trying to conceal it.

"So far you haven't sounded that way," he said. "But tell me more."

I said, "I know it has occurred to you that the ideal way to penetrate an intelligence service is through its counterintelligence division."

"And why would that be?"

I said, "CI is above suspicion by definition because suspicion is its turf. It has the need to know everything about everyone, but no one else has the need or the right to know anything about it."

"That's true in a twisted sort of way," Burbank said. "As you know, we've had some experience with being penetrated. We learned from the experience. It can never happen again."

"You believe that?"

"I *know* that."

"How do you know it?"

"Because the last fellow was a clown doing a clown's work and we now know how to take clowns seriously."

"Then one of the clowns is still inside the little trick car in the center ring, because I think it *has* happened again."

"Meaning what?"

"Meaning that I have reason to believe that Guoanbu has an agent within Headquarters, within CI."

"Do you now?" Burbank said.

He smiled a dead-eyed smile. He looked at the clock on his desk. He yawned. He turned the clock around so I could see it. Too many gestures, too much disinterest.

I said, "Will you listen?"

"All right," he said. "Tell me more. Five minutes, my friend."

He pronounced *five* as *fahv,* in an LBJ drawl.

Scientists have established the existence of a parasite called *Toxoplasma gondii* that is transmitted from the feces of cats to human beings, rats, and other mammals. *T. gondii* invades the brain and rewires it, rerouting the connections among neurons. It impels rats to run toward the cat that is hunting them instead of fleeing as instinct would command. In humans, the parasite causes its host to behave in wildly reckless ways, leading to such self-destructive actions as reckless adultery, deliberately crashing cars, or shoplifting. It is suspected of triggering schizophrenia. I had never gone anywhere near a cat turd if I could avoid it, but in Burbank's study I had a *T. gondii* moment. Something leaped in my brain from one neuron to another, and in the nanosecond this took I was transformed into a nutcase who didn't know the meaning of the word *consequences.* Had I been standing on a balcony thirty floors above the ground I probably would have leaped onto its parapet and gone for a walk.

I said, "This will take a little more than five minutes."

Burbank glared at me—*how dared I contradict him?*—and pushed back his chair with a squeal. He started to get to his feet.

I said, "Sit down."

Burbank, who probably hadn't been given a direct order in twenty years, looked startled. I was bigger than he was and years younger and my forearm was larger than his calf, and possibly I had a look on my face that gave him pause. In any case he sat down. Maybe he had a panic button under the desk that would bring a goon squad into his study in a matter of minutes, or some kind of concealed weapon that would fire an instantaneous knockout dart designed for tigers and suicide bombers into my body. I didn't care. I just wanted this whole masquerade to end—now and not a minute later. Enough was enough. Burbank sat down.

"Let's go back to the beginning," I said. I was a little surprised at how steady my voice was, how reasonable my tone. Burbank, apprehensive but cold-eyed, playing the man of stone, waited for me to go on.

"The original assignment," I said, "was to identify half a dozen Guoanbu agents who were giving us trouble and then find a way to denounce them to Beijing as American spies, yes?"

No response from Burbank. Maybe he wasn't listening—probably he wasn't listening. He didn't really have to listen because every word I spoke was almost surely being recorded. I was fine with that. I wanted this encounter to be on record. I was recording it myself with the spyware cell phone in the pocket of my shorts.

"However," I said, "what we wound up with was six B-list princelings who have never done America harm and probably never will. You seemed to be satisfied with that result. Why?"

Again no response. I lifted Burbank's desk a couple of feet off the floor and dropped it. The keepsakes on its surface flew off in all directions.

Outwardly at least, Burbank remained calm. Unperturbed. As if nothing unusual had happened to his desk he said, "Because you struck out."

"So why didn't you fire me?"

"Compassion. Patience. I thought that was not quite the best you were capable of doing and that we might as well see where it led us."

"But you thought I had failed."

"Everyone falters from time to time," Burbank said. "In this business, a lot of things don't work out. As I've told you over and over, it can take years to put an operation together. Your spoiled brats might not be dangerous now, but who knows what they might grow up to be? As often as not an operation never really comes together. It almost never turns out exactly the way we thought or hoped. But I supposed you'd learn from this experience and do better next time. After all, the operation was still alive. There might be a breakthrough, a game changer if you kept at it, believing you had a chance of coming through. I thought you should be given time and space to make something happen. I believed you could do that. That's why I gave you a free hand and the chance to be creative. Even now I think you can amount to something in this business. I really do."

So Burbank had had nothing but avuncular intentions toward me all along, and still had them even after I had revealed the real me to him in the last ten minutes. To give him his due, benevolent uncle had always been the part he played best. He was just staying in character.

I didn't ponder the alternatives. After an interval of heavy silence I said, "Are you familiar with the Dreyfus affair?"

Burbank's eyes widened, an unfeigned reaction at last. In a flat voice he said, "The what?"

I said, "The Dreyfus affair."

"I read Zola when I was a kid."

I said, "What's your recollection of the details of the case?"

"What does that have to do with the price of anything?"

"Indulge me."

He shrugged. If I insisted on being humored, he'd humor me. He summarized the Dreyfus case. Naturally he aced the details—the false (Burbank used the word *mistaken*) accusation that Alfred Dreyfus, a Jew from Alsace, therefore the perfect patsy, had passed military secrets to the German embassy in Paris. He knew all about Dreyfus's court-martial on a charge of treason, about his five years in solitary confinement on Devil's Island, about the attempts of the French army command to quash new evidence that showed him to be innocent, about the final vindication. He knew about Esterhazy.

"So now that you know I know all that, what do you think you know?" Burbank said.

I said, "I know that I'm Dreyfus. That you're Esterhazy."

I'd like to report that Burbank reeled in guilt and surprise. But his face betrayed nothing, his voice did not change, no muscle moved.

He said, "You're serious?"

"Absolutely. That's what this masquerade is all about. You're a spy for China. If the allegation is ever made, you've got a fall guy. He gets to wear the handcuffs, he goes to jail or the guillotine, you go right on doing what you do."

Burbank's smile broadened with every sentence I uttered. He said, "Ingenious. I was right about you. You really do have the knack."

"Thank you."

"However, you poor bastard, you're demented. Anyone can see that."

He got to his feet. "As of this moment you're on indefinite administrative leave," he said. "You are relieved of all duties. Your clearance is suspended. Your access to Headquarters is terminated, your ID is canceled. However, your salary will continue and your medical insurance will still be good. The Headquarters shrinks will be in touch with you first thing in the morning with the names of outside psychiatrists who are cleared to handle cases like yours. Unless you've got an imaginary Chinese submarine waiting for you offshore, it would be futile to attempt to leave the country. Now I'm going to bed. Get out of my house. Go home."

I said, "I'll leave, but I won't go away."

"I wouldn't be too sure about that," Burbank said.

He walked me out. Not a pinpoint of light fell through the windows. He opened the door for me and stood back to give me room, as if I were a guest departing after a good dinner and an interesting conversation. For a moment I thought he was going to shake hands with me, but that did not happen.

44

Alice Song listened intently while I told her all this. I had booked a private dining room at the club, so we were alone and Alice's elocution was not the factor it might have been in a crowded dining room. Like Burbank the night before, she was absolutely still. Nothing moved—not her eyelids, not her hands, not the muscles in her face. Her body did not shift in her chair. After a while the waiter arrived, looked at our untouched plates, and asked if everything was all right.

"Everything's lovely," Alice said. "Could you clear the table, please?"

As soon as the waiter was out of the room, Alice said, "Is that all of it?"

"So far."

"And the crux of the matter is that this mysterious character called Chen Qi wants to destroy you because you knocked up his daughter, and that this same Chen Qi is a Chinese spymaster who is spying on U.S. intelligence through the eyes of the man who is the chief of U.S. counterintelligence?"

"Yes."

Alice, still frozen in place, said, "Then I guess it's time to ask why are you telling me all this."

"Because I think I'm going to need legal advice."

"I think so too, unless this is some kind of joke."

Well, that was exactly what it was in its own way, but I didn't think I could explain that to a stranger to the craft, so I just said, "My hope is that you will agree to represent me. If you believe me."

"If I represent you it won't matter whether or not I believe you," Alice said. "And on the basis of what I've learned about spooks in the last hour, I have no reason not to believe you. Everything you've told me is so crazy that it doesn't even matter if it's the truth. But there are problems. For one, the case doesn't exactly fall within my area of expertise."

"I don't care about that."

"What do you care about?"

"Your smarts. Your courtroom manner. Your knowledge of me."

"But I just found out I don't know anything about you."

"No, you just found out that there was something about me you didn't know. Big difference."

"There's another issue," Alice said.

"Is there some kind of ethical question because we've slept together?"

"No. But I'm emotionally involved," Alice said.

I was thrilled by her words. Even though I knew I would probably never sleep with her again, I said, "You are? That's wonderful."

"Isn't it, though? In your interests I should recuse myself. I can find you an excellent lawyer."

"Thank you, no. No Ole Olsens. It's you or no one."

"If it's no one, you'll end up as dog food. A competent lawyer can at least raise enough doubt to keep you alive."

"That's the optimum outcome?"

"You be the judge," Alice said. "Do you have any proof that this creature you call Burbank is the traitor you say he is? Documents, tape recordings, witnesses, anything at all?"

"No witnesses. Tape recordings of everything except Chen Jianyu whispering Luther Burbank's name in my ear."

"So that includes what?"

"Every meeting with Burbank, every meeting with Lin Ming, with Chen Qi, with Mei and Chen Jianyu three days ago, everyone involved in the operation."

"Where is this material?"

"In the mail, addressed to you."

"Tape recordings are iffy things."

"Maybe to judges, but they're catnip to the FBI."

"Meaning what?"

"If the Bureau investigates me, they'll have to investigate Burbank," I said. "Even if I go down, he goes down with me. He can't be allowed to go on selling the country out to Guoanbu."

"That's the plan, stopping him?"

"More like a forlorn hope," I said. "But it might work."

"And if it does, everything will be right with the world?"

"Maybe not quite everything. But I'll settle for what we can get, as long as we get Burbank."

"The simplest thing for these enemies of yours to do is to kill you," Alice said. "People get murdered for no apparent reason all the time."

"Headquarters doesn't do that kind of thing."

"Tell that to al Qaeda," Alice said. "What about Burbank or Chen Qi or Guoanbu?"

"My sudden death is not enough for Chen Qi. He wants me to die by inches. "

Alice drew a deep breath, then another, as if oxygen was an antidote to exasperation. "Even if the plan works, the government will pursue the charges against you," she said. "You will have caused them too much trouble for them to do otherwise. Given the evidence you've laid out tonight, you'd need twelve twisted minds on the jury to get acquitted. In fact the jurors will be normal people to whom the activities you take for granted will sound like a day in Satan's workshop. In the end the jurors will think one of two things—either you're the vile traitor the prosecution will say you are and you're trying to save yourself by destroying your innocent boss, or you're insane. In any case, you'll be locked up. Forever."

I already knew that. I told Alice I just wanted to get the facts, deformed as they might be, on the record. In the short run, Headquarters might protect Burbank and sacrifice me to cover its own fanny. But the possibility that I was right about him would not go away. It would flit from mind to mind, inside Headquarters and inside the news media, and sooner or later, the hornets' nest would wake up. Burbank would be kicked out of Headquarters. Even if he didn't go to jail, even if Chen Qi didn't have him assassinated to make sure of his silence, he would do no more harm to his country. That was an outcome I could accept.

"You really mean that?" Alice asked.

"Yes. If I don't have a chance of beating the charges, and I know I don't, then I'll settle for getting the bastard in the end."

Alice thought it over, her eyes boring into mine. Then she said, "Okay, I'll take the case, but much as I might wish to do so, the firm probably won't let me do it pro bono. Given the complexity, the essential hopelessness of your situation, you're looking at maybe a couple of million dollars. Can you cover that, leaving aside the Chinese money, which the government will seize?"

"I can come close," I said. I had the house in Connecticut, the apartment in the city, and the stocks and bonds and jewelry Mother had left me.

"Okay," Alice said. "You may even have something left over in case of a miracle. Give me a list of your assets and I'll draw up the papers posting them as collateral. Are you all right with that?"

I said, "Go ahead. I'm assuming everything I've told you tonight or will tell you in the future will be protected by lawyer-client confidentiality."

"Correct. That's why it's costing you so much money. Now let's talk some more."

She opened her purse and rummaged around in it. "Want an energy bar?" she asked, tossing one onto the table for me. I unwrapped it and ate it. Somehow Alice ate hers without spilling a single crumb.

The rest of the conversation was Q & A. She was an even tougher customer than I had thought. It was very reassuring to imagine Burbank, who had been immune to questions for such a long time, trying to stand up under cross-examination by this remorseless inquisitor. For me it was liberating to tell the truth, the whole truth, and nothing but the truth for the first time in years, to hide nothing, to remember lies and crack them open to get at the facts within, and to do this because it profited me and advanced the operation. It was a strange process, baring the soul. I had been told about defected spies weeping with relief, wetting their pants, clinging in gratitude to their interrogators as if to a priest after spilling everything they knew, so great was their relief to cleanse their consciences.

At eleven o'clock the club closed. No gong sounded, Alice just knew what time it was. As we walked down the stairs together, the last two people in the place except for the watchman, Alice said, "We're hungry, no?"

"Yes. Want to go to Subway?"

"Let's go to my place and order a pizza," Alice said.

A last sleepover. My heart sang.

At the bottom of the steps that led from the sidewalk to the door of the club, two persons in black baseball caps and matching warm-up jackets waited. One of them flashed ID and said, "FBI." He then spoke my name as a question. I said yes, that was me. The other agent, a female, also flourishing a badge, repeated my name and said, "You are under arrest on suspicion of espionage under the provisions of 18 U. S. Code, section 793." She then read me my Miranda rights. The other one shackled me, wrists and ankles.

Alice said, "I am this man's attorney. Where are you taking him?"

They told her.

"I'll follow," she said. To me she said, "You know what to do. Say nothing to these people, repeat nothing, apart from stating your name, which you have already done. There is no need to be polite or congenial. Do you understand?"

Before I could do so much as nod in agreement, I felt a hand on my head as Special Agents XX and XY put me into the backseat of a large black Ford that smelled of Lysol. The plan had worked, but far more quickly than I had imagined. Being taken into custody by America's equivalent of the secret police was like slipping into unconsciousness after being wounded in combat. Would I ever wake up again? To my utmost surprise I suddenly felt bottomless fear, worse than anything I had known in Afghanistan or in the dreams I had brought home with me from that godforsaken place.

45

Eventually I got over being terrified. Thanks to Alice Song's skills and a criminal justice system that was more interested in big fish than in small fry like me, I did better than Dreyfus. About a year after my arrest, only dimly aware of how Alice had managed to lead the government to the fundamental, undeniable truth that Luther Burbank was the real traitor and I was merely the babe in the woods, I pleaded guilty to a single felony charge. I was sentenced to three years' imprisonment. As ritual dictated, I expressed my heartfelt remorse for my crime though I wasn't sure what exactly I was being charged with. With credit for the time I had already spent in jail, I served two weeks less than two years in a minimum-security federal prison camp in Tennessee. The experience was something like ROTC summer camp except that the guards were less drunk with power than the instructor NCOs had been and I didn't get nearly as much exercise. Otherwise, all was familiar—barracks that smelled faintly of dirty socks and armpits, good guys and bad guys, dumb jokes, tight routine, unseasoned food, time oozing by. My Timex had been confiscated. I never looked at the clock in the recreation room, just listened for the announcements to tell me when to eat, when to sleep, when to be counted. Gradually I regressed to a Stone Age consciousness in which measurement scarcely existed, knowing only day and night, long and short, rain and shine, cold and warmth, hunger and food, sexual arousal and self-help. After a spell in the kitchen scrubbing pots and pans, I worked on the paint gang, an enjoyable job.

Meanwhile the case moved toward conclusion, inch by inch. Alice called me when there were new developments, but isolated as I was, it was hard to splice the pieces together. I felt that I was watching through the window of my cell as disconnected snatches of an eight-millimeter movie based on the true story of my life flickered on a distant screen. At last came the moment when the climactic scene played, the screen went to black, the music stopped, and a series of captions detailing the after-the-movie life of the characters appeared:

Burbank was indicted on eighty-six counts of espionage, but he was not tried on these charges because he declined to do the patriotic thing and plead guilty and the evidence against him was too sensitive and too damaging to U.S.-China relations to be revealed in open court.

He was also indicted for evasion of income taxes on the millions Chen Qi had banked for him in Singapore, and a trial was scheduled.

Burbank, who was under house arrest while awaiting trial, was found dead, seated at the dinner table in his home in rural Virginia with the crumbs of a piece of key lime pie, his favorite dessert, on the plate before him.

Two months later, a tourist for whom she had once catered a dinner in New York sighted Magdalena in Suzhou, People's Republic of China. She was never seen again by American eyes.

Nor was Mei.

The captions dissolve into a final scene. Alice Song meets me outside the gates of the prison camp on the day I am released after serving my sentence—or if you prefer, after completing my penance for inconveniencing my betters. She is wearing shorts and sneakers and a Chinese red T-shirt with 雙喜, the character for "double happiness," printed on it, her hair cut shorter than before but otherwise looking just the same. I am thinner, calmer—the result, maybe, of 716 days of staring fixedly like a Zen monk at a certain invisible stain on the wall. We drive away, Alice at the wheel. It is late morning on a sunny day in spring—songbirds in flight, crows cawing, blue skies, puffy white clouds, and after we reach the Interstate, flowering trees in the grassy median strip. Somehow all this awakens the memory of Burbank and Magdalena dancing in the dark. And I wonder if Burbank, who knew so many things that nobody really needed to know, ever realized until he took his last bite of key lime pie, who his caretaker, his Ginger Rogers, his matchless chef really was.

"So how was it?" Alice asks.

"Not so bad," I reply.

"Your thoughts?"

"Mostly I thought about the power of coincidence," I say. "The bomb not killing me in Afghanistan. Mei crashing into me on her bike. Her father being the psychopath he was."

"And still is, don't forget," said Alice.

I pretend not to hear her. I go on with my thought: "Chen Qi's connection to Burbank. Burbank's connection to my father. Bumping into Lin Ming on a dark street in Manhattan. Running into you the first time I walked into the club. I could go on. People may scoff, but if you think about it, the unforeseen is what makes the world go around."

Alice takes her eyes off the road and looks me up and down, as if she had known me up to now only in a photograph.

"Say again? What makes the world go around?" she says.

"Coincidence."

"Ah, the white man's word for fate," says Alice.